STRIPPED BOUNTY

DOROTHY F. SHAW

PRAISE FOR DOROTHY F. SHAW

"*Unworthy Heart* reminded me of what I love about the romance genre."—The Book Tart

"*Unworthy Heart* by Dorothy F. Shaw made me think, made my heart happy, made me tear up and made me sigh in happiness. Shaw combines heat with heart almost flawlessly. I cannot wait for the follow-up books in this series."—Romance Novel News

"I fell in love with the series from book one…Grab your copy and buckle up for the ride. Dorothy Shaw doesn't do anything half way."—Beyond the Valley of the Books on *Defensive Heart*

"Holy smokes can Dorothy Shaw write a freaking awesome sex scene…"—Wicked Good Reads on *Defensive Heart*

"*Defensive Heart* by Dorothy F. Shaw is a good read which gives credence to the statement that opposites do attract."—Harlequin Junkie

"Even though there is plenty of sex in *Shattered Heart*, the author does not neglect the storyline at all – packing it full of romance, danger, trauma, healing, laughs, and the Donnelly family."—Crystal's Many Reviewers

"*Shattered Heart* is an emotional tear-jerker of a romance that had me reaching for the tissues on more than one occasion."—Romance Novel News

"Wow! What a sexy, steamy story that kept me reading from the first page."—Crystal's Many Reviewers on *Stripped Bounty*

"If you are into vanilla, forget this book! Characters larger than life and sex to die for. Dorothy F. Shaw painted a canvas that is both intriguing and close to hardcore."—Amazon Reviewer on *Stripped Bounty*

"Epic story! Rosie and Badger are amazing characters that pull you into the story. The sex is HOT and the ending is perfect!"—Book Addicts PR on *Stripped Bounty*

"I was blown away by how easily the story was told by Dorothy F. Shaw"—CeeriJays Smexy HotReads on *A Few More Rules*

"*A Few More Rules* (a femdom novella) is a super-hot romance that sets the foundation well for a probable HEA between Rig and Beth. This story is a winner."—Romance Novel News

"WOW!!! This erotic, sensual short story will have you panting for more! These two beauties are more than fang bangers. The dark world of lust and sex will feed any appetite you desire."—Bookaholic and More Blog on *Playtime*

"I like books that grab my attention so much that I read a line and end up gasping or commenting out loud... and this one did just that - a few times! I'll definitely be reading it again."—Goodreads Reviewer on *Playtime*

"True to Dorothy Shaw's form, *Avoiding the Badge* is full of everything I love about her writing."—Amanda at Wicked Good Reads

"I liked the way the author brought about the truths that they had been keeping from each other, and I really enjoyed the steps that the two characters took in order to overcome the troubles in their path."—Amazon reviewer on *Avoiding the Badge*

"*Redeeming the Badge* is a second chance romance that is hot as Hades and with a backstory that will twist your heartstrings." —Amazon Reviewer

"This is a tale of love and heartache, dealing with some tough issues such as infertility, endometriosis, and miscarriage. It will tear at your heartstrings and make you believe in true love." —Amazon Reviewer on *Redeeming the Badge*

"Jeff and Tish are a good couple with incredible chemistry that makes you jealous. I can't recommend this series enough." —Amazon Reviewer on *Trusting the Badge*

"*Trusting the Badge* is a quick read for readers who enjoy a focus on relationship building, characters with tragic backstories, and some steamy moments." —Amazon Reviewer

"It was written in a way that I got very emotional reading it, most books don't make me cry. This one did."—Amazon reviewer on *Jaded Heart*

Stripped Bounty

***Protecting her isn't an option.
It's a requirement.***

Badger finally got Rosie in his bed, but in order to keep her there, he has to figure out how to save her life.

After her drug-running husband gets himself killed, Rosie Santini figures Phoenix is a fine place to get a fresh start. Deuce's strip club isn't too fresh, but the money's easy. As she works the pole, the only gaze she can't ignore belongs to the club's head bouncer, Badger Baxter. But Rosie's seen her fair share of tall, dark, and dangerous, and no way is she heading down that road. Not even for a hot hunk of muscle like Badger.

When he's not bounty hunting, Badger runs security at Deuce's. Rosie should be just another piece of fresh meat in the club's stable of pole jockeys, but all her sexy parts add up to a ride Badger would like to test drive. Trouble is, Badger likes his women submissive, but not broken. She's definitely got baggage he wants no part of. But when her husband's killer shows up looking for stolen cash, she fits naturally under his protection—and it isn't long before she's hooked deep into his heart.

So deep, losing her now would make him bleed in more ways than one.

DEDICATION

For you…

ACKNOWLEDGMENTS

My shout-outs are as follows—in no particular order:

My darling, Shane Rice, aka my brother from another mother. My favorite cover model of all time. My convention partner in ~~partying and drinking~~ totally innocent fun… A million thanks for the totally awesome, very, *very* naughty hood of the GTO sex scene. Who knew you had such a dirty imagination? Well…I suppose I did, but that doesn't count, does it? Anyway, much love, my friend!

To Robert Gawe, aka my adopted Dad. Thank you for your extensive law enforcement information—including the lecture about never bringing a knife to a gunfight. As if I didn't know? Sheesh. Anyway, I love you and appreciate you more than I can ever express. Thank you for always being there.

My dear friend, Dawn Vasaeo. Thank you for letting me babble for far too long in your ear to figure out my plotting issue. Girl, you totally saved my ass! Seriously.

My ex-husband, Terry "Wookie" Hoffman. For discussing the plot of this book with me pretty much every two weeks, and sometimes in between, until I finally finished it. Also, for your extensive badass biker knowledge and as usual, your never-ending support and encouragement.

My awesome friend, Bill. For your willingness to share some majorly important things in order to give me details and facts about those kinds of things… (Don't worry, he'll know what I'm talking about.)

My beautiful cousin, Lisa Ruiz, for her medical scene information.

Anthony Garcia, for his Phoenix PD information.

Luis at 3-D Bail Bonds in Connecticut: Thanks for all the helpful info on your procedures.

My sprinting partner and pretty much favorite person on the planet, author Sidda Lee Rain. Jeez, where do I start? Where do I end? There's just so much. Okay, here goes: Plotting. Writing sprints. Never-ending encouragement. Late-night FaceTime talks that went on way too long while I babbled about where the hell this book was going. Then, me saying a trillion times that I JUST COULDN'T DO IT! And then when I finally did it, and it was all said and done, you read the book and told me what needed to be fixed. I seriously love you, woman.

My Megan Hart…just thank you. For all the things. All of them. And then more of them. I love you, Bebe. You are my confidant, my friend and my mentor and just…all the things.

To my wonderful beta readers: Marchelle Lagueux, Sherri Zak, and Samantha Pereira. As always, your feedback is invaluable! More love for Sherri Zak for being my typo-finding queen and to Sunnie Andrews for her pass of line edits. MWUAH! David Faulkner for proofreading the final version.

Last but not least, shout out to Pandorasparlour.com! Work it, Meredith!

CONTENT/TRIGGER WARNING

Be on the lookout for D/s sexual play, which may cause drooling and might have you reaching for the nearest man or battery-operated boyfriend.

Trigger Warning: *This book contains violent situations, including death due to physical altercations and gunfire.*

PLAYLIST

Type O Negative - *Christian Woman*
The Pretty Reckless - *Make Me Wanna Die*
Tesla - *Love Me*
Halestorm - *Unapologetic*
Karise Eden's cover - *It's A Man's World*
Godsmack - *Keep Away*
Amy Winehouse - *Tears Dry On Their Own*
Hozier - *Take Me To Church*
Beyonce - *Crazy In Love* (slow version)
Blue October - *Hate Me*
Kenny Wayne Shepherd - *Live On*
Sia - *Chandelier*
ZZ Ward - *OVERdue*
BANKS - *Before I Ever Met You*
Eminem - *Lose Yourself*

PROLOGUE

THE SOUND of the phone ringing split the silence of the dark bedroom, startling Rosie awake. She rolled beneath the covers and slapped at the nightstand in search of the cordless receiver on its base, missing it a couple of times.

"Fuck…really?" Finally getting a hold of the now torture device and flopping back onto the mattress, Rosie hit "Talk" on the handset and raised it to her ear. "Someone better be dead!"

"Rosie!"

She bolted upright in bed at the urgency in her husband's tone. "Joey? What's wrong?"

"Nuthin'." He coughed. "All good. Listen careful, baby girl." His voice was low and out of breath. "You listenin'?"

Christ, he was always doing that to her—scaring the crap out of her for no damn reason. And he accused her of towing the drama line. Whatever. Rosie swallowed down the panic-induced lump that had risen in her throat and looked at the digital clock on her nightstand. It was after three in the morning. Joey should've been home by then. What the hell had he gotten himself into now? "For the love of… Just get to the point. I'm listening!"

"I took something and hid it. If I don't come home, you need to get it and then, no matter what, you get the fuck out of town."

"What do you mean if you don't come home?" Rosie pushed her hair over her shoulder. "Are you getting arrested again?"

"No. Why do you always assume that? Fuck's sake." He grunted and then coughed again.

Why did she…was he serious? Rosie rolled her eyes. "Do you really want me to answer that question?"

"Whatever. Just listen. Go to the ladies' room at the train station. Under the sink, behind the pipes, you'll find a locker key taped to the wall. Grab it, and go to the self-storage lockers."

"Train station? Which fucking train station? What the hell did you take?" With a shove of the covers, she threw her legs over the side of the bed.

"I took our future, baby."

Good God, she could practically hear the smile behind his words. Rosie looked up at the ceiling, knowing this was going to lead nowhere good. The only place that damn ego of his ever led him was back to jail. Unless… *Oh fuck no.* Cold dread slipped down Rosie's spine, and she shivered. "You rolled the dealer, didn't you? Jesus-fucking-Christ! Are you trying to get us both killed?"

Joey let out a harsh sigh. "Keep your drama ass in check, Rosie! For real. I got this. That small-town fuck has no clue what he's doing. His crew is no better. Trust me, it's gonna be fine. Just take a damn breath for once and do what I say, got it?"

"Do *not* yell at me, *Joey!*" She got to her feet and paced in the small space between their bed and dresser. "You go do something insane, and you expect me to be calm?"

"Yeah, that's exactly what I expect."

Rosie ran her fingers through her hair. She wanted no part

of the world of drug trafficking he'd gotten himself into. And she'd made that *very* clear. Not that he ever respected what she wanted or needed. Too busy screwing up to bother. Regardless, Rosie had managed to stay far away from the people he'd been associating with.

What he'd gotten himself into was a one-way ticket to jail or the morgue. Joey had already been to prison one too many times. Jesus, he hadn't even been out more than six months from the last stint. At the rate he was going, it wouldn't be long before he was back behind bars. Or dead.

God, Joey had done a lot of stupid things, made a fuckton more stupid choices, but Rosie never thought he'd do something *this* stupid.

She should've known, though.

Always so goddamn greedy and always wanting more. Joey Santini thought he was a big-time hustler—big enough to pull something this insane off. But he wasn't. He was small-time. Small-town—small fucking potatoes. Especially in the drug world. He was nothing but a runner. A peon. And he'd just put both their lives at risk. She blew out a harsh breath. "Which station, dammit! Where are you?"

"Bridgeport."

Holy shit. That was nearly forty minutes away. The gravity of the situation hit her in the gut like a hard punch. She had no idea what to do. A tear dripped down Rosie's cheek, and she brushed it away. "Are you coming home?"

"I hope so."

CHAPTER ONE

Three months later…

"No Colors or Weapons Allowed."

Rosie Santini read the sign mounted on the brick exterior wall of the establishment. Shaking her head, she opened the solid wood front door and stepped out of the Phoenix hundred-and-four-degree heat and into the dimly lit, air-conditioned strip club.

Back in the day, "colors" meant a biker's patches—as in motorcycle club patches. Commonly found on the back of a leather or denim vest. Considering there was a pack of Harleys parked on the sidewalk out front, Rosie figured in Arizona, that's exactly what the sign referred to. Plus, as she'd learned pretty quickly after arriving in town, barring having a criminal record, people could carry a gun in AZ right out in the open for all to see.

She took a moment as her eyes adjusted, no longer sure if this was such a good idea, and looked around. Type O Negative's "Christian Woman" blared from the speakers as Rosie walked forward on the old green and white—or gray, rather—

linoleum-tiled floor. A small birdcage-style stage sat empty off to her left. To her right, the mahogany bar with its large, mirrored backsplash and various bottles of booze stretched along the wall. In the center of the large space sat a collection of small round tables, a tealight candle atop each one, with two pleather chairs arched around them. Doing a quick count, around twenty or so customers occupied the bar. Not uncommon for the middle of the day in a strip club.

Ahead of the tables was the main stage in the shape of an upside-down T. Mirrors lined the back wall with red curtains draped theatre-style at their edges. White rope lights ran along the edges of the narrow stage, leading down to the wide part, which held a pole on each end. There was also a spinning wheel mounted on the ceiling near center stage; she hadn't seen one of those in years. And, finally, another pole near the mirrors along the back wall.

Two girls had the big stage, clad only in their G-strings and stripper heels. One circling a pole, the other on her hands and knees as a patron stood behind her, dollar bill at the ready. Rosie shook her head. Dancers these days barely danced—hardly did anything to put on an actual show or striptease. That was the whole point, wasn't it? At least back in her heyday, it was.

She drew in a deep breath and blew it out. Deuce's Cabaret wasn't seedy…necessarily. But it wasn't plush, either. More that it needed a face-lift. Desperately. Not her first or even eighth choice for employment. But it'd do. At least the music was good.

Rosie circled in place, scanning the corners of the club, looking for cameras. And there wasn't a single one to be found. Anywhere. Hopefully, they had good bouncers. She'd spotted at least two of those throughout the space.

Hiking her big pocketbook a little higher on her shoulder, Rosie blew out a breath and stepped to the bartender. "Hi there."

The big man, clad in a black T-shirt, turned from the cash register and faced her. Rosie lost her breath when she caught sight of his face, but managed to get a grip on herself as he walked toward her. He dipped his chin, cocking his head to the side, as he wiped the bar top directly in front of her with a white bar rag. "You lost?"

Rosie swallowed past the layer of glue that'd suddenly appeared on her tongue. Jesus, he was breathtaking…speech-taking, too. Perfect nose, full lips, the bottom one a tad fuller. Incredible bone structure. Freaking guy could be a model. He was huge, too—muscular and at least six-one, maybe taller. She blinked a few rapid blinks and glanced away from his piercing light-brown gaze.

In an attempt to gain some control of her thoughts, Rosie plopped her pocketbook down on the closest barstool and, after a breath, looked back to him. "No. Not lost. Are you, by chance, hiring?"

He crossed his muscled arms, his biceps bulging, testing the limits of his T-shirt sleeves. "Bar or stage?"

"Bar." She managed a smile.

"Nope." His stare didn't waver, and Rosie took in the small lines around his eyes, but also his strong jaw, partly hidden by a goatee and way-more-than-five o'clock shadow. Yeah, definitely a good-looking man.

"What about waitress?"

"Nope." He dropped his arms and turned his back.

Wow! Had he really just dismissed her like that? *What the hell?* Rosie faced the stage and the dancers again. The Pretty Reckless's "Make Me Wanna Die" played now. She hadn't been onstage in about two years, and it was the last place she wanted to be again. But she was broke. Getting across the country from Connecticut to Arizona had cost Rosie more than she'd thought. She hadn't anticipated the freaking car dying. Twice. She hadn't anticipated her husband dying, either. *Jerk.* Rosie would never forgive him for putting her in this position.

Biting the edge of her barely existent thumbnail, she turned back around and faced the bartender. Desperate times called for desperate measures. "Okay, fine. Stage?"

With his back still to her, he glanced up from the bottle he was wiping down and caught her gaze through the reflection in the mirror. "You sure about that?"

Was she sure? Rosie'd already been to six other bars that day and three the day before. No, she wasn't fucking sure, but she needed a goddamn job. "Absolutely."

He turned, stepped to the bar top and rested both his hands on the edge. Did a muscle in his jaw just tick? Again he dipped his chin and cocked his head to the side—almost as if he was sizing her up and judging her abilities right there on the spot.

A beat of nervous energy rolled through her. Talk about feeling like a bug under a microscope. Jesus, she was uncomfortable. Rosie crossed her arms and jutted out her chin. The guy might be hotter than hell, but the last thing Rosie needed was bullshit from some stranger right now. "What?"

He pursed his lips, his firm gaze steady on her for another few moments before rubbing his palm along the side of his whiskered jaw and letting out a sigh. "Far side of the stage. Follow the hall to the back. Evie'll help you out."

"Oh." She cleared her throat. "Okay then." Rosie shouldered her bag, feeling a bit like she'd disappointed him. Which was pretty weird, considering she didn't even know him. "Thanks."

Turning on her heel, she stepped away from the bar. He was still staring at her. She knew it. Rosie could feel his gaze like a physical touch, skittering down her spine and over her skin as she made her way across the club in the direction he'd sent her. The screwed-up thing was, rather than creepy, the feel of his eyes on her was titillating.

Considering she'd only lost her husband three months ago, her body's reaction made her feel even more uncomfortable than she'd felt standing in front of him. Shrugging all of it off, Rosie walked through the narrow doorway in the far corner of the bar and down the empty, almost sterile hall.

And back into a world she hadn't wanted to ever visit again.

———

BADGER SHOOK his head as he watched the tall, slender brunette with the sad, dark-brown eyes walk toward the back hall. "Shame."

"What's that, Badge?" Deuce came up to the bar.

Badger glanced over to him. "Fresh meat."

The owner took a seat in his spot at the end of the bar. "Fresh meat's always good in my book. Nothing shameful about that."

Badger grunted and reached for a fresh glass. "You want something?"

"Eh, just a seltzer water. Evie's been nagging me about soda." Deuce clasped his hands together on the bar top and looked toward the stage.

Badger filled the glass with the clear carbonated fluid. "Hate to break it to you, boss. But this is soda."

"Like hell it is. It's water with bubbles in it. Smart ass. Now, grab me a lemon."

Badger chuckled and placed a lemon wedge on the edge of the glass. "We're fresh out of umbrellas."

"Kiss my ass." Deuce chuckled and sipped the drink.

"Maybe later." Badger grabbed the clipboard from the side of the register and went back to taking inventory.

Didn't matter what the boss said. Pretty girl like that one ending up being another stripper was a damn fucking shame. No two ways about it.

For a minute, since she'd asked about tending bar or waitressing, Badger thought, or maybe hoped, she might not be another pole jockey. So much for that. She had to have been on stage before. Sadly, you could take the girl out of the strip club, but you couldn't take the stripper out of the girl. Eventually, they came back. Especially if they still had some looks and a body. This one had both…in spades. Her eyes had gotten to him, though.

Badger looked up from the beer cooler to see her walking back across the bar toward the exit. She glanced over at him but quickly looked away before stepping out into the bright Arizona sun. Yeah, eyes were always a weakness or a warning for him. Hers were sad, like she'd seen some hurt in her days. But they were skittish, too. The skittish smacked of more than hurt in her past.

Regardless, he didn't mess with the strippers anymore. Those days were long gone. But even if she hadn't turned out to be a dancer, Badger would've steered clear anyway. There was enough "more" behind those sad and skittish eyes of hers for Badger to keep his distance. He didn't need the drama or the headache that came along with that amount of luggage.

The front door opened again, and the weekday bartender, Wendy, walked in. "Hey, Badger." She waved as she passed by him on her way to the office as if she wasn't over thirty minutes late for her shift.

"You're late, and I got shit to do besides cover your ass behind the bar."

She spun around, facing him, and shrugged, arms out at her sides. "Sorry. I had a flat." She continued walking backward before turning again and disappearing down the hall.

Badger grunted before staring down at the clipboard in his hands again. Damn bar staff were just as bad as the dancers. It wouldn't matter so much if he wasn't always the one on point to cover until they brought their asses in. He was supposed to just run security, not the bar staff, too, but the lines tended to blur. Mostly because Badger had a tendency to blur them.

Not that he'd admit that to Deuce if his life depended on it.

"You got some bounty hunter work to attend to?"

He glanced over at Deuce and nodded. "Yeah. Got a lead this morning on a skip I've been tracking."

His boss looked at his watch. "Good luck. See you back here 'round eight?"

"'Course." He set the clipboard down and jerked his chin at Deuce as he stepped out from behind the bar. "Earlier if I can. Order's ready to go. Don't wait up, honey."

"But, darling, we haven't had any quality time together."

"Yeah, yeah." With a wave over his shoulder, Badger chuckled and headed for the same hall he'd sent the brunette down. As he passed the dressing room, he gave a nod to Evie, Deuce's old lady. After a quick stop in the office to grab his gun, he stepped out into the daylight, lit a cigarette, and made his way to his pickup.

It was time to give his other career a little attention.

CHAPTER TWO

Later that night, Badger pulled his Harley-Davidson Dyna into the back lot of Deuce's Cabaret and parked in his usual spot near the back door. He pulled the bandana off his forehead and tucked it in his back pocket, and did the same with his shades. It was nearing the end of summer, and the late nights had finally started dipping just below the triple-digit mark, but seeing as it was just after seven thirty at night, the air temp was still pushing a solid one-oh-four.

Badger strode to the back door. "Evening, Jayson."

"Evening, boss." The bouncer nodded and held the door open for Badger to enter.

"Thanks." Badger stepped into the cool air of the back hall and made a hard right directly into the office. Deuce was at the desk, shuffling through some paperwork and stroking his long beard as Evie lounged on the couch to the right, book in her hands. "Evening, kids."

"Hey, Badger. You get the bad guy?" Evie smiled, and Badger moved to her and gave her a peck on the cheek.

"Not yet." He turned to Deuce. "Thought I told you not to wait up?"

Deuce snorted. "I got lonely."

"Awww." Badger clapped his boss on the shoulder and shot a wink to Evie. "Girls all present and accounted for?"

She gave him another million-dollar smile as she giggled. "Of course. Hey, how's your grandmother doing?"

"She's good. Saw her tonight before heading in." He removed his Glock 9mm and holster and locked it in the top drawer of the filing cabinet.

"You're such a good grandson. She's lucky to have you." Evie's eyes softened along with her smile.

"Thanks. More like the other way around, though." He looked back to Deuce. "You need anything, I'll be up front." With that, he left them to their business and made his way down the hall to the bar.

Evie and Deuce Stevens had been together damn near thirty years, maybe longer. His boss was in his mid-fifties, but the miles the old biker had weathered when he wore his now-retired MC patch on his back made him appear a lot older. Evie had been with him through all of it. The miles had weathered her, too, but she was still a damn pretty lady.

Badger strolled past the dressing room. The noise from all the girls getting ready for the night was loud enough to penetrate the closed door, as well as the dull echo of the music coming from the DJ in the bar. Damn, crazy ass, loud strippers. He shook his head and kept on his way.

The strobe and black lights were in full effect inside the main area of the bar as Tesla's "Love Me" played on the sound system. Two strippers had the main stage, and a few were scattered among the small crowd, working table dances.

Two of his security team flanked the open area on each side. He nodded to them both and then ambled past the bar and waved to Sadie, the night bartender. As he took a mental accounting of the lingering happy hour patrons, Badger took a seat on his perch between the front door and the bar.

It was Thursday night, so they'd draw a decent crowd over

the next four or so hours and maintain it until closing time, though Friday and Saturday nights were always better.

Within two hours, the crowd was in full swing. As Halestorm's "Unapologetic" began on the sound system, the deejay announced a new dancer, Arianna, on the center stage. New song, new dancer. No biggie. But a tingle at the back of Badger's neck had him glancing to the stage as he took a swig of his coffee…and almost choked on the lukewarm liquid. He cleared his throat and blinked. Twice.

It was her.

The goddamn brunette from earlier in the day.

Badger set the cup down. *Fuck me.* The very brunette he hadn't completely stopped thinking about all afternoon. He watched as she strutted down the stage in a black fitted skirt that came just above her knees, topped by a white button-up dress shirt. All that pretty long hair of hers was pulled up, and she had on a pair of sexy-ass glasses.

The woman looked like a librarian or schoolteacher—a fucking sexy-as-hell one.

Every hot-blooded male's wet dream. Blowing out a breath, Badger ran his palm along his jaw and kept his eyes on her. As if they'd be going anywhere else.

Arianna—not likely her real name—rounded the pole at stage left, turned, and with the bar against her back, arched her body so her petite, upside-down heart of a rear-end was pressed against the shiny steel. She ran her hands down the front of the white shirt, giving definition to the small but pert breasts beneath it.

Three beats of the song later, she ran a hand back up her chest to her cheek—her glossy red lips set in a pout—and pushed off the pole, strutting until she reached the other end. Arianna—or whoever she was—gripped the steel in one hand, hooked a leg around it and, lifting herself off the ground, spun a few times before dropping into a low squat, the post pressed between her parted thighs to her core. After stroking up and down, riding the pole a couple of times, she thrust her hips backward with a snap that had the audience cheering.

Men and women in the crowd began to rise from their seats and approach the stage. With the pole gripped tight in two hands, she bent forward before straightening—slow and sultry, unbelievably sexy. The curve of her ass in the tight skirt was enough to make Badger grind his back molars.

Jesus.

Holy shit.

Goddamn.

Fuck!

Badger crossed his arms and leaned his back against the wall. Tracking her movements like a hawk, he watched as she moved center stage, gliding on those long legs like the devil herself, pulling the skirt higher with each step. In an effort to save himself, he glanced away. He had to.

A few beats later, the crowd cheered again, and without giving himself permission, Badger whipped his head back around. She was just too fucking hot not to watch. Badger's mouth went dry as she turned her back to the crowd and made a show of tugging down the zipper of the skirt before sliding the fabric down her long legs and stepping out of it.

The hem of the white dress shirt hung past her ass, and as she strutted upstage to the back wall and, more importantly, the pole and mirrors, Badger knew this was only the beginning.

This woman was putting on a show, and by the time she was topless, Badger had a feeling it might be the best show the customers of Deuce's Cabaret had seen in a long-ass time.

For sure, it was already the best show Badger had ever seen.

——

ROSIE PRESSED her hands to the mirror upstage and rolled her hips around. She'd been beyond nervous since she'd gotten hired that morning. Evie, the house mom and apparently also the owner's wife, had been so sweet to her while she'd auditioned earlier in the day and again just now while getting ready. Rosie could've hugged her. She'd even brought Rosie a double shot of Jack Daniels from the bar. Thank God. It was enough to take the edge off but not enough to get her drunk —just what Rosie had needed.

The song ended, and just as she'd directed, the deejay queued up Karise Eden's cover of "It's A Man's World." If she had to get back on the stage, may as well do it with a bang. Rosie turned and slid down the mirror slightly, tugging on the ends of the shirttails as she rolled her hips, using her legs to propel her movements.

Two steps downstage, and she stopped, raised her fingers to the arm of the prop glasses she wore, pinched it between two fingers, and peered over the top of the frames to the customers. As she scanned the crowd, her eyes landed right on him—the bartender from that morning. Rosie couldn't make out the expression on his face, but his eyes were on her. She felt them.

For the whole day, and especially when she'd reported in for her shift, Rosie had been plagued with the feeling that she'd somehow disappointed him. It was stupid. Not like she knew the man—he sure as hell didn't know her. He had no right to judge her, and she had no reason to care. But really, why work in a strip club if he didn't like strippers?

With a wink in his direction, simply to bust his balls, she pulled off the glasses and tossed them aside. Raising her hands to her hair, she yanked the two strategically placed pins free and let the mass of dark thickness fall down around her shoulders. Fine. He didn't like strippers. Well, Rosie wasn't the average stripper, and she intended to show him that.

Without hesitation, Rosie reached for the pole, swung

around and pulled herself up, scissoring her legs into the air before curling herself around the cool steel as if she'd just done this deal yesterday. Technically, she had…

Rosie may've hung up her G-strings and stripper heels two years ago, but she'd continued pole dancing at a local fitness studio in Connecticut. It was strictly to keep her body in shape, as well as release the constant flow of energy that'd always plagued her. Good thing she'd kept at it, or her come-back to the scene might not have been so easy. All things considered, it wasn't going too bad.

But "easy" was a subjective term, really. None of what Rosie was doing was easy. Not emotionally, anyway.

The patrons went a little nuts as she spread her legs wide while suspended upside down. Rosie gazed out over the crowd before righting herself and sliding to the ground into a Russian split. Making a dramatic show of every movement, she cocked her head to the side and tugged open one button of the shirt. Then another. Rosie teased, popping her shoulders and revealing a bit of her cleavage before she let go of the blouse and moved her hands to her hair, shaking out the long length. It felt good, casting her spell on the crowd, the energy from them filling her insides, fueling her to take it another notch higher.

Shifting, she changed her position to a front split and arched backward. In that position, she undid the rest of the buttons on the shirt and peeled the two halves open. With her top discarded, she bent forward, rolled over and up to her feet.

She'd had just enough cash left to go and buy a black, strappy bikini-style top and matching G-string. The skirt and dress shirt she'd already had.

She'd worn them to her husband's funeral.

How apropos she now wear them to make a living—a living Joey had never had a problem with. He'd liked the money too much. *Selfish bastard!* Not like he had a say anymore. Years ago, he was the reason she'd quit. She'd done it to spite him. Now, he was the reason she was back on the pole.

Rosie shoved the thought aside and strutted, slow and easy, downstage and right to a group of men waiting, dollar bills in their hands. Her ass might be hanging out, but she hadn't removed her bra top yet. And already she was making money. Relief washed over her as she turned and squatted down in front of the small group and let them tuck the money they held in the side straps of her G-string. "Thank you."

Rising, she smiled over her shoulder and shot them a wink before stepping away to the other pole. She gripped the steel in both palms, swung her body and flipped herself upside down. As she rotated, Rosie hooked a knee around the bar and let the momentum of the movement spin her.

Keeping her arms out to accentuate the motion of her body, she completed a few more revolutions before rising and righting herself once more.

Godsmack's "Keep Away" began, and as Rosie allowed her body to slow in its revolutions, she extended out of her position until, once again, she was on the floor. She pushed up off the ground and moved center stage. Rosie scanned the crowd, searching for him again.

And found him.

He hadn't moved, and he was still watching. Good.

In the next moment, she unhooked the back clasp on her bra as she scooped up the skirt she'd discarded earlier with her free hand. In one seamless motion, she slipped off the strappy top and slid the black skirt in front of her bare breasts.

Rosie teased the crowd. As she'd always done. As dancers were meant to do.

That was the whole point of a striptease, wasn't it? Maybe she'd shown him that. She sure as hell did the crowd. Whistles sounded from the club floor, and more patrons lined the sides of the stage—dollar bills at the ready.

Still on her knees, she spun away, giving them her back,

but then arched backward to lie on the stage. With one hand tangled in her hair, the other still holding the black fabric to her chest, Rosie undulated her hips, her long legs extended in the air.

After twining them together at the knee and then apart a few times, she slammed the soles of her feet down on the ground, thrust her hips high in the air and tossed the skirt aside. Rosie rolled backward, her legs coming over her body as she pushed herself over and up to her feet.

Adrenaline pulsed through her, and her body hummed from the energy in the crowd. With her hair hanging over one eye, she turned and faced the crowd, finally giving them what they wanted: her bare body. Bare except for the strappy, black G-string.

Rosie walked forward, stopping to roll her head, swinging her long hair around. She'd missed this. The show. The response from the crowd. The high that came from gaining their attention. *All* of their attention. The feeling was unexpected, but no less true. With a bounce and pop of her hips, she swayed in time with the hard beat of the song before moving to each customer lining the stage. As the song played out, she let the searing sound of the guitar and the deep tone of the singer's voice roll through her as each man at the edge of the stage tucked dollar bills in the straps on her hips.

When the song ended and the deejay announced the next dancer, the crowd clapped and whistled right over the top of him. They clapped, for God's sake! Loudly and with vigor. Yeah, she'd missed this. Unable to stifle the pride that automatically rose in her belly, Rosie gave herself a mental pat on the back and gathered the additional dollar bills that'd been tossed onto the stage for her performance.

The next dancer mounted the stage, and just as Rosie was about to step down, she glanced over her shoulder.

His eyes were still locked on her.

But now she could clearly see he wore that same hardened

stare she'd been subjected to that morning. And just like earlier, she felt it like a physical touch. The tingle she'd experienced came right back, too, skittering down her spine. Titillating. The same as it'd done that morning.

And Rosie didn't like it. Not at all.

CHAPTER THREE

Badger watched her the entire time she'd danced. Yes, danced. Unable to take his eyes from her, he watched her until she disappeared down the hall after she'd finished dancing. Yes, dancing.

Strippers these days? They didn't dance anymore. They walked around the stage, took off their tops—almost immediately, maybe did a few spins on the pole, and then rolled around on the floor with their ass in the air in front of a customer, but they sure as fuck didn't dance. They didn't "strip," and they sure as fuck didn't tease.

But this girl—this woman, Arianna, danced. She stripped. Jesus, fuck, *and* she teased.

Badger had been right; she'd put on the best show he'd ever seen. Even in Vegas. Which was saying a lot because those clubs and those bitches? They cost a pretty penny. But not as pretty as Arianna…or whatever the fuck her name was.

Leaning toward the bar, he hollered to Sadie for a shot of JD. She slid it his way, and he tossed it back. Badger didn't normally drink while on the job, but he needed something to help settle the fire that'd started in his gut.

He stroked his palm along the side of his jaw. Strippers

weren't on his "to-do" list. He'd seen too much over the years and been burned one too many times by their brand of fucked-up baggage. If he wanted to get his dick wet, he did it outside the scene. If he wanted something more cozy...well, scratch that.

He didn't ever want more, and he for sure didn't do cozy.

Not like he had time for it anyway, so it didn't really matter. Except this broad... Christ, she had his cock stirring behind his zipper, all ready to come out and play. And that shit was just not happening. No way. No how.

Badger glanced to the hall. She'd be coming out soon to work the bird cage stage—the one that was oh-so-close to his perch.

Which meant he needed to get ghost...

As soon as the thought finished its trip through his mind, the brunette appeared at the mouth of the back hall. Badger froze as she glided across the floor—her black skirt clinging to her narrow hips and the black, strappy top back in place. About five guys got to their feet in steady pursuit of her while others waved her over, vying for her attention. *Shit.*

She paused a moment, a small smile curving her lips as she addressed them. After a moment, she broke through the crowd and continued forward on her black-and-clear platform heels. Badger nodded to one of his guys nearest to her, letting him know to get closer. She stepped behind a customer, out of Badger's line of sight, but she appeared just as fast before jerking to a halt, her arm extended behind her as she spun around.

Then he couldn't see her.

Badger was up and moving. Someone had grabbed her, obviously, and that someone was about to get his ass tossed out on the sidewalk. After Badger educated him on the error of his ways. His man, Stevie, had gotten there first but hadn't grabbed anyone. What the fuck? Badger moved around another patron and stopped dead in his tracks at what he saw.

There was a customer, ass planted in the chair with Arianna bent over him. Dude must've grabbed her, but that grab didn't last long. She was the one doing the grabbing now. She had the guy's wrist in some sort of twist hold, and his face was contorted in pain. Arianna was bent close, almost nose to nose with him, saying something Badger couldn't hear.

Wasting no time, Badger stepped beside her, started to touch his palm to her lower back, but then thought better of it. "Hey, babe? I got it from here."

She didn't look at him. Just kept right on talking. "Listen closely to me. You do not *ever* put your hands on me uninvited. You got me?" She tweaked her hold a bit, and the guy responded with a frantic nod and a loud groan. She glanced at Badger, her dark brown eyes sharp as a hawk, before focusing back on the dude. "It's your lucky day, asshole." Then she released him, straightened, and hit Badger with a look filled with black fire so hot that every muscle in his body went tight. "He's all yours."

Frozen in place, Badger watched her. Completely ensnared in all that he saw—but couldn't decipher—in her gaze as she strutted past him to the small stage.

Holy. Fucking. Shit.

He ran his palm along the back of his neck and glanced back at Stevie, who looked about as shocked as Badger felt. "Eighty-six, this asshole. Find me when you're done."

Stevie nodded, and Badger turned and walked with measured steps back to the bar. What the fuck. She danced, she teased, she stripped, *and* she knew how to take care of herself? *Who* in the *fuck* was this chick, and *where* in the *fuck* did she come from? He wrapped his knuckles on the bar top. "Sadie? Glass. Bottle. Now."

The bartender jumped and then did as he requested. "You okay, Badger?"

He poured, drank, and poured another. Downed that one,

too. Wiping his wrist across his lips, he slammed the glass down. "Yep."

"Oohkay then." Sadie reached for the bottle.

"Leave it." He crossed his arms in front of him on the bar.

Sadie pulled her hand away and tugged the rag hanging from her back pocket free, and wiped the mahogany top down. He glanced over his shoulder to the round stage…and there she was. Of course. Where the fuck else would she be? He turned away and ran his whole palm over his face. After a few beats, he pushed away from the bar and walked toward the front door.

Stevie was on his way back in, and Badger motioned for the bouncer to follow, and they both stepped outside. Badger walked a few feet away from the entrance and pulled his Zippo from his front pocket, his hard pack of reds from the other pocket, and lit up. Once he'd gotten a satisfying drag, he leaned against the brick exterior wall of the club. "What the fuck was that?"

"That was some crazy shit, is what that was. We've had girls shove a customer off, but we ain't never had a girl put a guy in a hold that damn near had a dude pissing his pants."

"Right." Badger took another pull. "What'd he do to her?"

The kid leaned against the wall and ran his palm over his bald scalp. "He tagged her arm as she walked by. Near as I could see, that was it, but I'm guessing he startled her or maybe tugged a little too hard on her. But by time I got over there to handle him, she had him like you saw."

"Shoulda pulled her off."

"Yeah, you're right. In another second, I would've, but I was just so fucking shocked."

Badger took another drag, eyeing his man as he blew out a steady stream of gray smoke. "Fuck." He shook his head. "What's her name?"

"Rick called her Arianna when he announced her."

"Her real name?"

Stevie shrugged. "Dunno, boss. I'll find out, though."

Badger took one last drag of his smoke before flicking it out onto the street. "Nah. All good. I'll get it. Get back inside." He moved around Stevie to the entrance and walked into the club.

By the time he got back to his perch, Arianna had finished her turn on the round stage and was out in the crowd, already doing a lap dance for a customer. Badger did his best not to look at her again. No easy task, considering she'd damn near set him on fire with her gaze when she walked away from him.

He saw something in her eyes. Something more than the sadness he'd recognized that morning. It'd piqued his interest something fierce, and Badger seriously wanted to know what it was, but knew better than to dive into the deep end of that particular pool.

Didn't mean he wasn't curious. He just wasn't stupid.

Arianna's pretty, deep-brown eyes and whatever the hell was behind them were going to have to stay a mystery.

———

ROSIE SAT in the corner of the dressing room, ankle propped on a knee, tying up the laces on her twelve-year-old red Chucks. After tipping out the bar, the door, and Evie, plus the house fee, she had over four hundred bucks in her bag. Four hundred more than she had five hours ago. She'd had better nights back East when she worked the clubs there, but overall, considering it was a Thursday night in an older but clean club in Phoenix, Rosie hadn't done too bad for herself.

She stood and slung the strap of her duffel bag over her shoulder. Most of the girls had already left, heading for food or after-hours parties, which, being the new chick, Rosie wasn't invited to. In truth, being left out stung a little, but she'd get over it.

Not like she was interested in any of that crap anyway. As a woman in her mid-thirties, Rosie felt like her party-girl nights were long gone. Or should be. Late-night drug parties were definitely long gone. No question about that.

Regardless, Rosie wasn't there to make friends. She was there to work and get her rent paid. Perfectly content to just head back to the small studio apartment she'd rented, enjoy a bowl of cereal—because it was all she had in the house—and curl up with a juicy romance novel. And eventually, get some sleep.

She stepped out into the empty hall and moved toward the back exit. Guess she wasn't getting an escort to her car. Whatever, she could definitely take care of herself. She pushed the drop bar on the door and stepped out into the lukewarm, arid night.

"What the hell was that all about?"

Rosie had barely made it two steps into the parking lot before the rumble of his voice hit her like a sledgehammer. She didn't have to look to know exactly who was talking to her as a tingle slid up her spine and spread over her scalp.

After her first set, she realized he was a bouncer, not a bartender. Later in the night, she found out he wasn't *just* a bouncer. He was the king bouncer. She should've figured.

Slowly, she turned her head in his direction. He stood with his ass leaned against the concrete wall of the building. Leg bent with his booted foot propped on the wall. His head was down, a cigarette pinched between his lips and his hands in his pockets.

Though there was lighting in the parking lot, where they stood had very little light, so she couldn't see his face, but she was still close enough to make out his features. Even shadowed, he was just as breathtaking as he'd been that morning and every damn time she'd looked at him while she danced. It should be illegal for a man to be that good looking with a body that incredible. Dude probably snagged pussy anytime he wanted it. Especially in a strip club.

Rosie pivoted to face him and took a deep breath while she did it. "What was what all about?"

He drew on the cigarette, the tip glowing red, before pulling it from his lips and flicking it across the parking lot. "Don't play coy. It doesn't suit you." He pushed away from the wall and wrapped a bandana around his forehead.

How in the hell would he know what suited her? Jesus, he was arrogant. A welcome agitation coursed through her; it was better than the unwelcome attraction she felt. Rosie crossed her arms and cocked her hip to the side. "And pompous doesn't suit you."

"Big difference between pompous and confident."

"Yep, and big difference between coy and a genuine question, too." Done with this and him, she turned, heading for her car. Gorgeous or not, king bouncer was an asshole.

"Arianna?"

Again, barely making it two strides away, she stopped. But rather than turning to face him, she merely looked over her shoulder.

"You got a problem. You let my boys handle it. We clear?"

Oh, *that*. Yeah, okay. Rosie shook her head. So she'd taught some stupid asshole a lesson. Which sent a message to every other dude in the bar that she was not one to be fucked with. It wasn't a big deal. Not all bouncers were created equal, and as a result, she'd always taken care of herself in the clubs —never thought twice about it, either. And because she held her own, the clientele learned not to misbehave with her. Annoyance beat through her, and she turned and moved toward him again. "What's your name?"

He swung a leg over a motorcycle parked to their right. "We clear?"

"Sure. I'll play along. Yeah, we're clear." She gripped the strap of her duffel bag and shifted it. "Name?"

"Badger."

Interesting nickname. She rolled her eyes. "How about your real name?"

"Not something you need to know, *Arianna*." Her stage name rolled off his tongue, sounding like something out of a porno, with an added layer of disgust threaded through it. Then he started the bike and rapped the pipes.

The loud rumble echoed around the empty parking lot, and Rosie narrowed her eyes. Was that a sneer pasted on his lips? Why would he be sneering? He didn't even know her. Fucking hell!

He jerked his chin. "That yours?"

Rosie followed his gaze to her green Toyota before looking back to him. "Why?"

"Get moving. I need to get ghost."

Get ghost? She furrowed her brow. "Yeah. Okay, *Badger*." She tried like hell to match his tone as well as his sneer before pivoting and walking to her car. He probably couldn't even hear her over his motorcycle pipes. But Jesus, why was she baiting him? Not the best way to start out a job. A job she freaking needed. Annoyance at her own behavior settled in her stomach like a sour meal. Ugh. She *should not* care what he thought about her. It didn't matter. He didn't matter.

But dammit, he was watching her. Again. The whole time, as she walked away. She knew it. Not only because he was sitting there on his bike and had given her the order to get gone, but because she felt it like a physical touch.

Again.

CHAPTER FOUR

BADGER DIDN'T TURN around when he heard Rick announce Arianna to the stage. Didn't turn around when he heard the song start playing, either. Fucking Amy Winehouse—Rosie loved to dance to that stuff. It was so goddamn different, just like Rosie was. All the little dresses she somehow managed to make work while she worked the stage, right down to the insanely sexy G-strings and tops, as well as garter belts she wore beneath them. Every bit of it…different.

"Tears Dry On Their Own" echoed through the bar. The only reason he knew the names of the songs was because he'd had a month of listening to them. A whole goddamn month of Rosie and her brand of different up on that friggin' stage. Out on the floor, too. Plus, she worked almost every night. The girl never took a break. Translation: Badger never got a break from her.

He stroked his palm over his beard—which he'd let grow in—scratched his chin, and sighed through his nose. Hell would freeze over before he laid one fingertip on that woman's tight, slender, and completely natural body. But fuck him if there weren't moments he found himself praying for a nor'easter to blow through the scalding desert and make all that touching he kept wanting to do possible.

After taking a swig of his coffee, he turned and surveyed the crowd, careful to avoid her—but he knew she was on one of the poles, damn near touching the ceiling. It was Tuesday night, so there wasn't much doing, but Rosie—or Arianna, rather—had started to attract quite a following with her style of routines. For a weeknight, they were fairly busy.

Business had always been good. But it seemed now, since her arrival on the scene, it was real good. She had to be making a mint, at least as much as anyone could in a club like Deuce's. Satisfied that his two men on the floor had everything covered, Badger headed out the front door to inject some much-needed nicotine into his frayed nerves.

The door closed with a whoosh, sealing the sounds of the music away inside the club. Badger moved a few feet down the sidewalk, leaned against the wall and lit a cigarette. Evie had nothing but good things to say about Rosie, not that he cared to know or had even asked. Evie, for whatever fucking reason, found a way to bring Rosie up any time he was in her presence for more than two minutes. The devil herself needed to save him if the woman was trying to play matchmaker.

Badger finished his smoke and promptly lit another. When he was satisfied she'd be off the stage, he went back inside. Sure enough, she was done with her set and already in the corner giving a lap dance to one of the local patch holders. A flame of jealousy curled in his gut when he saw her long, dark hair splayed across the guy's arm. *Fuck me.*

That was another reason he didn't fuck with strippers. Badger didn't share what belonged to him. Ever. He barely even talked to this woman, didn't know shit about her really, but seeing her rubbing up on some other guy had him ready to spit fire. Not good. Badger jerked his chin to Sadie. "Be back."

She nodded. "Grab me ice?"

"Yep." Badger walked away, making a beeline for the back hall. He needed to get his shit tight and do it fast. It appeared Rosie wasn't going anywhere anytime soon. Neither was he. Getting a hard-on for a pole jockey who may or may not be oh so much more than just a pole jockey made it real fucking hard to stay focused. Distracted was dangerous. People got hurt when there wasn't focus. Badger couldn't afford that. Neither could Deuce or his cabaret.

When Badger got to the ice machine, he realized he'd forgotten the ice buckets. "Goddammit!"

"Looking for these, boss?"

Badger glanced over his shoulder. Rig, one of his bouncers, was standing there, goofy-ass look on his face, bucket dangling from each hand. Badger blew out an exasperated breath. "Apparently."

Rig stepped forward and opened the lid of the machine. "I got you, boss. All good."

"Thanks." Badger clapped him on his back and left him to it. Rig was one of his new guys. Country boy moved there from Arkansas. Fuck if Badger knew what the hell his name meant, but whatever. The kid showed on time, was polite and built like a fucking Mack truck. Then again, the name Rig fit the dude perfectly.

About to enter the office and find some paperwork to bury his face in, Badger stopped short when he heard Evie's voice. Hell no. Nope. Not going in there because the last thing he needed, on top of his already agitated state of mind, was Evie talking about Rosie some more.

Badger glanced up one end of the hall to the other. Sonofabitch, he had nowhere to go. It wasn't like he could leave. *Fuck me!* Badger leaned his back against the wall, covered his face with his hands and let out a loud groan. *Get a goddamn grip, chump!*

"Badger? Are you okay?"

He froze. Oh, fuck. *Fuuuuck! Fuck me!*

———

Rosie moved down the hall, her dress hanging over her arm and a wad of cash in her palm, toward Badger. He looked like someone had just kicked his dog. Not that she could see his face or anything because he had covered it with both hands. "Badger? Did you hear me?"

He dropped his hands but didn't look at her, just stared straight ahead at the wall across from him. "Yep."

Clipped answers and one- or two-word sentences was all she'd ever gotten out of him. He was so damn aloof all the time she really had no idea what his deal was. Rosie shifted the dress and money as she got closer to him. "You sure? I mean, I don't mean to pry, but you look upset."

In the next moment, Evie appeared from the office. "I thought I heard someone out here." She looked to Rosie with a smile. "You need something, honey?"

Badger let out a grunt and ran a palm down his face. Rosie frowned, looking at him. "I'm fine, Evie. Thank you."

"Oh! The new dress! Did it work out okay?"

Rosie focused on her and smiled. "It did, yes. Thanks again for the sewing."

"Anytime, honey. Don't even mention it." She smiled, waving her hand at Rosie. "Badger, isn't it neat all the different and sexy little dresses Rosie wears on stage? I never thought a dancer could work in them, but our Rosie, she does it. Just perfect."

Badger cut his eyes to Rosie, and she swore she felt the disapproval in his expression straight to her toes. "Sure is."

A shiver sped down her spine at the gravelly tone in his voice, and her skin got warm. As always, the effect of his good looks rocked her to her core. In addition to being really fucking good-looking, he was also really fucking intimidating. That, and he was perpetually in a bad mood. And no matter how often she smiled or tried to be sweet to him over the past month since starting at the bar, he always looked at her like she disgusted him.

His gaze stayed on her, assessing, condemning…judging. *Hello, uncomfortable?* Feeling a bit raw and exposed, Rosie fidgeted with the dress, then tucked a stray lock of hair behind her ear before wrapping her arms around her waist. "I wouldn't go that far, Evie. It really just takes a little thought to figure out what'll work and what won't."

"Oh, phooey, let me tell you, honey. I've been in this business for a lot of years. The girls are sweet, but not many of them 'think' much like you do. I still don't know what the hell you're climbing a pole for. But I'll be damned if Deuce or me is ready to let you go should you decide to up and come to your senses." She cocked a hip to the side as a grin tugged at the corners of her lips. "Besides, Badger would miss you."

Badger's head snapped in Evie's direction so fast Rosie swore she heard his neck crack. "Seriously, Evie?" He let out an exasperated sigh.

Holy crap! *Hello, uncomfortable on steroids?* Rosie bit her bottom lip and shifted her weight to one foot. Could she just turn around and run? God, short of him actually telling her how much she disgusted him, the moment could not get any worse.

Evie let out a giggle. "Come on, Badger. Don't be such a hardass. You'd miss her, even if you won't admit it." She winked, turned around, stepped back into the office, and closed the door.

Badger was still staring at the spot Evie no longer stood. The silence stretched, and Rosie started to wonder how it was she was going to make an unnoticed exit. In a desperate attempt at emotional self-preservation, she shoved aside her mortification and shored up her emotional walls.

So what if he didn't like her? Not everyone in the world liked one another. It shouldn't bug her, but it did. More than she'd ever admit. Rosie took a breath and a step back. "It's okay. Evie was just being nice. Glad you're okay. And sorry if I intruded."

He looked back to her, a different expression in his eyes now. One she hadn't the first clue how to read. He blinked, paused a moment or two and then nodded. And Rosie took that as her cue to get moving. She turned but got no more than two steps away.

"I'm fine, Rosie. Thanks for asking."

With her breath held, Rosie glanced over her shoulder. His eyes appeared softer, almost sad. Maybe a little confused, too. It was hard to tell. Either way, she wasn't going to spend any time trying to figure it out. He was a brick wall she didn't need to bang herself against. With her nerves still jumping beneath her skin, she forced a smile. "Anytime."

He nodded, pushed off the wall, and strode past her. The scent of his cologne mixed with a trace of cigarettes and leather wafted into her lungs. Rosie pressed a hand to the wall to steady herself, trying for all she was worth to gain control over her body's response to him while at the same time being tormented by the sight of his beyond-perfect ass.

For fuck's sake, he was just too much. Tall, dark, and dangerous. Plus, deadly sexy with a masculine scent to die for. With her feet rooted to the floor, she watched as Badger continued down the hall and disappeared into the club.

She'd never been with a man like him. Not that she'd been with many men in her life—she and Joey had been together since just after high school. Her husband had been tall but slender, not at all what someone would call a big guy. Though he was definitely good looking and she'd always been attracted to him. She loved him a lot at one time, but sadly, that had faded over the years into more of a platonic kind of love.

But Badger? Christ, Badger inspired a whole other level of what being attracted to a man felt like. Rosie had certainly danced for plenty of guys that looked like Badger and, in the last couple years, served drinks to them. So it wasn't like she'd been under a rock. She'd just never paid much attention before. She couldn't help but pay attention now.

But regardless of how attractive she found him, Rosie was damn sure he didn't think the same of her.

The fucked-up thing was Rosie had heard all about him from Evie. Stuff she probably could've gone her whole life not knowing. For example, apparently, he didn't date the strippers. Like ever. Which was probably why he didn't like Rosie.

Also, Badger was a former patch holder in one of the local motorcycle clubs. According to Evie, he was a really ambitious guy and rose pretty quickly in the ranks. Now he was a bounty hunter, which Rosie thought was pretty fucking cool, though she didn't express that to Evie.

In addition, he ran all the security at Deuce's, which was also pretty cool. He'd been working for Evie and her husband for the last fifteen years. That part had made Rosie's heart swoon just a little bit—knowing that such a hard man could be so loyal.

Oh…and he was single.

Ideas and feelings Rosie had no business entertaining had swirled in her mind and tummy regarding his dating status, but she refused to pay them mind, give them light or let them out of the closet. Hell. No.

It *did not matter* if Badger was available because Rosie was a stripper. Actually, none of anything she knew about him mattered, and frankly, she had no idea why Evie had filled her in on all the Badger deets. But she had.

Rosie shook herself from the thoughts and got her feet moving toward the dressing room. She had at least four more sets to do that night, and if no other girls showed, she might get more. Plus, lap dances were putting her over the top and making rent real easy to cover. She was getting back on her feet, and she was doing it all by herself.

Rosie sure as hell didn't need tall, dark, and dangerous

getting in her way. No matter if he was loyal and happened to be single.

Ugh. Badger was a distraction. And the last thing Rosie needed was a distraction. But damn, the scent of him still lingered in her nostrils as she laid out the costume for her next set. Distracted was apparently going to be her best friend that night, whether she wanted it to be or not.

CHAPTER FIVE

Badger stood in the far back corner of the bar, near the head of the stage, watching the crowd. It was Halloween, and damn near every customer was in costume. Lots of masks, some gruesome, some playful. Someone had a full toothbrush costume on—finding a seat for that moron had been interesting. Every inch of the bar was covered in the standard holiday decorations of bats, cobwebs, and pumpkin lights. Badger had come in early, Evie's orders, to help decorate…which, of course, meant his boys had all been in early, too. After all their hard work, the Halloween party appeared to be in full swing. Badger ran his palm along his jaw. He was fucking exhausted.

The majority of the dancers were wearing the typical stripper Halloween costumes: Bunny ears with a puffy tail, devil horns with a devil's tail or a halo—minus the wings because a lap dance with wings could be a problem. He hadn't seen Rosie yet, so her costume was still a mystery. Though he had to admit, only to himself, of course, he was curious. A few of the guys had started calling out bets regarding what she might pick. Naughty nurse, school teacher or librarian were in the running. One even said Cat Woman.

Badger disagreed with them all, though he didn't so much as make a peep while they speculated. He knew better. She wouldn't pick something so predictable. Rosie would be in something no one would expect. It would be different, and every guy in the house would be drooling at her feet.

Except him.

He wouldn't drool, not visibly anyway. But he'd watch. Not only because that's what he was paid to do, but because that's what he always did when it came to her, even when he tried like hell not to. It was unavoidable and confusing as fuck, so he'd given up forcing himself to not watch nearly a month ago.

There was just something so…well, just unique about Rosie. He couldn't help but watch her. Maybe it was those pretty yet sad brown eyes and the mystery behind them. Or the care she took with each of her dance sets, the outfits and dresses, her moves…fuck him, her moves. Every bit of it was enough to make a sane man lose his ever-loving mind to lust and intrigue.

But whatever it was, whichever thing, didn't matter. She was just different, and all that different made him want things he shouldn't want and wouldn't take. So, instead of touching her, Badger watched her. He watched when she danced onstage but didn't watch when she was on a customer's lap because the sight of that made him want to crack a mother-fucker's skull open.

Outside of that, he avoided her like the fucking black plague.

"Ladies and less than gentlemen, let me hear you make some noise for the best Halloween bash in the valley!" Rick's voice boomed over the sound system, and the crowd went nuts. "Are you ready for your favorite dancer?"

The crowd cheered again and Badger shifted his weight, settling with both feet braced apart, arms crossed. She was coming, and he knew it. Not because Rick had just called out what had become her standard intro, but by the way the knot curled tight in his gut and his skin itched.

"I can't hear you." Rick paused, and the crowd got louder. "Come on, Phoenix, you better make our girl feel welcome. You've been waiting for her. Let me hear you now. Shout your love for *Ariannaaaa!*"

As the customers yelled out, calling her name, whistles sounding from several people, the lights dimmed…and then the crowd went quiet. The first words of Hozier's "Take Me To Church" cut the silence, and Badger watched as the two small spotlights came up and—

Badger's breath caught in his throat.

She stood just past the up-stage pole, shrouded in a hooded white cloak. Two black silk drapes hung from the handles on the old spinner wheel, mounted in the ceiling center stage. No one used that thing anymore—except Rosie. The young breed of strippers were more or less happy to play on the poles rather than mess with the spinner.

It seemed tonight, Rosie had something different planned for it.

He watched as she danced, keeping her body hidden under the cloak. She glided between each pole downstage, her movements loose yet deliberate and definitely titillating. As she grabbed hold of a pole with both hands, she swung herself around, the cloak flaring out behind her as she twisted her body and somehow managed to not get tangled. Half the time, Badger thought he was going to have a fucking heart attack watching her. But she never faltered. Not once.

Rosie dropped down and walked back to center stage. As the song ended, the lights dimmed again, and Beyonce's "Crazy In Love," the slow version, began. In the shadow, Badger saw the cloak drop to the ground but couldn't make out what she wore beneath it. He tracked her movement and saw the silk drapes hanging from the spinner sway. The lights came up slowly, in time with the beat, and Badger's eyes went wide.

Clad in a second skin—a red and nearly transparent body suit—Rosie had both scarves gripped in her hands and began climbing upward, using her legs and feet as leverage to propel herself upward. When she'd risen at least three feet in the air, she somehow hooked an ankle, pulled the silk fabric tight over her thighs and suspended herself sideways.

Badger stood frozen, arms still crossed over his broad chest. He didn't want to blink, didn't want to miss a moment of this display. Rosie went through a series of what he could only call aerial acrobatics, the kind of shit he'd only seen on YouTube or in Vegas. She wasn't Cirque du Soleil, but she was pretty fucking amazing nonetheless. Splits, flips, and spins. Amazing. Un-fucking-believable.

They'd throw money tonight for her. She was going to bring the rain—an old saying in the business. There wasn't a doubt in Badger's mind. Hell, even he'd give up his hard-earned pay for what he was playing witness to at that moment.

Then it happened, just as he'd predicted, dollar bills flitted through the air, covering the stage below her. Hundreds of them as the crowd went absolutely insane while Rosie spun, her body parallel to the stage and wrapped in black silk.

She unrolled herself as the song ended, and Blue October's "Hate Me" began. Rosie stood center stage again and slowly peeled off the top half of her body suit and then the bra top, baring her breasts. She moved to one pole and executed another intricate move, then as she strutted to the other, she unpeeled the bottom half of the bodysuit, revealing a red G-string.

Badger's mouth went dry, and he ran his palm over his jaw and then the back of his neck. Her dark nipples were fully erect as she, again, mounted a pole, hooked it with the back of one leg, and with a swing, arched her body in a perfect arc around it, one arm extended in front of her. Spinning, spinning, spinning…as money flew around her.

She was fucking beautiful.

Not an angel or a devil, but something in between.

Pure temptation.

———

As ROSIE's third song neared the end, signaling the end of her set, she closed her eyes and let the motion of her body spinning on the pole take her away—if only for a few seconds. She knew she'd made a killing.

Rosie remembered the first time customers had thrown money at her. The sound of those bills flying through the air —like nothing she'd ever heard in her life. She was just a kid, barely twenty years old, dancing at an upscale gentleman's club in Danbury, Connecticut. There was a lot of money to be made there, and the older strippers who had been on the scene too long had taught her how to make it. Now, she was the old one on the scene, but it didn't matter, right?

At thirty-six, Rosie wasn't necessarily old, but on the scene, she definitely was. Old or not, she was leading the parade. And it was fucking raining money…

Rosie slid down the pole and spun away. The dramatic ending of the song came over the sound system as Rosie walked along the edges of the stage, pausing as customers stuffed bills in the sides of her G-string. She blew them all kisses, nodding, winking, and smiling at many of the regulars that were there for her. Just for her.

It was crazy, but it felt good. *Really good* to be wanted or sought after. Appreciated even. Though it was a fucked-up way to earn that admiration, she'd take it. Not like she had anyone special, or anyone at all really, to shower her with praise or compliments. Women wanted to feel that admiration, even if they didn't need it. They all deserved it.

Speaking of admiration, she'd seen Badger standing beside the head of the stage during her set. He'd watched her the whole time. She wasn't surprised because the behavior wasn't new. It'd become something that went on whenever he was on shift now.

He watched. She danced.

And she did it knowing his eyes were on her the whole time.

Although Rosie had grown accustomed to his gaze on her, she had no clue why he watched her. But she'd be a liar if she said she didn't like it. She did. Badger's eyes on her were as good as if he was touching her…his gaze was *that* penetrating. And she'd begun to crave the feel of his stare on her body. Because of that, she'd also be a liar if she said she didn't sometimes, if not all the time, dance *just* for him now.

In the beginning, Rosie felt like she had something to prove to him—to show him she was different, especially after realizing the reason he didn't like her was likely because she was a stripper. So completely unfair. She wasn't *just* a stripper. Rosie was so much more than that.

And at that moment, she was a stripper who'd just… Made. It. Rain!

Rosie turned to gather the rest of her money off the stage. Her eyes went wide at what lay before her. The stage was covered, absolutely coated in various bills. Movement to her right caught her attention, and suddenly, Badger was on the stage.

With her.

Oh God.

Quickly, she scanned the floor of the stage, locating the bra top of her costume. As she grabbed it, desperate to cover her body in front of him—which made absolutely not one bit of sense—she felt her cloak cover her shoulders.

"Givin' you a hand."

A shiver ran down her spine at the low rumble of his voice

at her ear. Cursing her body, she glanced over her shoulder at him. His offer to help, as well as cover her with her cloak, both shocked and touched her, but also confused her. Rosie nodded. "Thanks."

He jerked his chin once and then set to gathering her money. Rosie quickly fastened her top, and instead used the cloak to pile money into. When they'd finally gotten it all, Badger gathered up the cloak, took her by the back of the arm and escorted her off the stage.

The deejay announced the next dancer just as Badger rounded the corner of the hall, his fingers still wrapped tight around her upper arm. Maybe he was worried someone would try and grab her money? His strides were so long in comparison to hers…for every step he took, Rosie took three in order to keep up. Was he rushing? Was he annoyed?

She glanced at his profile. Eyes straight ahead, lips pressed in a hard line, jaw set firm, so much so that a muscle ticked in his cheek. Jesus Christ, she still couldn't read this scary, beautiful man. But she wanted to.

Especially because in a matter of a few minutes, he'd successfully knocked her off her high "look at me and how kickass I am" horse. She felt her face get hot as foolishness settled like a rock in her stomach. Rosie went to move into the dressing room, but Badger kept hold of her and continued down the hall. She faltered but caught her footing, thank God. "Hey, uhhmm…where we going?"

"Office."

Shit. He practically growled the word at her. No way she'd done anything wrong. No reason for him to be so harsh in his tone to her, either. So, fine. Whatever. Maybe her ego *had* gotten a little bigger than necessary. There was no reason to be such a dick to her. And frankly, she'd had it with him. Rosie scowled, ready to lay into him. "Why? Did I—"

"Too much cash. It'll be safer in the office."

What? Safer? *Oookay*, that was unexpected. She frowned.

"Oh… Uhmm." It was pretty damn smart of him, actually. Rosie hadn't even thought about it. "Thanks."

Badger stayed silent as he stepped into the office. Pulling her with him, he shut the door. After letting go of her arm, he crouched low next to the far side of the desk. Rosie watched, shifting her weight on her stripper heels, as nervous energy boomeranged through her body.

She glanced down. Clad in only her G-string and the bra top, the rest of her body suit still up on the stage, and she suddenly felt very…naked. Which was just as stupid as her thoughts on stage because, hello, she'd been naked in front of him a million times, and he'd watched her damn near every one of those times.

Rosie glanced away from him, and whatever he was doing that she couldn't see. The difference was being alone with him, she felt completely bare—naked at a soul-deep level.

Swallowing past the knot that'd formed in her throat, she crossed her arms over her stomach, wanting nothing more than to shield herself. A loud thud in the room brought her focus back to him.

Badger got to his feet and smoothed his palms down his denim-clad thighs. "All locked up. You can get it end of night." He moved for the door—the very one she was blocking. "'Scuse me."

"Sorry." She froze for what felt like forever, wanting to say something, anything to him. He just waited. Staring. Nearly expressionless. Forcing herself to move, Rosie stepped aside, and he opened the door. Desperation kicked in, and she said the only thing she could think of. "I… I left my costume on the stage."

Badger glanced at her over his shoulder. "I'll grab it."

"All ri—"

And then he just walked away.

"He watches me, but he hates me. Like, *really* hates me." Rosie blew out a breath and stepped into the hall. She wasn't a woman who ever gave a shit if someone liked her or not. Badger didn't like her, big deal. But hate? Jesus. That stung.

She shouldn't give a shit. He was no one to her.

But she did.

She really fucking did.

And that sucked.

CHAPTER SIX

With her small, off-white purse tucked under her arm, Rosie managed to get the back door to Deuce's open. But it wasn't easy. She held a homemade lattice-top apple pie tight in her hands, along with a grocery bag filled with Cool Whip, a bottle of something special, and fresh strawberries to go with the something special hanging from her wrist.

The simple, high-heeled sandals she wore echoed on the linoleum floor of the long back corridor leading to the main bar. As she neared the end of the hall, the soulful sound of Kenny Wayne Shepherd's "Live On" filled her ears. When she emerged, Rosie was beyond surprised and stopped short, completely in awe of what she saw.

Deuce's Cabaret had been turned into a beautiful dining hall. Four long tables set in a square formation took up the main area, all draped in white tablecloths. Each had center-pieces filled with candles and flowers, as well as place settings at each seat. Along the wall, opposite the bar, were two more tables covered in an array of dishes for their feast. Above the bar hung a sign proclaiming "Happy Thanksgiving."

One of the other dancers, Sabrina, came over. "Hey, girlie. Wow, you look pretty! Then again, you always do. Let me take that for you." She bent and gave Rosie a peck on the cheek before grabbing the pie from Rosie's hands.

"Thanks. So do you." Rosie smiled and followed her to the food tables. Sabrina was one of the few girls Rosie had gotten friendly with since starting at the bar a few months ago. Mostly because Sabrina had always been sweet to her. Rosie set the bag down and removed its contents. "This is incredible. Do they do this every year?"

"I guess so, yeah. I was here last year, and it was the same. Wait 'til Christmas. Evie goes all out." Sabrina pulled the foil off Rosie's pie and set it near the other desserts. "Holy crap, that pie looks *deelish*!"

"Thanks. My grandmother's recipe. It's to die for, provided it came out right." With a smile, Rosie smoothed the front of her dark green wrap dress. "I've never known bar owners like Deuce and Evie before. Well, not any that owned a strip club anyway."

"I know, me either. It's cool that those of us who are otherwise unattached have a place to go for the holidays. I guess Evie takes in strays, too. But don't tell anyone I said that." Sabrina winked. "Ready for a drink— Oh, wait, you brought something, right?"

"Yeah. It's no big deal, just being polite."

Sabrina laughed. "Definitely polite. I never would've thought to do that." She took Rosie's hand and led her to the bar. "Cute sandals, by the way. You do realize it's winter, right?"

"Winter? Sabby, this isn't winter. In fact, I wake up every day and look out the sliding glass door in my little apartment and think, 'Oh, look! Another sunny day.' I plan on wearing sandals as much and as often as I can."

"I give it a year, and your blood will thin out. You'll be wearing boots and a turtleneck this time next year, talking about how cold out it is."

"Never gonna happen." Rosie shook her head with a

laugh and set the bottle of Verdi Spumanti on the bar along with the strawberries.

"If you say so. Just mark my words so I can say I told you so." Sabrina turned and knocked on the bar. "Hey, sweetness. How about getting two pretty ladies a drink?"

Rig, the newest of the bouncers, looked over from behind the bar. "Absolutely!" With a wink, he strode in their direction. "By the way, pretty's an understatement. What can I get you two beauties?"

"Aw, you're so sweet." Sabby leaned over the bar and pinched his cheek. "Give me a shot of Jose, and I'll chase it with a vodka cranberry." She turned to Rosie. "You?"

"How about a glass for this?" She held up the bottle. "And your small cutting board and paring knife for these, please?" She smiled.

Rig flipped the white bar rag he held over his shoulder and smiled at Rosie. "How 'bout instead, *I* cut up the berries and take the bottle and stick it on ice for you, ma'am?" He grabbed the bottle and held it out in front of him, eyeing the label. "Wow, looks fancy. Verdi…Spoo-what?"

"Spumanti." Rosie laughed. "It's just sparkling wine. Not all that fancy, really."

"Looks pretty fancy to me." He smiled and walked to the other end of the bar.

Rosie dug in her clutch for some money. By the time she'd separated a twenty, Rig was back with Sabrina's drink. Rosie went to hand him the cash. "Let me get Sabrina's."

"No, ma'am. *These* are on Deuce and Evie." He smiled.

"Oh. Well, okay. At least let me tip you." She slid the twenty his way.

He slid it back and winked. "Respectfully decline. No tips, either."

"Jeez." She smiled. "How about a thank you then?"

"Seeing you all dressed up is thank you enough, Miss Rosie." He winked and stepped away.

"*Ooooh*! Someone's got a crush. Lucky you." Sabrina bumped Rosie's shoulder with her own.

"Are you kidding? I've got at least ten years on that kid, maybe even fifteen." Rosie laughed and watched while Rig sliced up the strawberries.

"First of all, you're not *that* old. Second, young is fun! Or so I hear. Plus, he's a country boy. I bet you could corrupt the hell out of him." Sabrina grinned before tossing back her shot of tequila.

"Miss Rosie, what'm I supposed to do with the berries?" Rig called to her.

Rosie shook her head at Sabby before focusing on Rig. "Toss a few in my glass and set the rest on ice in the container."

"Toss a few in the sparklin' spoo stuff?"

"Yes. With the spoo stuff." She giggled. Lord, he seriously was entirely too cute with his Southern accent.

Rig walked her wine glass filled with sparkling wine, strawberries floating at the top, over to her. He smiled his bright smile. "Here you go, Miss Rosie."

"Why, thank you, sir." Rosie took the glass from him and looked to Sabby. "Shall we toa—"

"Woman, only you'd wear a dress like that and be holding a wine glass with fruit floating in it."

Rosie froze at the sound of his voice, and a shiver raced down her spine. Dammit, would she ever stop reacting that way to him? With great effort, she put a lid on her ass-backward physical response. He'd never said so many words to her in one sentence, but worse, when he did speak to her, his words always carried such a harsh undertone. Now was no different.

Gathering her courage, Rosie twisted around to face him.

Badger's eyes locked directly onto hers...like a predator who'd found its prey. Another shiver skittered down Rosie's spine and then sped through her body. She cleared her throat and quickly avoided his sharp gaze. But instead of looking away, her traitorous eyes landed on his body. God help her.

Of course, he was dressed different from his usual T-shirt and jeans, and Rosie bit her lip at the sight of him. Sage-green button-up shirt, which hugged his broad chest and narrow waist to perfection. Black jeans and black motorcycle boots.

Why the hell had she picked *this* color of dress from all the others in her small closet? Christ, they looked like a matching set. "Sorry you don't like it." Rosie blew out a breath and turned back around to face the bar.

Happy fucking Thanksgiving!

She tilted her glass to her lips and took a long swallow. Could she just run now and save herself the humiliation?

"Didn't say that." Badger stepped beside Rosie and rested his forearms on the bar. She was always so goddamn skittish around him and pretty much never met his eyes. He didn't know what to make of it, except that he didn't like it, and he sure as shit didn't trust it. When a person couldn't meet another's gaze, it usually meant they had something to hide. That something usually being past baggage. In any and every form, and none of it being good.

She sure was pretty, though. Too goddamn pretty. He shook his head. So different. All the other strippers came to these shindigs in what they considered their best attire. Translation: A flashy short dress that was better suited for clubbing and not a holiday dinner, paired with the same damn platform heels they wore onstage.

But not Rosie. No, she wore a dark green dress. Not slutty, not flashy, and definitely not club-ready. Just simple, classy, and pretty. On her feet was a pair of high-heeled sandals of the elegant variety—as in, minus the platform.

She sipped her drink, and Badger watched, smoothing his palm over his beard. "What are you drinking exactly?"

She set her glass down and briefly glanced at him. "It's just spumanti." She looked down and brushed something invisible off her lap. "With strawberries in it."

"You want a shot, boss?" Rig asked.

"That'll do." He shifted and faced her. "Spumanti, huh? Not sure I'm familiar." He lifted the glass from her palm. "Mind if I take a sip?" Before he had the edge to his lips, her eyes were on him. Perfect. Though she wore a bit of a scowl. Holding her gaze, Badger tilted the glass and took a small sample. The sweet flavor spread over his tongue, and he swallowed. Resisting the urge to drink more, he set the glass down. "Not what I expected."

She blinked. "Nothing ever is."

He quirked one brow. "Cynical much?"

"Maybe." She set the glass down. "Did you like it?"

He did. A lot, actually. "It's all right. A bit fancy for my tastes."

"Suit yourself." She shrugged and took another sip.

Badger watched her full pink lips close over the edge of the glass, and his dick thickened behind his zipper. The small rumble of a growl escaped before he had a chance to catch it, and he covered it by clearing his throat.

A vision of what they would look like wrapped around his cock had every inch of his skin tight. Blowing out a breath, he jerked his chin to Rig, who was busy talking to one of the dancers. "Rig, you forget something?"

"Huh? Oh! Shit. Yeah. Sorry, boss." Rig moved like a fire was under his ass and set a shot glass down in front of Badger and filled it.

"Leave the bottle."

Rig nodded and stepped away. Badger tossed the shot back and refilled the glass.

As he was about to toss back the second, Rosie shifted off

the barstool and smoothed the front of her dress. "If you'll excuse me."

Without giving himself permission, Badger reached out and circled her upper arm with his fingers. "Hey." She turned, glanced down at his hand and then to his face. The expression she wore looked a whole lot like "get your fucking hands off me," but Badger ignored it. "Your dress?"

Rosie shifted her weight. "What about it?"

Badger glanced down her body. Her nipples were hard. The tight points making their presence known through the thin fabric. Jesus fucking Christ, she was killing him. He grunted, trying to get his mind back on track. "Go easy, woman. It's pretty. You look real pretty, Rosie. Beautiful even. That's all I meant."

He let go of her arm, faced the bar and downed the shot. He'd meant what he said. Every woman deserved to be told they were beautiful. Especially when it was true, but that was about all she'd get from him. Anything more was too risky. Especially with those precious nips of hers calling his name.

God, what he'd do to those perfect handfuls. He'd never really been a breast man, which meant the bigger variety never did much for him. But he sure as hell was a nipple guy —especially small areolas tipped with nipples the size of raspberries. Perfect for biting. Badger let out another grunt as he cleared his throat.

"Thanks. I think."

He glanced at her as he poured another shot. "You think?"

"I don't know. I just…I can't read you, Badger. Frankly, it's confusing. But it's very clear you don't like me. I just don't know why." She shrugged.

He let out a small chuckle and tried his damnedest to block out the sadness radiating from her eyes. "Never said I didn't like you. And not many can read me. Don't stress yourself trying."

"*Ooohkay*. Never mind then." She stepped away.

Badger lifted the shot glass and sipped. He was not going to turn around to see where she went.

Was not.

He didn't care.

Fuck! Dammit. Yeah, he did.

Which wasn't good.

Badger spun on the stool and glanced around the bar. She was nowhere in sight. Sonofabitch, did she leave? He stood and moved toward the back hall.

"Lose something?"

Badger stopped and looked at Deuce. "Not last time I checked."

His boss stroked his hand down his long beard. "Maybe you should check again."

"Deuce, the fuck are you talking about?" A beat of annoyance rolled through him, and Badger crossed his arms.

"Uh-huh. Have a seat with me, brother." His boss patted the table in front of the open chair.

Badger braced his hands on the back of the chair and bent low. "Listen…I don't know what you're gonna say, but I got an idea. So, save it."

Deuce laughed, his body shaking as he continued to stroke his beard. "She's different, Badger."

Badger straightened and crossed his arms. "And?"

"That's it. I figure you'll figure out what to do with her from there." Deuce tilted his beer to his lips.

With a grunt, Badger shifted his weight and stared at the hall Rosie had disappeared down. "Yeah. She's different. She's also got baggage, likely the complicated kind."

"Might be worth it."

"Doubtful." Badger clapped Deuce on his shoulder and stepped away.

Blowing out a harsh breath, he made his way down the hall—looking for her but telling himself the whole time he wasn't *really* looking for her. He neared the dressing room and peered inside. Lights were off, and it was empty. Badger continued down the hall on his journey of not seeking out Rosie. When he neared the office, he slowed his roll as the sound of Evie's voice echoed through the corridor. It was quickly followed by Rosie's laugh—the sound of it rippling over Badger's skin like she'd touched him with her fingertips.

Badger stopped and pressed his back against the wall. This whole situation was fucked and would turn into a shit-storm if he gave any more gas to his attraction to her. She couldn't read him, thought he didn't like her. Stupid woman. She just wasn't paying attention.

Then again…it wasn't like he was putting out any vibes for her to pay attention to. He'd been gruff and short with her pretty much from the minute he'd laid eyes on her. Her laugh echoed around him again, and Badger fisted his hands at his sides as the sound resonated straight to his balls.

Fuck. Fuck. Fucking fuck! He bent his head and ran his palm over his beard. *Walk away. Walk the fuck away.* Too complicated. Too much baggage. He just knew it—felt it in his gut. Badger pushed away from the wall and moved back down the hall to the open area. Another shot of Jack might help him get his head on straight, or…it might have him thinking with the head south of his belt…

One way or the other, his head would be warm and cozy.

CHAPTER SEVEN

THE SOUND of Rosie's cell ringing drew her from the deep sleep she'd been in. Reaching blindly for the little side table, she found the charging cable and tugged the device onto the bed. Rosie squinted at the screen and cleared her throat. It was a local number she didn't recognize, but hit "Talk" anyway and put the phone to her ear. "Hello?"

"Hey, girlie girl. Wake up, and let's go shopping!"

Whoa! Way too much enthusiasm at that early—Rosie glanced at the clock—okay, late hour. It was almost twelve-thirty in the afternoon. She closed her eyes and rubbed her forehead. "Um, who is this?"

"Oh, sorry." The woman giggled. "It's Sabby. Evie gave me your number. I hope you don't mind."

Oh, wow! So much for employee privacy. Okay then. "No. Not at all." Rosie tugged a pillow over her face, knowing she was just being grumpy because she was tired.

"So, what do you say? Wanna come shopping with me? We can have a late lunch…or early dinner. You're not working today, right?"

Rosie pulled the scrunchie from her hair and dragged her fingers through the long length as she sat up. Did she have work today? Rosie glanced around, trying to orient herself. "What day is it again? Oh wait…it's Sunday, right? Yeah. No, I'm off. Hang on, aren't you working?"

"Yes, it's Sunday." Sabby laughed again. "Nope, not going in today. I didn't get everything I wanted last week on Black Friday, and this week's been a blur, so I figured I'd take the day off and give Metrocenter a twirl. Was hoping maybe you'd want to come, and we could make it a girls' day."

Rosie stood and wandered to the bathroom. A girls' day. Ever since her husband was murdered, she'd existed in autopilot mode. Moving through each day like a robot, doing the next thing in front of her that needed doing. Rosie couldn't remember the last time she'd really taken any time for herself. A girls' day was absolutely what she needed. "You know what? I think that sounds great! Need to grab a shower, though. Is that okay? I'll be quick. Promise."

"Of course. Is an hour enough time?"

Rosie laughed. "I'm not planning on anything fancy, so thirty minutes'll be fine."

"Perfect! Give me your address, and I'll head over a little before one."

After relaying the address, Rosie set the phone down and jumped in the shower. Once done, she did a quick and light makeup job and piled her hair in a messy bun. Donning a pair of jeans, flip-flops, and long-sleeve T-shirt, she headed to the small kitchenette in her studio apartment.

She had just enough time to microwave a cup of yesterday's coffee when the doorbell chimed. With mug in hand, Rosie walked the three steps of distance from her small kitchen to reach the entryway, peered through the peephole, and, seeing who it was, opened the door. "Hey there!"

"Hey, girlie. You ready?"

Rosie took a sip of the semi-hot coffee. "Yes. I'm kind of hungry, though. Can we eat first?"

"Sure. Since I woke you, do you want breakfast or lunch? Or brunch? It is Sunday, after all." Sabby smiled.

"Brunch sounds fantastic." Rosie stepped to the side, placed the mug in the sink, and grabbed her purse from the small counter. "You driving?"

"Definitely driving. There's some places over by the mall we can grab brunch *and* mimosas. I know I'm still a little hungover from last night's shift."

"All right. Lead the way."

After locking the door behind her, Rosie followed Sabby out to the front of her building and then stood next to the open passenger door of a fire-engine red, incredibly sporty-looking coupe.

"Crap. Sorry. Let me get this out of the way." Sabby grabbed four different pairs of stripper heels along with several costume pieces from the front seat and floorboard and tossed them to the small space behind the front seats. "I swear I'm more organized than this."

Rosie slid into the leather front seat. "This is an amazing car. I mean, a *really* amazing car." She closed the door. "What kind is it?"

"Thanks! I just got it in October. It's a Nissan 370Z." Sabby beamed and reached to—

Whoa! She pushed a button, and the car started with a rumble. Holy wow! Rosie couldn't stop the giggle that bubbled out of her. "It's gorgeous and still smells new."

Sabby groaned as she backed out of the parking space. "I know! I love it!"

"The car or the smell?"

"Both!" She shifted into gear and zoomed through the parking lot to the exit.

"Agreed." Rosie reached back and grabbed for the seat-belt. She'd been so distracted by the car she'd forgotten to put it on. And by the looks of how her friend was tearing ass into traffic, she was going to need it.

They arrived safely at their destination. The restaurant her friend picked was a nice little modern American-style eatery, which, amazingly, only served breakfast foods but in a million different ways. And as Sabby had wanted, mimosas.

Once settled at their quaint two-person table in the back of the dining area, full plates in front of them, Rosie took her first sip of what tasted like the most glorious coffee in the world. She closed her eyes and let the sounds and scents of the restaurant weave around her.

"You're funny, Rosie."

Rosie focused on Sabby. "Thanks, I think. How so?"

"You got this look on your face…like this is the best thing that's ever happened to you. I know that can't be true." Sabby bit into a piece of bacon. "I think it's sweet, actually."

Rosie set her coffee cup down on its saucer. "Maybe *it is* the best thing that's ever happened to me." She shrugged.

"But you're—"

"A stripper?" Rosie cut into her Belgian waffle covered in whipped cream and strawberries.

"Older."

"Gee, thanks." Rosie laughed and took a bite.

"No, I mean. Believe me, you're fucking hot. Totally hot, especially onstage. You're making a killing out there and showing the rest of us up. What I meant was you're older than me, so you've had to have done cool things in your life. Especially because you're a stripper." She shoveled in some eggs and spoke around them. "I mean…how have you not been getting wined and dined by customers?"

"Well." Rosie swallowed her mouthful of food. "I stopped stripping over two years ago. And I mean no offense, but letting customers wine and dine me wasn't really my thing back then. It's still not."

"None taken. So, you got out. Why'd you come back?" Sabby sipped her mimosa.

Rosie shrugged. "I moved here for a fresh start, but things

didn't go as smoothly as I wanted. And I needed the money. Fastest way to make it is the stage."

"Yeah, I get it. I started a couple years ago just to put myself through school, but eventually, it got harder to get up and make my classes. Sometimes, I don't think I ever want to quit dancing now. The money's too good." She took another sip of her drink. "I mean, seriously, look at my car? Wouldn't have that if I wasn't dancing."

"Take it from the old lady." Rosie winked. "You should go back to school."

"Old lady? Whatever. But yeah, you're probably right." She glanced around the restaurant, a resigned look in her eyes. "I'll go back someday."

"I hope you do." Rosie pursed her lips. "What did you want to be?"

"Justice and Law Administration. I wanted to work in Juvenile Probation." Her friend smiled.

Rosie nodded. "That sounds really, really cool. Money's probably not as good, but you'd be doing good in the world, helping kids, and that's worth a lot more."

"Thanks. That means a lot." Sabby raised her mimosa. "Here's to our future!"

With a smile, Rosie picked up her mimosa, which she hadn't touched yet, and clinked the edge to Sabby's. "Our future."

They each had a sip, or rather, Sabby downed the remainder of hers before digging back into her food. Rosie watched her friend for a moment and finally attended to her own meal. It was strange, listening to her new friend talk about her future. As young as she was, she had so much to look forward to, but she'd have to act soon. The longer a girl waited, the harder it became to leave the stage.

Rosie had started her dancing career at the age of nineteen. And she'd known many girls just like Sabby, best of intentions that never went anywhere. The lure of the scene was a hard thing to resist, and many never got out. But Rosie had been with Joey, so the "scene" never held appeal for her. The wining and dining from customers was limited to what they gave her in the bar. If a customer wanted her to sit next to him while he steadily tipped her and bought her drinks, she'd do it. If one paid for lap dance after lap dance, she'd do that, too.

But once the customers were gone and the lights came up, Rosie would go home to her boyfriend—who, not long after, became her husband. Joey had no issue with her stripping. Years later, when things weren't so great between them, she'd realized it spoke volumes that he didn't have a problem with it. He actually pushed her to keep at it. Joey liked the money. Plain and simple.

She'd spent fifteen years on the stage, in many different clubs around the state, dancing topless for customers. Every time she thought Joey might have a job good enough for her to hang up her heels, he'd end up getting arrested again and eventually going back to jail. She'd been trapped. Trapped by him and by the money.

"So, what's going on between you and Badger?"

Rosie almost choked on a mouthful as Sabby's question both pulled Rosie from memory lane and shocked the shit out of her. She swallowed and wiped her mouth. Holy crap, where had that come from? "I…um…nothing." She shrugged. "What makes you think something's going on?"

Sabby leaned forward. "Seriously? Girlie, he watches you like a hawk when you're onstage. Don't tell me you haven't noticed. I mean, you'd have to be dead to not notice how that man watches you."

Oh, she'd noticed, all right. "How do you think he watches me?"

"There's really nothing going on? Damn…I thought for sure." Sabby slid her glass to the edge of the table, and the waiter refilled it for her. "For real, he watches you like you're his woman."

"Like I'm—" Rosie frowned. "No way."

"Yes, way. Let me tell you, it's totally fucking hot, too. Crystalline said he even growled one night a week or so ago." Sabby took a sip of her mimosa and continued. "How have you not noticed this?"

"I've noticed. Sure. But I know the man can't stand me, so I doubt there's anything other than disgust behind it."

"Disgust?" Sabby jerked her head back. "There's no disgust in his gaze when he watches you, Rosie. That man has a hard-on for you. In a big way."

Shock plowed through Rosie at her friend's words. It had never occurred to her that Badger could have a thing for her. And yeah, she thought he was attractive and sexy and dangerous…but it wasn't like she was interested. Was she? "Maybe you're right. I guess I never gave it much thought."

Sabby forked up a mouthful and spoke around it. "Girlie, if that were me, I'd be jumping all over that man. In a hot minute."

"I'll keep that in mind." Rosie laughed and took another sip of her mimosa.

Maybe she *was* interested in Badger. She set her glass down and focused on her plate. Technically, she was single. Still mourning—sort of—for her dead husband, but definitely single.

There had been days early on that she'd missed Joey with an ache so fierce it was physical. But as the months passed, it'd lessened. Considerably. On occasion, a memory would hit her, and she'd find herself fuming at him rather than wishing he were still with her.

Remembering all the bullshit, remembering how many chances she'd given him—none of it without wishing she'd done things differently—or how many times they'd been evicted because he'd blown their rent money. She was grateful she didn't have to live that way anymore.

Over the years, the love she had for him had died, at least the in-love part did. But she'd stayed with him anyway. Christ, they'd been together since forever. How could she not? Rosie had been his home base. The place he came back to after each stint behind bars…

She blew out a sigh and picked at the waffle on her plate. All of that was done now. And although she wouldn't have picked for it to end the way it did, it had, and she'd found a way to move forward.

Rosie had come to Phoenix on a mission to start fresh. Change her future. Since she'd ended up back onstage, things hadn't exactly gone as planned, but that didn't mean she couldn't still change it. She could. And she would.

But now she wondered if Badger would somehow play a part in that future. Rosie took another bite of waffle and decided it didn't matter whether he did or not. She'd do whatever she needed to do to move forward.

Rosie was a fighter. A survivor. She'd learned early on how to be.

CHAPTER EIGHT

ROSIE SWUNG UPSIDE DOWN, one leg hooked around the slim pole, her back arched as she formed a perfect arch with her body. The powerful lyrics from Sia's "Chandelier" flowed through the club's sound system, wrapping around Rosie as she let herself get lost in the beat.

It'd been about two weeks since Thanksgiving. And Badger hadn't said a word to her. Ever since Sabby had brought up Badger watching Rosie while she danced, she hadn't stopped thinking about the attempted conversation on Turkey Day.

Now, the only thing she was getting from him was a whole lot of grunts or groans. A couple grumbles, too. But that was it. No words, not even clipped ones laced with disgust.

Rosie didn't get it. And really, she'd grown damn sick of trying to figure it out—figure him out. He wanted to be an asshole? So be it. All she needed from him was to keep the crowd in line. Really, she didn't need that, either. She was perfectly fine taking care of herself.

She let go of her foot and extended both arms out as she continued to spin. The song ended, and ZZ Ward's "OVER-due" started. She'd picked the songs that night for Badger.

Though she'd told herself the whole time that wasn't what she was doing. Did he listen to the words while he watched her dance? Was he watching her now?

Rosie curled her body around the pipe, her torso and thighs holding her suspended. She let herself drop, sliding down the pole and stopping only right before she hit the floor. The crowd went nuts. Considering it was Friday night, they were packed, and the roar from their cheers was damn near louder than the music.

Rosie got to her feet and walked around the pole. Arching back against it, she popped her hips, along with her legs, keeping her movements tight but sensual. She walked forward and pulled the slip dress she wore over her head.

Yeah, he was watching.

Catching Badger's eyes as she walked, she tossed the costume to the side and stopped at the end of the stage, cupped her chest in her hands and rolled her hips, then turned and bent forward, swinging her long hair around.

She went to her knees and crawled along the edges of the stage, allowing the customers to show their love…in the form of dollar bills. By the time Rosie got to the other end, her next song began. After getting back to her feet, she moved upstage and unlaced her white string bikini-type top.

The slow but solid beat of BANKS's "Before I Ever Met You" fueled her. After giving her ass a little shake, Rosie arched backward and executed a back walkover. When she was upright again and facing the crowd, she rolled her head and flipped her hair over one shoulder. Rosie cupped her breasts in her palms before making a show of pinching her nipples. More hoots and whistles from the men in front, a few hollered her name. But what was better was Badger's reaction. His eyes had gone wide when she'd tugged on her nipples, and he'd run his palm over his face.

If he'd ever reacted visibly to her before, Rosie had never

witnessed it. But she'd seen it now. And damn if lust didn't fill her limbs like warm honey because of it.

She let a knowing smile arch her lips and made eye contact with a few patrons. But as she turned to move to the other end of the stage, she caught another set of familiar eyes.

What the?

No. It couldn't be him.

Rosie rounded the pole there and hoisted herself up to get a better view— *Oh my God.* In the back of the crowd, standing in a far corner opposite the bar, was someone she was so sure she'd never see again. Rosie spun, meeting his eyes with each revolution. Nothing but revenge emanated from his expression. That, and hate. Pure, unadulterated hate.

Lust forgotten, fear settled in Rosie's stomach like a lead weight as sheer panic raced through her limbs like an inferno. How the fuck had he found her? The music ended, and with that, so had her three-song set.

She was supposed to head to the small cage stage next, but there was no goddamn way that was happening. Without gathering up her discarded costume pieces or the rest of the money that'd been tossed on stage for her, Rosie stepped off the platform and headed down the back hall in a rush.

She had to get out of there. Immediately.

———

BADGER WATCHED as Rosie made her way off the stage and high-tailed it down the back hall like her ass was on fire. Something had happened about three-quarters of the way through that last song and freaked her out. In the last four months or so, Badger had done nothing but watch Rosie, and in that time, he'd gotten real familiar with "Arianna" and her many expressions when she was onstage.

"Freaked out" wasn't one he'd seen from her before, but

regardless, he'd noticed the change immediately in her expression as well as her demeanor. In a matter of a nanosecond, her eyes had gone from the normal brightness inhabiting them whenever she performed to—if he wasn't mistaken—fear. Maybe a customer had made a nasty comment; it wasn't uncommon. But knowing how Rosie normally handled that sort of thing, it wouldn't make sense for it to upset her or, worse, scare her.

From his usual perch near the bar, Badger scanned the crowd. Nothing seemed off from his perspective. Deejay Rick did a second shoutout for Arianna for the small cage stage as the next song played for the girl on the main stage. Badger watched the mouth of the hall, waiting for her to emerge. He glanced at Rick. Rick shrugged. Where the fuck was she?

Badger gave his guy closest to the back hall a chin jerk, indicating he needed to head down the hall in search of Rosie. Charlie nodded and headed that way. He knew the routine with the girls, knew she was late. As Badger did another scan of the crowd, he moved toward one of the dancers on the floor. Again, he found nothing out of the norm.

Charlie emerged from the hall, shaking his head. The fuck? Something was wrong. Really wrong. Maybe she was sick. Badger clasped the closest dancer not engaged in a table dance by the arm and asked her to work the cage stage, and then moved down the hall.

Uncaring who was in what state of dress, Badger walked directly into the dressing room. A couple of the girls gasped and covered their bare breasts. Badger rolled his eyes and turned to Evie. "Hey, where's Rosie? She sick or something?"

Evie glanced up from sewing whatever the fabric was in her hands, pink-framed reading glasses perched on the edge of her nose. "Rosie's onstage, Badger." She raised the thread and bit it with her teeth.

"If she was, you wouldn't be staring at my ugly mug right now, Evie. She ran down the hall after her set and hasn't come back." He glanced among the girls in the room and into the small, attached bathroom. "Any of you seen Rosie?"

"Who?" One of the girls ran a brush through her hair.

Goddamn stage names. None of the girls really ever knew each other. "Arianna." He let out an exasperated sigh. "You seen Arianna? About this tall—" Badger raised his hand to show Rosie's approximate height. "Long, dark hair. Petite tits, pretty much petite everything except for her long legs."

"Oh yeah, I saw her." The girl grabbed a can of hairspray and started fogging up.

"When?" Tired of this game, Badger stalked to the girl and snagged the can from her hand. "When did you see her?"

She jerked back from him. "Jesus! What's your problem?"

Badger tossed the can down and gripped the girl's upper arm. "I don't have a problem. What I do have is a missing girl." He pulled her closer. "Now, take a second, jiggle some brain cells so they start firing, and tell me when the fuck you saw her last." The last was said on a growl. Though he hadn't meant for it to slip out.

The girl's eyes got wide before she started glaring. "Take your fucking hands off me."

"Badger. Easy now…"

He glanced over his shoulder to find Evie beside him, her hand resting on his forearm. The look of concern on her face gave him pause, enough to rein his shit in and let go of the ditz he was hell-bent on getting an answer from. Badger let out a breath. "I'm cool. All good, Evie. You see Rosie, let her know I'm looking for her, yeah?"

"Sure, honey." Evie patted his arm with a meek smile. "Sure."

Badger took two steps backward before turning and leaving the room. Where in the fuck was she? He ran back toward the bar. Charlie was still at the entrance to the hall. "She come out?" Charlie shook his head, and Badger did a one-eighty and headed for the office. Barging inside, he found it empty. A cold chill zipped up his spine and made the hair on the back of his neck stand on end.

Badger ripped his keys from his front pocket, unlocked the filing cabinet drawer and pulled out his gun. After holstering it in place on his side, he stalked out the back door of the club. Her POS Toyota was still in the lot. *What the fuck?* He took two steps forward and listened. After a moment, a faint sound of something scraping on the pavement off to the right near the dumpster caught his attention.

Badger pulled his gun from its holster and racked the slide. Keeping his steps light, he slowly walked toward the big green trash bin. Moving to the side of it, he pressed his back to the hard metal. He paused long enough to draw in a deep, calming breath and then pivoted around, arms extended with his gun gripped firmly in his hands. Badger's eyes went wide at what he found.

"Oh, fuck! Holy shit, Badger. Don't shoot." Rosie shrank farther down into the crouched position she had herself in, shivering like crazy, her arms wrapped tight around her bent legs.

Badger flipped the safety and holstered the gun. "Holy shit is right. What's wrong? What the fuck are you doing out here, Rosie?"

"Will you just…" Her voice shook, and she cleared her throat. "Fuck!" She gripped the side of the dumpster, got to her feet and, with visibly shaking hands, slipped her platform shoes off. "Just go grab me a T-shirt from the office? Please?"

Christ, she wasn't shivering. She was shaking, as in from fear. She looked scared out of her mind, and Badger's protective nature roared to life, setting his insides on fire. Resisting the urge to move to her and pull her close, Badger crossed his arms and tilted his head to the side. "That wasn't an answer."

"Please? I'm cold."

Badger gritted his teeth. The expression in her eyes was about enough to take him to his damn knees. "Fine. But I swear to the devil herself, you move from this spot before I'm back, and I *will* take it out on your ass when I find you."

"Where the hell'm I gonna go? All my shit is inside in the dressing room." She crossed her arms over her chest and glared at him.

He grunted. "Point. But my warning still stands."

Badger turned from her and went back inside. Goddamn drama. Fucking baggage. He had no fucking clue what was going on with her, but he intended to find out.

CHAPTER NINE

Rosie wrapped her arms tighter around Badger's waist as he exited the freeway off-ramp and made a hard right turn onto the main road. She was fucking freezing, the T-shirt he'd brought her doing very little to keep her limbs warm. The fact that she was on the back of his Harley, pressed up against his hard body, her bare legs spread around his lean hips, had her other parts—the ones she should so *not* be paying attention to—overheated.

Rosie had no idea where they were going. The man of many words hadn't told her. Just tossed the shirt at her, started his bike and ordered her onto the back of it. She'd complied, though it wasn't like she'd had much of a choice. Running out of the club without grabbing her things—like her car keys and some clothes—hadn't been one of her brightest moments.

But she'd panicked.

Swear to Christ, Alvaro, the fucking drug dealer who'd murdered her husband, had found her. She couldn't believe it. The last Rosie knew, he was in jail awaiting trial without bail. He'd either been let out or escaped, or—she really had no idea. Rosie swallowed down the wave of fear that rose in her throat. All she knew was the crazy bastard was standing in the far corner of the bar, watching her. And by the look on his face, he hadn't come to pay his condolences or express his regret.

Badger turned off the main road into what appeared to be an older but well-kept neighborhood. Forcing the anxiety back, she focused on the houses. Older brick, stone, or wood-sided ranch-style homes lined the well-lit streets, and Rosie glanced at each one, taking in their immaculately kept exteriors as they passed by each, making a series of lefts and rights, until finally, he pulled the bike into a long, wide driveway.

He dropped the kickstand and leaned the bike to its side. "Hop off."

She did as he said, careful not to catch her too-tall heels on the pegs or fall when she got her feet on the ground. Badger dismounted his cycle and punched a code into a small keypad by the two-car garage door. The panel raised as he mounted the bike again and then rode it inside.

After shutting down the engine, he got off and removed the folded bandana he'd tied around his forehead, then his clear shades. He glanced over at her. "You coming or gonna stand out there in the cold?"

Without answering, Rosie blew out a breath and moved toward him. Christ, it didn't matter if he was being Mr. Quiet-Aloof guy or a dickhead barking orders at her, he was still hot. She hated that. A lot. At least he served as a decent distraction at that moment.

He was just so fucking…alpha. There really wasn't a better word for it.

But what she hated more was the fact that she kinda liked it, too. A lot.

As the garage closed down behind her, Rosie followed him through a door, which opened into a far too neat laundry room and beyond, into a kitchen. He flipped on a light, and Rosie glanced around, grateful for yet another distraction.

Three walls were lined with dark pine cabinets—old but in pristine condition. All the appliances were modern, stainless steel, and a decent-sized, oval table with four chairs around it sat in the center, just past the cabinets.

Terracotta tile spread along the floor and beyond into what appeared to be an open family room. From where she stood, she saw a red leather couch facing a huge stone fireplace with a rough-cut, dark wooden mantle. Mounted above it was an extremely large flat-screen TV.

"You want a beer?"

Pulled from her appraisal of his home, Rosie turned to find Badger with his head stuck in the refrigerator. "This is your house?"

He glanced at her over his shoulder. "Beer?"

She sighed. "You have anything stronger?"

He nodded and closed the fridge door. Reached above it, opened the cabinet and pulled out a bottle of Jack Daniels. "Strong enough?"

"Perfect." She glanced away and chewed her thumbnail. Good old Jack would get the job done and definitely take the sharp edges off the nerves poking around her insides; would get the residual shaking still wracking her body to stop, too. Jesus, what the hell was she going to do?

Badger set two stout glasses down on the counter. "Ice?"

"No. Straight, please." She tugged on the hem of her T-shirt. "So, you have some sweats I can maybe borrow or something?"

He shifted his eyes to hers, down her body to her legs, before looking back to the glasses as he poured. "Not that'll fit. But I'll get you something else."

After handing Rosie her drink, he walked out of the kitchen and through the attached den. She stared at his back until he disappeared down a hall to the far left of the room. He'd looked at her legs in almost a clinical way. And as though he really didn't like what he saw. When he looked at her in that way, she felt more self-conscious than a teenager heading into puberty.

Shaking off the thought, with glass in hand, she wandered into the living room. Rosie ran her palm over the soft leather of the back of the sofa. Before she had a chance to take more than one sip of her drink or do any further exploration of the room, Badger was back with a pair of boxer briefs and thick socks.

"Here." He placed the items on the back of the couch. "Bathroom's first door on the right."

"Thanks." She watched him as he brushed past her to a sliding glass door she hadn't noticed yet. After opening it, he stepped outside. "Okay then."

Rosie turned on the toe of her shoe and found the bathroom. There was nothing special about it, really. Except that it was clean. More so than she'd have expected. Basic toilet. Older vanity made of the same wood the kitchen cabinets were. Formica countertop. Bathtub/shower combo. Clean towels hanging on the towel bar. Maybe this was the guest bath…she closed the door and made quick work taking off her shoes and G-string and pulling on the briefs and socks.

Rosie took a moment and stared at herself in the mirror. Her face was still caked with her stage makeup. She looked like a damn circus freak. Turning, she found a narrow linen closet and opened it in search of—bingo, a washcloth. After wetting it down, she grabbed the bar of soap by the sink and lathered the cloth. And set to scrubbing her face clean. Somehow, being makeup-free in front of him, in his home, felt a whole lot better than all glamoured up like some sort of…well, like some sort of stripper.

She still couldn't quite figure out why he'd brought her there to begin with. It was clear to her, from the very start, where she stood with him, which was to say, nowhere. After all, the man barely talked to her. Even now, in his home, he barely answered her questions, and when he did speak to her, he kept it short, as usual. She was sure he had his reasons, but as far as Rosie knew, she'd never done anything to cross him. At least not anything she was aware of. The man made no sense.

Satisfied that she'd cleared away the evidence of her employment, she rinsed out the washcloth and draped it over the side of the bathtub to dry. She picked up her glass of Jack and downed the double shot in one swallow.

She was going to need it to get through the next…well, however long it was, she was going to be stuck there.

———

AFTER SHOOTING a quick text to Deuce letting him know he'd taken off, Badger stood in the darkness of his backyard. With a cigarette dangling from his lips, he stared up at the stars. He was jumpy. His skin itchy. She was in his house and about to be wearing a pair of his goddamn underwear and socks.

What the fuck was he thinking bringing her there? He hadn't been thinking, and that was the problem.

Every damn time he got near the woman, his fucking brain short-circuited. All rational thought vanished, and he got stupid. Putting her fine ass on the back of his Dyna was just that. Stupid. Worse, the feel of her arms around his waist and the fact that she fit against his back so perfect struck something deep inside him, making him want to just keep riding. At least riding, he didn't have to talk. He just got to feel.

"Can I get you more Jack?"

Badger exhaled the smoke he'd just drawn into his lungs, dropped his head and peered over his shoulder at her. She held the bottle of Jack in one hand and her empty glass in the other. She'd removed all of her heavy face paint and was completely makeup-free. Perfect was the only word he could think of to describe her. He had to take another drag off his cancer stick before he could answer, and then another, because in addition to her naturally beautiful complexion, she looked so fucking sexy in that T-shirt paired with his boxers, his socks bunched at her ankles, he worried the instant hard-on he'd acquired might bust through his zipper. His dick was ready to shout out a salute of praise.

In an attempt to play it cool, he walked over to the small outdoor table and stubbed out his smoke and then downed what remained of his booze. "Sure."

She moved to him, refilled his glass and her own. After setting the bottle down, she raised her glass to her sweet lips and took a sip. Badger watched. He wasn't a man of many words, but fuck him if he didn't trust himself not to say something insane like, "So, I got something you can wrap those fine lips around." Because, yeah, that'd go over about as well as a bride getting caught fucking the best man in the backroom of the church. *Jesus. There's a visual!*

She took a few steps away from the table. "It's really peaceful out here. What city are we in?"

"Phoenix."

"Oh. It seemed like we'd—"

"City limits stretch pretty far." He swallowed a mouthful of alcohol and then lit another cigarette.

She glanced back at him. "Thanks for coming to my rescue."

Right. Perfect timing and an opportunity to get his mind off of…her. "Yeah. About that." He leaned his ass against the table. "You wanna share what the fuck happened?"

She faced him and tilted the glass to her lips, her pretty brown eyes locked on his, and Badger ground his molars together. She was stalling by way of distraction, and it was fucking working. But goddammit, he knew in his gut she was in a heap of trouble. Something or someone had spooked her onstage, and Badger intended to find out what was behind it.

Clearing his throat, he took a swig of the booze. After

another drag of his cigarette, he blew out a long stream of gray smoke into the sky and then prompted her again. "Rosie, one way or another, you're going to tell me what happened."

"What happens if I don't?" She moved back to the bottle and topped off her glass.

"You will." Rather than turning to face her, Badger picked a spot he couldn't see on the brick wall bordering his property to focus on and let out a grunt.

"I'm cold. Can we go back inside?"

"Suit yourself. I'll be in as soon as I finish my smoke." With his focus still trained on the back wall, he listened as the sliding glass door opened and closed. He'd give her a minute before he headed inside. Though being inside with her felt so much more risky than being out back. Inside, he'd be subjected to a clearer view of her perfect face and the scent of her sweet perfume. Badger ran his hand over the back of his neck and stared down at his boots.

At some point, this woman had turned into an Achilles heel for him. She was a weakness, and Badger didn't tolerate weakness in anyone. Including himself. Ever.

He downed the remains of his drink, and the warmth of the whiskey settled nicely in his stomach. It'd take the edge off, helped him regain a bit of control. After one last drag, he smashed his smoke out in the ashtray and moved back into the house. He looked around the den and found it empty. As he passed by the coffee table, he set his glass down and moved down the hall toward the bathroom. "Rosie? You down here?"

The bathroom door was open, light off, and he continued farther down the hall to the bedrooms. Lights were all off down there, too, but he checked each room before he made his way back to the main part of the house. "Rosie?" Where the hell was she? Badger moved through the den, and as he entered the front formal living and dining room, he saw the front door closing. "What the *fuck!*"

Badger threw the door open and burst out to the front

yard. She'd made it to the end of his driveway when he caught up to her. He grabbed her arm, halting her movement. "What the hell do you think you're doing?"

She yanked her arm from his grip. "I'm leaving."

"Like hell you are."

"Badg— Aghh!"

In one motion, he grabbed her wrist, bent forward and tossed her over his shoulder. At that moment, there wasn't anything that needed to come out of her mouth he was interested in hearing. She was coming back into his house whether she liked it or not.

"Badger, put me down!"

"Woman, I'm not gonna tell you again. You better close those sweet lips of yours before I give you something to occupy them with. You push me on this, and I swear to Christ, I'll tan your ass while quieting your mouth. We clear?"

She went stock still as she let out a gasp, and the sound of it made Badger's dick go instantly rod-hard again. This was not good. So not fucking good. Fuck. Fuck. *Fuuuuck*! Not. Good.

CHAPTER TEN

ROSIE DIDN'T KNOW if she was filled with shock and disgust at being manhandled by him and being threatened with having her mouth occupied—she could only assume he'd meant with his dick—as well as having her ass tanned or completely and utterly turned on at the sexually depraved promise of it.

Badger had just taken alpha male to a whole new level. How about badass-biker hot extra-strength-alpha male? Yep, that was the level he was at, and it was a level Rosie had never spent time on before.

She bit down on her palm in order to keep herself quiet… the urge to push him and see if he'd deliver on his threat raced through her like lightning, and she figured the better option was to just shut the hell up. Which was insane. No one, not any-fucking-one, talked to her that way. Rosie didn't take orders. *She* did the ordering. *She* made the decisions. And she did whatever the hell she wanted when she wanted.

However—it appeared that would not be the case with Badger. Rosie was so clearly not in control of the situation, and that little realization, along with the Jack she'd consumed, had her head spinning.

Badger marched them straight back into his house and

kicked the door closed behind them once they'd cleared the threshold. Faster than she could track, he bent forward, and Rosie's feet hit the floor. And then he was in front of her, backing her against the wall with his big, hard body.

The space around her disappeared, and all she could see was him.

Rosie drew in a deep breath, and every one of her senses came alive as his masculine scent flowed through her. With his eyes locked on hers, he placed one hand on her side, his thumb and fingers framing her waist. He rested his other palm on the wall, alongside but above her head. Rosie raised her hands and placed them on his chest as a bolt of pure, undiluted lust spiked through her system, and her damn knees went weak. *Shit.* "Badger…"

"Shhh." He slid his palm up her side to just below her breast, and Rosie bit her bottom lip in order to keep herself from moaning. His hardened gaze dropped to her mouth and then back to her eyes. "Goddamn. Can't figure you out. Been trying since you walked in the bar that first day. So fucking different. Something behind your eyes, too. Hurt. Pain. Anger. Whatever it is, it's baggage…" His voice was low, almost a whisper, but with a gravely tone to it that vibrated through her entire body, settling between her thighs.

He'd been trying to figure her out? How? When? That statement made no sense to her. The man barely looked at her. Rosie frowned, trying to sort out the confusion racking her brain. But her mind flew in a whole other direction when Badger moved his other hand from the wall and ran a fingertip along her jaw and down the side of her neck.

Rosie lost her breath at the intimate touch, but then he clasped his hand around her throat. She gasped and automatically arched against him. He wasn't hurting her or constricting her breathing, but definitely holding her tight enough for there to be no mistaking his presence. In reaction, Rosie's nipples went instantly hard, and she knew he had to be able to feel them against his chest even through their layers of clothing because he let out a low growl. Which arrowed straight to her clit.

As Rosie tilted her head back slightly, his hand still firmly locked on her throat, his eyes dropped to her lips again. Was he going to kiss her? Holy fucking shit… God help her, she wanted him to kiss her. She was half out of her mind with the anticipation of it. Rosie had never been so desperate for a kiss in her life.

"Badger," she breathed and slid her hands down his sides to his waist, and gripped his shirt.

"Fuck me… I shouldn't… But I have to." Badger slammed his lips down on hers, and Rosie moaned into his mouth as his tongue dominated hers. Tangling, stroking, and taking what he wanted from her.

He tasted of JD, cigarettes, and something wild. He tasted like sweet sin. And Rosie wanted more.

From the bottom of her feet to the top of her head, her entire body lit on fire. She ran her hands up his wide back and pressed her body tighter to his. Since Halloween, this man had consumed her thoughts. For months, she'd existed in a constant state of self-consciousness, and because of how he'd treated her, did her best to stay out of his way—completely convinced he hated her. But based on the fact he now had his tongue down her throat and his hard cock pressed against her pelvis, there was no way he hated her. Apparently, he liked her. A whole hell of a lot.

Badger released her neck and moved his hand, fisting it in her hair as he tugged her head back farther. As if he'd been holding himself back forever, his kiss felt fueled by desperate need. And lust…lots of fucking lust.

It was the hottest goddamn kiss she'd ever had in her life.

Wanting more of him, Rosie rubbed her body against his and slid her hands under his T-shirt, over the bare skin of his muscled back. He yanked from her lips, and she gasped for breath as he moved his mouth to her throat. "Need to fuck you," he growled as he made his way down the side of her neck, nipping and sucking at her skin. "Need to fuck you so bad, I'm out of my goddamn mind with it."

Shivers zipped down her spine and radiated outward, making every inch of her skin tingle. Holy shit...out of his mind with it? Was this really happening? The situation was totally out of her control—not in a way where she couldn't stop it if she wanted to. She could. He'd stop if she told him to.

But she didn't want him to stop. Rosie wanted to be fucked, but more so, she wanted to be fucked by Badger.

———

BADGER FISTED her hair tighter and pulled on the soft strands. She let out a little kitten moan, and his dick got harder, aching behind his zipper. Fucking hell, she was sweet. All responsive and giving. Like he feared she would be. Tasted better than ambrosia on his tongue, and he wanted to devour every heavenly inch of her. There was no going back now.

Her perfect nipples were next. Man, he'd wanted to suck on those fucking hard berries from the very first time he saw them. Small breasts with areolas the size of a quarter, tipped with nipples made for biting. Far too many nights, he'd stroked his cock, fantasizing about her tits.

Badger released her hair and pulled his mouth away from her neck. She was breathing heavy, her gaze heady and filled with lust. He took both of her wrists and raised her arms above her head. "Keep them up." When she didn't respond to his order, he gripped her chin and bent his head so he was almost nose-to-nose with her. If she didn't get it, she'd learn. He was all too willing to teach her. "When I give you a direction, you say, 'Yes, sir.' When I ask you a yes or no question, your answer is, 'Yes, sir' or 'No, sir.' We clear?"

She sucked in a breath, her eyes wide. He grunted and shifted his hips forward, grinding his erection against her. "We clear, Rosie?"

She nodded and then whispered, "Umm… Yes."

"Yes, what?"

She blinked. "Yes, sir."

"Good girl." He pressed a quick kiss to her lips, nipping her bottom lip as he pulled away. Badger let go of her arms, and surprisingly, she left them where he'd told her. Taking hold of the bottom of her T-shirt, he pulled it off of her and tossed it aside. "Fuck me, your tits…" Badger smoothed his palms over her breasts, reveling in the feel of those hard points on his palms. "Perfect fucking tits."

He squeezed the petite mounds, and she let out a moan that had him almost coming in his jeans. Shifting his hands so he had them both cupped in his palms, he bent his head and sucked one perfect, tight areola into his mouth. She let out another moan, this one more high-pitched, and her body jerked against him.

Something primal let loose inside of Badger, and he knew, in that moment, with her hot body tight to his and her sweet nipple on his tongue, that he was well and truly…fucked.

"Oh God…"

He pulled away from her nipple, biting the tip and tugging. Then he let the hard peak go and dragged his tongue over it. With his other hand, he pinched its mate, rolling it between his finger and thumb. She whimpered, writhing against him, hot as hell and making his cock ache to get inside her. He yanked his mouth away. "You like that, don't you." Badger pinched both nipples and tugged on them. "A little bit of pain?"

She was panting, moaning, and rubbing her hips against his dick. "Yes."

Her answer came out on a moan, and his balls drew up tight, the head of his cock throbbing at the sound.

"Yes?" He tugged a little harder, stretching the points away from her body, and she arched against him.

"*Oh, fuck! Yes! Oh God!* Yes, sir!"

"Mmm…such a good girl. Knew you'd be a good girl. Knew you'd like it rough, too." He gazed down at the taut points, reddened from his handling, and lust spilled through him like gas on a fire. "I could play with your perfect tits all goddamn night, Rosie. But tell me, how wet is your pussy right now, hmm?" He kissed her before she could answer and dragged one palm down her soft skin to the boxer briefs he'd given her to wear.

Badger slipped his hand inside the waistband and found her bare lips. Sliding two fingers over her clit to the drenched mouth of her cunt, he growled and tore away from her kiss. "Fuck yeah, baby. You've soaked my boxers. Best get these off you." She nodded and bit her bottom lip. Badger quirked one brow. "Like that lip. I'll bite them for you. Drop your arms and slide the boxers off." She did as he asked, damn near immediately.

Oh yeah, she needed this. Needed to be told, ordered, dominated. Someone else to take control. He'd give her that… and more.

"Press your palms against the wall at your sides and spread your legs wider." He watched as she complied, and Badger took one small step back to look at the beauty before him. Then he went to his knees and gazed up at her. "You ready?"

She nodded, and he tilted his head to the side. "What was that?"

"Mmm." Her whimpered moan vibrated down his shaft to his balls. "Yes, sir."

Badger stroked two fingers through her wet folds again. "First, I'm going to eat this fine pussy 'til you come on my tongue. And if you're a good girl, I'm going to fuck your mouth." She sucked in a breath, and he licked his lips. "Then, I'll fuck your cunt. You want that?"

She nodded. "Yes, sir."

"How do you want it, baby? You want it rough?"

"Never had it rough before."

Badger moved his thumb to her clit and rubbed little circles over the tight nub. "I want to take you hard and rough. I want to fuck you 'til you scream my name so loud the neighbors hear you." She rocked her hips. "Yeah, like that, baby. Like seeing you want my touch. You want me to fuck you hard and rough?"

"Oh God…" She panted. "Badger, I'm going to come."

Badger pulled his thumb away. "Not yet. Not until you tell me how you want it. Your call, baby. You make it." He leaned back and unbuttoned his jeans and slid the zipper down. Her gaze dropped, and she watched as he reached down his boxers and adjusted his cock. He took a moment and stroked himself a couple of times. "Want this, baby?"

"Mm-hmm. Please?"

"Rough and hard?"

She drew in a deep breath, her eyes locked on his crotch. "What if…what if I can't take it so rough?"

"You want a safe word, you can have one. You won't need it because you're gonna want everything I give you. But if it makes you feel better, pick one."

She let out what he assumed was a nervous laugh. "Fuck, I don't know."

Badger pulled his hand free of his boxers and went back to toying with her clit. "All right, word is berry."

"Berry?"

"Yeah. For those berry-size perfect nipples."

"Okay." She let out a giggle, and again, Badger felt it straight in his balls. "That works."

"Yeah, it does." He slipped two fingers inside her cunt again. "Nice and tight. Sloppy wet. Fucking perfect." Badger leaned forward and licked over her clit. A high-pitched sound came out of her as she sucked in a breath. He urged one of her legs over his shoulder, pulled his fingers free of her channel and slid his tongue through her warm, wet folds.

Her taste hit him like a pile driver to the gut. His cock jerked in his boxers, and wetness from his pre-cum dripped down the head of his dick...and Badger's mind went into a haze of animalistic desire. Her arousal coated his tongue, and he swallowed her down before he covered her clit with his lips and sucked, lapping at her opening with his tongue every couple of seconds.

Jesus fuck, she tasted like the sweetest goddamn honey he'd ever had. He'd known she was different, but he had *no* idea exactly *how* different. All of it was coming together now. The months of angst whenever he had to deal with her in the club or whenever he had to watch her incredible body on the stage. How whenever she spoke to him and his skin got tight. Fucking hell, damn near five months of making a deliberate effort to avoid her like the damn Black Plague...

With his mouth between her fine thighs, with her delectable scent infusing itself in his lungs, he was starting to wonder if this woman was just the kind of different he'd been missing.

CHAPTER ELEVEN

ROSIE SUCKED in breath after breath—her hands pressed so hard to the wall like she might break through the drywall—in between moans and whimpers of pleasure as Badger ate her pussy like a man who'd been starving to death.

For her.

He growled, his lips wrapped around her clit, and the vibration of it sent a spasm ricocheting through her entire body. Rosie's head spun, her vision going a little blurry, and she gave in to the urge to steady herself by grabbing his shoulder.

Badger pulled away from her. "You okay?"

She nodded. "Sorry, I just…" She licked her lips. "Don't stop, please? I just got a little dizzy."

His hard gaze softened, and he took her hand from his shoulder and laced their fingers together. "I got you, Rosie."

She nodded, but the tenderness in his expression, action, and words shot straight to her heart, and Rosie shoved it aside as fast as she could. There was no place for that in her world, and besides, this was just sex. Nothing more. Wild and crazy, untamed, and incredible…but nonetheless, just sex.

There wasn't a cold chance in hell it would ever be more than that.

In the next breath, his gaze went stone hard again, and with his eyes still locked on hers, he snaked out his tongue and licked over her tingling clit. Rosie squeezed his hand. "Badger…I need."

"Mmm." He licked over it again, teasing her. "Ask me for it." He dragged his tongue through her folds before moving back to her clit and sucking it between his lips. With his free hand, he slipped two fingers inside her channel.

Ask him for it? He wanted her to ask for what? *"Oh God!"* Rosie's clit spasmed, and she sucked in a harsh breath.

He nipped her clit with his teeth. "You need to come?"

"Yes. Fuck!"

He pulled his fingers free. "Yes, what?"

Rosie whimpered as her pussy clenched in on itself. She needed his touch again. Now. "Yes, sir."

"Good girl." He slid his fingers back into her channel, gazing up at her, one corner of his lips raised in a slight grin. "Ask me for it. Ask me to let you come."

"Please let me come. Please?" Jesus, she sounded so pathetic. She hated that, but goddammit, she was desperate for release.

"There you go." Badger latched back onto her clit and sucked, pressing his tongue to the tingling bundle of nerves as he worked his fingers in and out of her cunt.

Rosie pressed the back of her head to the wall and squeezed his hand. The vibrations of her impending orgasm flooded her system with heat. She panted for breath, moaning, rocking her hips, completely uncaring of how she sounded or looked as he worked her pussy and clit, bringing forth a blaze of heat that spread through her body like a wildfire.

Her cunt clenched, her clit spasmed, and then it hit. Rosie's climax broke free, and her moans turned into loud, mewling whimpers as wave after wave crashed through her. "Oh God! Badger, I can't…" She lost her footing, but he caught her, holding her up as he continued his delicious assault between her legs.

When he finally let her go, Rosie's body shook from head to toe. Caught in the daze of what might be the best orgasm she'd ever experienced, Badger eased her down and onto her knees. And then he kissed her. She moaned as her taste and wetness coating his beard flowed into her mouth. She sucked at his tongue, dragged her lips over his beard. Took everything he gave her, and she knew he wasn't done. There'd be more. His cock would be next.

And she wanted it. All of it. Starved for him, like he'd been starving for her.

Badger gripped her by the back of the hair and pulled from her lips. "Want this hot mouth wrapped around my dick."

Rosie swallowed. "Yes, please. I want that, sir."

"Fuck, Rosie." He shook his head, closing his eyes for a moment as he did. "Perfect."

He pushed his pants and boxers down to his hips, freeing his cock. The curved, hard shaft bobbed against his belly, the swollen head leaving a spot of wetness on his skin from the arousal oozing from the tip. Rosie licked her lips as a whimper escaped. She'd never minded sucking cock, it wasn't a "thing" for her like it was for some women, but she definitely enjoyed it.

Seeing Badger's above-average thickness had Rosie craving a dick in her mouth like a woman gone mad. The bulbous head was beyond flushed, swollen and clearly needed her tongue and lips to relieve the pressure.

He got to his feet and wrapped his fist around the thickness. "Rosie?"

"Hmm?" She was transfixed, unable to tear her gaze away as he lazily stroked the length.

"Crawl for me, baby. Hands and knees. Show me how bad you want it."

Crawl? Fuck yeah, she'd crawl! Never had before for anyone, never wanted to. But for him? For that cock? She'd crawl across the hot desert to have it between her lips. Badger took a single step back, then another. And Rosie followed, licking her lips as she went while her pussy throbbed and flooded with her arousal.

"That's it. Come to me. So fucking gorgeous." Badger stopped in the middle of his formal living room behind one side of the large sectional.

Rosie moved on hand and knee until she was in front of him, at his feet, with his cock just above her. Tucking her knees beneath her, she rose up and rested her ass on her feet. She gazed up at him. And waited.

She wanted to beg, wanted to ask. Wanted to take control…but she knew that wouldn't do. He'd not allow it.

For the first time in Rosie's life, the idea of someone else making the decisions for her, someone else running the show, had a sigh of relief blasting through her. The dynamic he'd put in place between them let something loose inside her she wasn't aware had been locked up.

When the night was said and done, Rosie wondered whether or not she'd regret giving him this kind of power over her. But she couldn't worry about that now. In part because the amount of lust pumping through her veins was probably contributing to her loss of sanity, but also because his cock was in front of her face, and she wanted it in her mouth. She'd deal with any regret later.

For now, it didn't matter. She didn't have to make any decisions. She didn't have to manage anything. Right now, it wasn't up to her—in this situation, nothing was. All she had to do was wait to be told what to do and when to do it.

"Something behind your eyes just changed. Can't read it yet, but whatever it is, I like it." With his cock still gripped in his fist, Badger cupped her cheek in the palm of his other hand and smoothed his thumb over her lips. "Want my cock?"

God, she did. Like she needed air to breathe. "Yes, sir."

"Open for me." When she did, Badger inched closer and ran the edge of the bulbous head over her lips and down her chin.

Rosie snaked out her tongue, licking the salty bead of arousal from the tip as well as off her lips. He continued to tease her, letting her lick the rim, the tip, and again, rubbing the head down her chin until finally he slipped it inside her mouth. She closed her eyes and her lips around the rim and moaned.

"Fuck yeah, baby. Suck me. Right there." He still had a grip on the shaft, not allowing her to take any more of him into her mouth, but she'd take it and whatever else he wanted to give her.

Rosie sucked the flushed, swollen crown, rolling her tongue and tasting the little spurts of arousal she was rewarded with from each pull of her mouth. Jesus Christ, he tasted good. She glanced up at him, and another blast of arousal ricocheted through her at what she saw. His brows were drawn together, his jaw set tight, lips pulled in a straight line. And his eyes—his eyes were locked on hers with undeniable lust swirling in his gaze.

With a growl, he let go of the shaft, fisted her hair tight and pulled her forward as he drove his cock to the back of her throat. Rosie moaned and gave herself over to him. Allowing him to fuck her mouth…fast, hard, and so fucking primal she practically came all over her legs. She sucked the head, moaning each time he drew himself out and then tightened her lips around his wide shaft as he drove back in.

With one hand still in her hair, controlling her movement, he moved his other to her throat and took hold. Clasping her tight enough to make his presence known but not enough to restrict her breathing. Just enough to let her know who was in control, and it sure as fuck wasn't her.

She wanted him to have it. All of it. He could take what he wanted. Do what he wanted. In exchange, she wanted to make him come so hard down her throat she'd practically choke on it.

God help her, she wanted all of it so much she could barely stand it.

———

BADGER WAS beside himself with all that had happened and *was* happening. She was on her knees, with his dick in her mouth, sucking him like a goddamn queen of cock. He was a dominant man in all things, especially in bed. It was part of his life, part of how he lived. Always had been. As far as the sex went, it was always rough. He preferred it that way. He preferred to be in control, too. Not that he couldn't be soft. He could. There just had never been a desire for it…or someone he wanted to be that way with.

He could see being soft with Rosie, but not right then. The realization hung out in the back of his mind, and he swatted it away. Not that night. Maybe not ever. Spanking, biting, scratching…hair pulling. Fucking her face, fucking her sweet cunt. Slapping her ass until it glowed red. Biting her nipples until they were so hard they could cut glass. All of it. He wanted to give her all of it.

He knew she was no submissive, not a genuine one anyway, but she *was* submitting to him. No question of that. Apparently, she didn't know she had it in her, either, because there was definitely a slight bit of hesitation when he'd laid it out for her. Rough or not? It'd taken her about a half a second to decide. It appeared she'd settled on her choice just fine because her lips were wrapped tight around his dick, and she was loving everything he was giving her.

Rosie moaned, slurping as she sucked. He let up a little on the tight grip he had on her hair. "You dripping down your legs for me?"

She nodded, sucking the head. "Mmm."

He pulled from her mouth, but that didn't stop her. She kept going and licked down the side of his shaft to his balls. Gazing up at him, she sucked his sac into her mouth, and her eyes fluttered closed. "Goddamn! So fucking sweet. Play with your clit while you service my cock. Make yourself come when I shoot down your throat and then all over your tits."

She nodded and licked over the sensitive skin of his balls and up his shaft again. As she swallowed the head between her lips, she moved a hand between her closed thighs and rubbed her pussy. Badger reached out and grabbed the back of the couch to hold himself steady. His orgasm tingled at the base of his spine, radiating straight to his dick. He was going to come so hard he'd probably see spots.

She worked him and worked herself, moaning and whimpering around his dick, taking him higher. Badger gripped her hair tight once again and rocketed in and out of her mouth fast and hard. "Take it. Fuck yeah, take it. Work that cunt for me. Work my cock. Here it comes."

Badger thrust forward, and his climax let loose like a blaze of lightning. His cock jerked in her mouth, exploding down her throat. Then he pulled free and spurt down her chin and her tits. Her guttural moans, as she brought herself to orgasm with her fingers, took him higher as he coated her skin, marking her with creamy lashes.

Rosie found his cock head again and licked over the rim before taking him into her mouth once more.

"Fuck, woman! Yes!" With one final hard thrust, he finished, spurting the last remnants of his orgasm down her throat.

Just like he thought, his vision got a little dim, and he was damn grateful he'd positioned them by the couch so he had something to hold onto as he caught his breath. Holy hell, that was incredible.

Pulling free of her mouth, Badger groaned at how sensitive his dick felt. She moaned, panting for breath as she nuzzled his thigh, her hand still between her legs. He was spent, but he was nowhere near done with her. He smoothed his palm down the side of her hair and cupped her chin, raising her face to look up at him. "You okay?"

"Mmhmm." She rested her cheek against his palm, a tender, sated expression on her face.

Badger bent down and kissed her. Her swollen lips were soft and giving, and he couldn't get enough of them. The taste of his orgasm lingered, and he sucked it from her tongue. A man shouldn't expect a woman to swallow his come if he wasn't willing to deal with the taste of it, too. Share and share alike. They'd tasted and swallowed each other, and Badger was all about give, take, receive, and give again. He pulled away. "Mmm. Damn, baby, my cum on your tongue is perfect."

She smiled, all soft and dazed from his kiss, and Badger practically had to cover his heart with his hand to stop the feelings she inspired from oozing out. Those goddamn eyes of hers got to him every time, and when she smiled, he was left defenseless. She could have anything she wanted, looking at him like she was in that moment.

His only solution? Bury it. Fuck her senseless. Fuck them both senseless.

Badger got to his feet and, pulled his shirt over his head and tossed it aside. "Stand up. Bend over the back of the couch. Ass in the air. Gonna get you ready for me, then fuck you nice and hard once you're begging."

He put out a hand, and she took it, rising to her feet. "Yes, sir."

Before she did as he asked, she pressed her lips to the center of his chest and then turned and got into position.

Badger drew in a sharp breath, and his cock jerked, coming back to life. Not that he'd gone completely soft to begin with, which was different for him. Especially considering how strong his orgasm has been. Instead, he was half-hard and quickly getting harder as he took in her long and lean body stretched over the back of his sofa. "Up on your tiptoes. Spread your legs as wide as comfortable." Before he shed his jeans, he pulled a condom from his wallet and set it beside her on the back of the couch. "Link your arms behind your back, Rosie."

Again, she did what he asked. Jesus, she was amazing. Badger dragged two fingers down her spine to her linked hands, and she arched against him. "Stay here."

Badger moved to his bedroom and retrieved exactly what he needed. Returning to her, he tied her wrists together with a cotton bandana. He bent over her, his lips to her ear. "Too tight?"

She whimpered and rubbed her ass against him. "No."

"What was that?" Badger pulled away and cracked her on the ass with his open palm.

"*Fuckkkmmmm!*" She tucked her hips forward. "Fuck, that stung."

Badger smoothed his palm over her reddened ass cheek. "No, what, Rosie?"

"Not too tight."

"Is that how you're supposed to answer?" Was she taunting him on purpose? Hmm… Badger smacked her ass again. This time a little harder.

"Oh fuck! *Fuck! Badger!*"

Damn. He ran two fingers through her folds. "Sopping wet again. Like that, did you? You want me to punish you, Rosie? Need me to beat this fine tight ass 'til it glows pink with my handprints?"

"I don't…I…" She moaned and writhed against his fingers.

He pulled his fingers away and stroked them over her tight

little asshole. Another moan ending in a whimper as she arched, pressing against his fingers. Badger's dick went stone hard, and he growled. Fucking hell, if he'd known this was what he'd been missing, he would've stopped avoiding her months ago.

He dipped his fingers in the mouth of her cunt again and once more spread the moisture over her ass. Again, she pressed backward, and he slipped them inside her tight hole. "Like that, too, I see. Goddamn, Rosie. The things I'm going to do to you." Withdrawing his fingers, he landed another hard slap to her ass cheek, and Rosie let out a guttural moan, but this time arched higher, seeking more from him. "Shouldn't have fucking wasted so much time."

"Badger, please? I need…"

He worked his fingers back into the tight ring of muscles of her asshole and worked her clit with his other hand. "What do you need, baby? Tell me."

"I need you to fuck me. Please, sir. Please fuck me."

"Good girl. All ready and begging for me." Badger pulled away from her, tore open the condom and sheathed his prick. Taking his shaft in his hand, he stroked the head through her folds, once, twice…then positioned at the wet mouth of her pussy. "Hold on, baby. Taking what's now mine."

Mine? *What the fuck am I saying?*

Badger thrust forward. Not slow. Not easy. Fast, hard, and with no mercy until he was buried balls deep inside her tight, hot cunt.

Oh yeah, this is mine.

CHAPTER TWELVE

Rosie inched herself, or tried to anyway, from beneath Badger's arm—which was slung over her waist and had been nearly all night. She needed to get back home, find her extra set of car keys, get her car, and get the hell out of Dodge.

Never mind that she'd just experienced the greatest sex of her life with this larger-than-life man—*God help me*—lying next to her on his stomach, snoring.

But it didn't matter. It didn't.

Who snored while lying on their stomach anyway? Normally, snoring kept her awake and drove her insane enough to want to punch the offender in the throat to shut them up. But not this time. Nope. Badger's snoring hadn't really bothered her at all, and it also wasn't the thing keeping her awake, either.

Through the course of the night, *after* the badass-biker hot extra-strength-alpha male and, let's not forget, much to her surprise, dominant sex, Rosie'd started to doubt her own eyes. Had she really seen Alvaro?

The guy was in jail, and bail hadn't been set. Wasn't supposed to be set, anyway. Unless his high-dollar attorney had somehow gotten the judge to change his mind, and that's how the lunatic was out. A guy like that could easily come up with enough cash to secure a bond from a bondsman. Plus, he had property… Fuck, she needed to go. Rosie bit her lip and slid another inch away from Badger.

If that *had* been Alvaro last night in the club, there was no way she could stay in Phoenix. Yummy dominant biker lying next to her or not, it didn't matter. It didn't. *Ugh*—

Badger moaned, slid his hand down her stomach, and curled it around her hip. Shit…she'd only made it halfway out of his grip, and now he'd locked on again. Talk about possessive. Jeez. He'd held onto her all damn night, including when he was fucking all the sense out of her brain, as well as back into it. Then, fucking her some more, and until she screamed his name. Like he'd promised.

Good grief, she'd "Yes sir'd" her way to several orgasms. A tingle spread through her lower tummy and arrowed straight to her clit. She'd done and said so many dirty things. Things she'd never said or done in her life. Ever. Rosie stifled a moan…he'd done things to her body she'd never let anyone do. Hell, no one dared to try, but if they had, no doubt she would've told them to screw off.

Rosie was no stranger to that sort of world. Dom/sub play. His world, apparently. She'd seen and heard plenty from other strippers about it, definitely read it in books before, and yeah, it was hot…in print. It was even hot when it was happening to someone else and they were telling her about it. But not Rosie. No way. Not her thing. And if Joey had ever tried to go all alpha on her like that? She'd have laughed his ass right out of the bedroom.

Badger was a whole other ballgame. She wasn't sure she was capable of telling the man no. It was almost as if she recognized his dominance over her on a cellular level. Which was fucking crazy and another reason why she had to get the hell out of there before he woke up. Because no way in hell he'd just let her go…and she needed to go because…Alvaro.

Rosie rolled over, and Badger's hand slipped to the top of her hip. Just as she let out a sigh of relief, contemplating her next move, he shifted, snuggled up behind her, his big warm body curling around her, as he—*really?*—tossed one of his legs over the top of hers. For fuck's sake! She blew out a breath and tried her best to ignore the fact that his dick was pressed against her ass and how easy it would be if she just... *Dammit, stay focused!*

Over the next thirty minutes, or maybe it was just five, either way, it felt like forever, Rosie managed to inch out of his embrace. Getting off the bed was another exercise in slow movement. She didn't want the bed to jiggle or dip or anything. He had to be used to sleeping alone, right? Seriously, how much did one man cuddle? Especially a hot, scary, badass biker guy?

Badger was a walking anomaly. And pretty much everything she'd avoided her entire life. Besides, she'd had enough issues with her husband getting into trouble; she sure as hell hadn't needed a biker in the mix. Trading a wannabe bad-boy for a real deal bad one wasn't on her to-do list.

Finally free, Rosie managed to find his wallet in his jeans. She swiped a couple of twenties and then tiptoed out of his dark bedroom. She'd pay him back, somehow. Her clothes, which consisted of a Deuce's Cabaret T-shirt, a pair of Badger's boxer briefs, and her stripper platforms, were in the entryway hall where she'd left them. The sun wasn't up yet, and amazingly enough, she managed to get dressed without any lights on.

In the dimly lit formal living room, Rosie's gaze lingered on the couch before she turned away and headed to the front door. Hot lust pooled in her tummy at the memory of being bent over the back of it, hands bound behind her back as Badger fucked her harder than she'd even been in her life.

With a hard swallow to stifle a moan, she opened the door just enough to sneak past it and then closed it quietly behind her. So far, she'd managed to get away. But she knew, until she was far enough away, she wasn't out of the woods yet. It wasn't until she cleared his driveway and made her way down the sidewalk that she finally breathed a sigh of relief. Rosie took a guess and made a left onto the next street, hoping like hell she'd soon find the main road. Her next goal was to hopefully find a gas station and beg to use the phone to call a cab.

Talk about doing the walk of shame—or, in this case, if she was lucky, the cab ride of shame.

CHAPTER THIRTEEN

IT'D TAKEN LONGER than she'd hoped, and by the time Rosie had gotten a cab to pick her up, the sun was high in the sky and blaring down on her, highlighting the fact that she'd definitely spent the night somewhere other than her own bed.

Using the money she'd taken from Badger, she paid the driver and headed for her apartment. As she walked past the kids playing in front of her building—in her clear with glitter, platform stripper heels—the mothers all stopped what they were doing to stare. Rosie avoided their eyes, feeling, for the first time in a long time, an ice-cold blanket of shame wrap around her. Frazzled, instead of heading to the office to ask for an extra key, she hurried around the corner to her apartment door—and came to a dead stop.

A shiver bolted down Rosie's spine. The door was closed, but it had definitely been kicked in at some point. *Fuck!* The lock was bent, and below it, a dent in the metal door, clearly the size of a foot, and the wood around the frame was damaged. With a shaking hand, Rosie pushed the door open wide. It didn't appear anyone was still in there, but she waited a moment, listening for any sounds. When nothing moved, she took a deep breath and stepped inside.

Rosie covered her mouth with her hand as a whimper escaped. Her small one-room apartment had been trashed. Completely and totally fucking trashed.

The bed was flipped on its side, the sheets and blankets hanging off it. Dresser drawers had been pulled out and lay dumped on the ground, a few of them broken. Her clothes scattered about. She looked into the small kitchenette as the tears filling her eyes breached the edges and dripped down her cheeks. Christ, the silverware and utensil drawers had been pulled out, the contents strewn across the tile floor. Dishes and glassware broken. Even the cabinets, holding the few pots and pans she owned, as well as food stock, had been dumped.

"What the fuck!"

A scream erupted out of Rosie, and she spun around so fast she lost her balance. Badger rushed forward and caught her before she fell on her ass. She flung her arms around his neck, a complete blubbering mess of tears. "Badger…I… Oh God!"

He stroked the back of her hair and held her tighter. "Baby, shh. It's okay now, I got you."

She sniffled and pressed her face against his neck. He'd scared the shit out of her, but she'd never been happier to see a man in her life as she was right then. "What'm I gonna do?" Her breath hitched on a sob. "I don't know what to do."

Badger smoothed his hand down her back before he pulled away and cupped her chin in his hand. "First thing you're going to do is find a bag and grab some clothes. The second thing you're going to do is walk your ass out to my truck and get in it. We'll figure out the third move once we're back at my place. We clear?" Still crying, she tried to focus on his eyes as he swiped a tear off her cheek with his thumb. "We clear, Rosie?"

The tenderness of his tone and his actions sent her already dramatic state into a maelstrom of emotional overload. First, the crazy wild sex, then the all-night cuddling? And now tenderness? For fuck's sake, the dude had layers! "Yes," she whispered, working to get her teary display under control.

And then he went and pressed a kiss to her forehead.

"Jesus, Badger!" Rosie burst into another round of tears.

"Shit." He cupped the back of her head and pulled her to his chest. "Go easy, woman. Deep breaths."

"Okay—" She sniffled and wiped her face. "Okay, I got it. I'm good."

He gripped her shoulders, and his gaze traveled over her face. "Good. Now do as I instructed."

"Yes, sir."

Badger's eyes flared, and so did hers. The words had come out before she'd even thought about it. Jesus Christ, she was in trouble. And not just because her apartment had been trashed —most likely by Alvaro and she was obviously no longer safe. But because at some point between when she'd run off the stage and hid behind the dumpster to this very moment, she'd given Badger a whole lot of power over her.

A power she wasn't necessarily comfortable with him having.

———

AFTER LOADING three duffel bags full of Rosie's clothes in the back of his pickup, Badger stopped by Deuce's and also grabbed the things she'd left behind the night before, as well as her money. He'd threatened to handcuff her to the steering wheel to ensure she didn't try and skip out on him again. She hadn't, thank fuck. But he was pretty sure it was only because she was still too shaken up at the condition of her apartment.

Now back at his place, he stood at his kitchen counter, loaded the coffee pot up, and started on some scrambled eggs. Rosie was in the shower, and any minute now, she'd be out. He planned to feed her, then find out what the fuck was going on.

As he finished placing her plate on the table and set to filling each of them a mug of coffee, Rosie appeared in the den. He straightened from his task and took her in, grinding his molars the whole time.

She'd applied only a little makeup. Her hair was pulled up in a tie piled atop her head. Covering her body was a basic but fitted mint-green T-shirt—Christ almighty, from the looks of it, she wasn't wearing a bra, either—faded jeans which hugged her hips and long legs and a pair of white Chucks on her feet.

Different.

Perfect.

Fucking gorgeous.

"Badger?" She cocked a hip to the side, raised her fingers to her mouth and nibbled her thumbnail.

He cleared his throat. "Hungry?"

"Mmhmm." She furrowed her brow.

"Then get in here and sit." He set the coffee pot back on the machine. "Hope you like eggs."

"Eggs are great. Thanks."

When he turned, she was seated at the kitchen table and was folding her napkin on her lap. He grabbed the half-and-half from the fridge and set it on the table along with her coffee. "Sugar?"

She glanced up. "No, cream is enough." She smiled.

Badger blew out a breath as he stroked his hand over his short beard and then smoothed his palms down his thighs. Nervous tension bounded through him like a pack of wild horses. The last thing he needed was caffeine in the mix, but he grabbed his cup anyway and took a seat at the table.

"Aren't you eating?" She stirred the cream in her coffee.

"I had some already," he lied. He was too amped up for food at that moment. Again, her brow furrowed, and he wanted to reach out and smooth the lines away. Instead, he let out a grunt and glanced away. "Eat, Rosie. It'll help."

"Help? How does that work exactly? Are these magical

eggs or something?" She scooped up a pile of eggs and put them in her mouth.

"Are you always this mouthy?"

"Yes." She sipped her coffee. "Are you always so cryptic?"

"Stop." He let out a sigh. "I'm not being cryptic."

"Mmhmm." She took another bite of her eggs. "Badger can't be your real name."

"You assume a lot."

She shrugged. "Maybe."

"Badger's my name." He leaned back in his chair and crossed one leg over the other, propping his ankle on his knee. "Got uses for that mouth." Her eyes went wide as she chewed. Raising his arms over his head, he stretched and let out a groan. "When you finish eating, you'll be using it to tell me what the fuck is going on."

Rosie broke their eye contact, licked her lips before wiping them with her napkin. Then took a swig of her coffee. Badger did everything he could not to watch her, but no matter how hard he tried, his eyes always gravitated back to her. He was a fool for even trying, but he'd be a bigger fool to let himself stare at that pretty face and brown eyes of hers for too long. For real, the feeling that if he looked too deep, he'd be lost forever was like a stone in the pit of his gut that he couldn't cast off.

"Badger?"

He snapped his gaze to hers. "What?"

"I'm sorry, but I don't want to get you involved. So I don't want to tell you what's going on."

He took a swig of coffee. Jesus, he needed a cigarette. "Too late. I'm already involved."

"You're not. Not yet, anyway. And you don't have to be. And I don't want you to be. I can take care of myself."

Badger dropped his foot to the floor and leaned forward. "I'm well aware you can take care of yourself. But that line just ain't gonna work for me, baby. So, eat your eggs. When you're done, you'll tell me, and I'll decide from there what's gonna go down next. We clear?"

The expression on her face went stone hard. She dropped her fork, and it clattered on the plate. "No. And no offense, but fuck you. We're not clear." She stood, the chair screeching on the tile. "I don't know what makes you think you can order me around like I'm some sort of slave or something. Yeah, you helped me out. Twice. And, yeah, you fucked me. More than twice. But what the fuck ever. I'm not your whore, *or* your woman, for that matter. And FYI, buddy, even if I was yours, I don't care for being told what to do. That shit ain't *ever* gonna work for *me. Bayyby*."

At her tantrum, Badger's dick went steel-hard. Fucking hell, she was hotter than molten lava and feisty as hell. Rosie tossed her napkin down on her plate and stormed past him. Doing his best to stifle the grin that'd formed on his lips, Badger snagged her by the wrist and yanked her down onto his lap. Her tight little ass landed right on his dick, luckily not hard enough to hurt. But he knew she could for sure feel it.

"Goddammit! Let me go!" She struggled to get herself up.

Badger let out a chuckle and locked her tighter against him. "Take it easy, Rosie."

"Fuck you. No." She pushed against his chest.

Badger cupped her chin in his grip and forced her to look at him. "You keep wiggling, and that's just what you'll be doing. My cock is hard enough to pound nails right now."

Rosie's eyes went wide as saucers before she closed them and pressed her lips together.

"That got your attention, didn't it?" He shifted his hips, pressing into her to emphasize just how serious he was, and she opened her eyes and glared at him. "I know you liked my dick in you last night. I liked it, too. I know you'd like it again, just like I would. But there's shit to handle, and as much as I want to bend you over the table and fuck you hard while I spank your ass red, we need to handle that shit first." With her jaw still locked in his hand, Rosie groaned but kept quiet, so he continued. "No, you may not be my 'woman,' but the way this goes is: I'm the only one fucking you right now, and believe me, I intend to keep fucking you because that pussy of yours? Yeah, damn sweet, baby. Fucking perfection. But because of who I am, I'm also gonna get you out of whatever shit you got yourself into. Now… Are we clear, Rosie?"

She stayed silent, her gaze boring into his and, fucking hell, his dick throbbed, aching to be wrapped inside her heat again. After a moment, she shifted against him and made an exaggerated show of rolling her eyes.

Badger chuckled once more. "You want it, don't you?"

"Fine. We're clear, but for the record, I think I hate you."

"Yeah, but you still want it." With a smile he couldn't help, he kissed her.

Badger could deal with her hate. He could deal with her tantrums. He just hoped like hell he could deal with whatever mess she was in because he'd meant what he said to her.

He was nowhere near done fucking her yet.

CHAPTER FOURTEEN

Rosie licked her lips, savoring the flavor that was all Badger. This time, instead of tasting of whiskey, he tasted of coffee and just a hint of cigarette mixed in. She didn't mind it; her husband had smoked. Once upon a time, she'd smoked, too. But for her, it'd always been more of a recreational sort of thing. Drugs. Booze. Nicotine. They all fell into the same category with her: take it or leave it.

Except for Badger…with that yummy cock of his pressed against her ass, she feared he could be a habit she might not be able to kick. Maybe because he'd just told her he wasn't done with her. Damn. She sighed and smoothed her hand down the side of his beard. "You don't play fair."

"Never." His lips tipped into another grin.

Jesus, talk about potent. A smoking-hot badass with a smile sexy enough to drop panties. Lord knew she'd dropped hers. Though technically, she hadn't been wearing any when he took over and dominated every square inch of her body. Rosie blew out a breath and put a lid on her libido. "Fine. You want the story, you got it. But don't say I didn't warn you."

She went to slide off his lap, but he pulled her back to his lips. Moaning into his mouth, she wrapped her arms around his neck and took what he gave her…which was pretty much a kiss that rocked her from head to toe, not missing anything in between.

After a moment, he broke from her lips and then patted her ass. "Now you can get down. Take your seat and tell me. I'm all ears."

"And apparently all cock, too." Feeling a tad dazed, she grinned as she slid off his lap and resumed her seat across from him.

He snorted but said nothing. Just picked up his coffee mug and took a sip.

"My husband was murdered."

Badger jerked his head back and wiped his mouth. "Fucking hell, woman. When?"

"Almost seven months ago."

"What happened?" He leaned forward, crossing his arms on the table.

Rosie drew in a deep breath and stared across the table at him, having no idea what Badger would think of her after she got done laying this out. She didn't want to tell him the story. She didn't want to tell anyone the story. It was gross, and as far as she was concerned, although she'd suffered a loss, Joey's actions were a complete and total reflection of her. Her husband, who she'd stayed with for far too long and for reasons she could no longer remember, was dead. And he was dead because he was stupid.

"Rosie?"

"Jesus, Badger. Give me a minute. This isn't easy for me to share." She took a sip of her coffee, set it down, and stared into the creamy liquid before willing herself to continue. "The club the other night…I saw someone. Someone I didn't ever expect to see again."

Badger grunted. "I gathered. Who?"

"My husband, Joey, he was…well, he was an idiot. He was

a runner. And I don't mean the kind that wear Nikes and nylon shorts."

"Got it. Since your husband's dead, it wasn't him you saw. Who was it?"

"Badger, please…just let me get this out."

"Fine. Apologies. Continue."

"Thank you. As I said, he was an idiot. He had a bright idea one night." She shook her head, breathing out a cynical-sounding laugh. "So typical for him, always looking for the quick ride." Unable to look at Badger, she glanced away. "Except this brilliant idea of his was far more dangerous than any of the ones before it and ended up getting him killed. He rolled the dealer."

"He take the product?"

"No. He took the money and ran. Or tried to anyway. He hid it but didn't get very far. The dealer found him before he got wherever he was planning on going." Rosie shook her head again, this time recalling the last time she'd spoken to Joey. *"Are you coming home?"* she'd asked him. *"I hope so,"* had been his reply. She focused on Badger again. "His body was found a few days later. They'd dumped him in the Pequonnock River."

"The Pequo-what? Where the fuck is that?"

That's what he wanted to know? Rosie was so caught off guard by his question she didn't know if she should laugh or scream. "Wow. So not the response I thought I'd get from you." She shook her head and took a sip from her mug. "It's in Bridgeport, Connecticut. It runs into the Long Island Sound."

"Yeah. Okay sorry. Anyway." He blew out a growly sigh. "Where's the money?"

"Joey hid it." Rosie chewed her thumbnail.

"Any idea where?"

She shifted in her seat. "He called me that night. Told me where to find it in case he didn't come home."

"And did you go get it?"

"No."

"Rosie, come on."

"What? I didn't." She crossed her arms. *Fuck. Fuck!*

He dipped his head and stared at her. "Don't bullshit me about this. He told you where it was, and you didn't go get it?"

"Fine. I went and looked, but it wasn't where he said it would be."

"Right." He sighed through his nose. "Fine. So, the dealer is here now, and he's looking for his cash. That's who you saw, right?"

"Yeah, but he's supposed to be in jail. They arrested him."

"Then he either escaped or he's out on bail, and obviously he wants his money, Rosie. Why does he think you have it?"

"How the fuck should I know? Maybe he's assuming! Or maybe he's just got a vendetta!" She pressed the heel of her hands to her eyes as frustration pounded through her like thunder. "From what I heard, word got around pretty fast in that world because he got careless trusting a runner he didn't know well enough. That's how he got caught. People talk."

"That's one hell of an ego hit for a dealer. What's his name, and how big time is this guy?"

"Alvaro Balzan. I don't really know how big he is. I stayed away from that shit, wanted no part of it."

"Let me tell you, baby, regardless of whether or not you wanted it, your man dragged you right the fuck into the middle of it. How much money are we talking?"

She slammed her hands down on the table. "Again, how the fuck should I know, Badger?"

Badger blew out a harsh breath. "You need to calm your ass down and quit talking to me like I'm the goddamn enemy. You got a dealer after you, and from the sounds of it, he's carrying a pretty fucking bruised ego. Because of that, he's wanting his money back to ease it. Apparently, he thinks you have his cash."

"Well, I don't fucking have it."

He smoothed his hand over his jaw, eyes boring into her like a hot poker. "Then, how about we call the police? If what you're telling me is true, they should've already been protecting you."

She stared at her blunt fingernails and jagged cuticles. "Yeah, well, they're not. I declined their protection. The scumbag was locked up with no bail set. What the hell did I need protecting from?"

"Oh, hell. I don't know, Rosie." He shrugged. "Considering he's here and not in Connecticut, locked up, protection might've been a good idea, don't you think?"

"Maybe. But you can't call the cops, Badger."

"Why not?"

"Because you can't."

He stood and leaned over the table toward her. "Rosie, you better come up with a better reason than that and do it quick."

Fuck! "Just, please. Look, I didn't tell them Joey called me that night. I didn't tell them anything I knew. I didn't want to be brought into the trial. I didn't want any part of it, and I still don't."

A groan sounding a lot more like a growl erupted out of Badger, and Rosie swallowed past the knot that'd formed in her throat. He straightened, grabbed his coffee cup and moved to the counter. "Fucking hell, woman."

"I told you I didn't want to involve you. I told you!"

"Too late for that. Already involved. This guy? He ain't gonna stop until he gets what he wants, which is likely you dead."

Rosie dropped her head in her hands as bile rose in her throat. She'd lied—lied straight to Badger's face. Self-loathing crawled over her skin like a bunch of fire ants, and her stomach folded in on itself.

She never should've taken that fucking money. Or better, she should've just given it over to the cops when she found it.

Talk about stupid. Joey wasn't the only idiot in this game. But she'd already lied about hearing from her husband. And then they'd arrested Alvaro, and Rosie'd just…

She'd gone to the train station on her way out of town, heading for Arizona—dead set on starting fresh, expecting to find nothing. But sure enough, she found the key Joey'd hidden for her. Like a robot fueled by fear and anger, she went to the lockers and found what he'd sworn was their "future." What a joke. She'd actually laughed when she opened that stupid locker, and the black leather duffel bag was there.

Without another thought—which was always the case when she wasn't thinking straight and did something that landed her on a road called stupid—Rosie pulled the bag from the confines of the metal cube, let that small yellow door slam closed and walked out of the station like it was no big deal. And then got in her car and headed west.

The fucked-up thing was she hadn't touched one red penny of that money. Not when her car broke down multiple times. Not when she'd arrived and had to set up house, either. She'd counted it, though. Fifty thousand dollars was in that black bag. It now sat hidden in one of the thousands of storage units located in the greater Phoenix area.

A fifty-thousand-dollar future…one she had no intention of ever touching. Or giving back to that fucking sleazebag dealer, either.

———

BADGER STOOD AT THE SINK, rinsing his empty coffee mug out. Rosie was lying. *Had* to be, but from what he could figure, she was sticking to her story. Not that he could blame her. He'd probably do the same thing if he were in her shoes. Just because Badger knew she could trust him didn't mean she knew that. Not yet, anyway.

Thing was, shit wasn't adding up. The girl worked six days

a week spinning on that chrome pole, so if she had the money, why do that? Why work that much when there was a pile of money to kick back and live off? It made no sense. So, maybe she was telling the truth. Setting the cup in the dish drainer to dry, he wiped his hands and faced her.

She had her hands clasped together on the table, staring down at her knuckles like there was a hidden message there. Badger cleared his throat. "I'm grabbing a smoke."

"Okay. What should I do while you do that?"

"Two empty drawers in my dresser. Room on the right side of my closet. May as well unpack because I think you're gonna be here for a while."

She stood. "Wait, I don't—we're gonna live together? Badger, this isn't—"

"You got someplace else to go?" Badger pushed away from the counter and stepped toward the back door. "Somewhere else you think you'll be safe?"

"No. But…"

He opened the sliding door and stepped outside. Rosie followed. He went to the table, slid a cigarette from the pack and lit it. The first drag was always the best, the burn in the back of his throat soothing rather than irritating. He exhaled a stream of smoke and glanced over at her. "But what?"

"We hardly know each other. Hell, we're not even dating. And you think I'm just going to move in?"

For fuck's sake, the woman's life was in jeopardy, and she was worried about details and dating status. He took another drag and exhaled the smoke through his nose. "Like I said, you got someplace else to go? Somewhere else you think you'll be safe?"

"No, but—" She shifted her hips from side to side and raised her fingers to her lips, chewing her nails. "What about if I stay in your guest room? You have one, I think, right?"

Badger turned and faced her. "You planning on taking somebody else's dick besides mine?"

"What? No!" She jerked her head back. "Why would you ask me that?"

"Like I said, I'm not done fucking you. Until I am, you're in my bed. Not my goddamn guest room. We clear?"

She crossed her arms and shot him a glare. "What happens when you're done fucking me?"

"Cross that bridge if we come to it." He drew on his smoke. "Now, we clear?"

She threw her arms up in the air and let them drop, flopping them against her hips. "Fine."

"Best get to unpacking then." He took another drag off his cigarette. Rosie stormed back in his house, and Badger's lips twitched in a grin. Fucking drama queen and her temper tantrums. A damn target on her head, and she's worried about where she's sleeping? Different. So fucking different.

Didn't most women want to have a guy let them move in? Let the dude take care of them? It was like Rosie was wired wrong or some shit. Badger shook his head and stubbed out his cigarette.

After heading back inside, intent on making some calls, he peeked in his bedroom. She was there, busy unloading her clothes, finding the spots he'd told her to use. Good. Badger moved to the spare room he used as an office. The first two things on his list had been accomplished. Rosie unpacking her shit and getting settled had become the third.

Now, it was time for the fourth. Badger needed to do some discreet investigating in Connecticut to find out if Mr. Alvaro, the drug dealer, had skipped bail. If he had, then this whole situation would be wrapped up nice and quick.

But Badger had a feeling nothing about this was going to be nice or quick.

CHAPTER FIFTEEN

Rosie flipped through the channels on Badger's television, buzzing with nervous energy from head to toe. She'd finished unpacking her things hours ago and even cleaned his already-clean kitchen. Nothing on TV was holding her attention, and Badger hadn't come out of his office for hours either.

Tossing the remote on the coffee table, she got up and stretched. She needed to burn some of her anxiety off. Run laps, do jumping jacks…have sex. Ugh! Rosie glanced around the den for about the fiftieth time since she'd parked her ass on the sofa. Badger had a bookshelf in one corner of the room, stuffed full of books and photo albums. He appeared to have a love of sci-fi novels and horror. Neither were her favorites. She went straight for the photo albums and sat back down on the couch with a stack in her lap.

Just as Evie had informed her, Badger had once been a member of a motorcycle club. Several of the albums were filled with pics of him and the other club members. Evie hadn't told her why he'd left the club. But seeing the pics, Rosie was pretty damn curious to know the reason. He was younger in all the photos, though how young she couldn't tell. Hell, she had no idea how old he was now. In fact, she had no idea about a lot of things where Badger was concerned. Except that he was a bounty hunter and amazing in bed. And dominant as all get out. In some of the pictures, there was a woman either on his lap or next to him. But it was never the same woman twice. Apparently, he didn't keep them around long.

Rosie tiptoed down the hall, not wanting to disturb him but too curious not to find out what he could be doing for so long. Besides, it was almost five p.m., and she was getting hungry. Also, she needed to be at work in another couple hours. Rosie peered around the corner of the doorway, doing her best to be quiet.

Badger glanced up briefly from a notebook he was writing in, but quickly focused on it again. "You need something?"

"Yeah, I'm kinda hungry." She stepped inside the doorway and approached his big wooden desk.

He continued writing. "Fridge is stocked. So're the cabinets. Go fix something."

Rosie rounded the side of it and rested her bottom against the edge beside him. "Okay, in the mood for anything?"

He gave her, or rather her hips and where her ass was pressed to the desk, another quick glance and again went back to his notebook. "Surprise me."

"Surprise you?" She crossed her arms and sighed. "I don't even know what you like. Hmm, okay then. I have to be to work soon, so I guess I'll see what I can make that's quick."

Something she'd said got his attention, and Badger stopped writing, put the pen down and looked up at her. "Rosie, you're not going to work."

"Yes, I am—wait. Why not?"

He leaned back in his chair and linked his hands over his tight stomach. "Oh, let's see, baby. Maybe because there's a drug dealer after you?"

"I can't just sit around here and do nothing. I have to work. I have to support myself."

"Guess you're gonna have to *just sit* around here and do nothing because there's no way in hell you're going to work. In fact, while I'm thinking about it, you best call Evie. Tell her your grandmother died or something, and you won't be in for the next week."

Was he out of his damn mind? She had bills to pay. Plus, there were regulars who came into the cabaret just to see *her*. She had an obligation to be at work. Rosie blew out an exasperated breath. "A whole week? No. I'm not doing that. I have to support myself, Badger. What? You planning on supporting me now? Jesus Christ, I have responsibilities, you know."

The glare he gave her almost made her flinch, but she managed to keep it together. Badger growled and got to his feet. "I swear to the devil, you are the only goddamn stripper I know that actually has a work ethic. What the fuck is that about, woman?"

What in the hell did he mean by that? Lots of dancers cared about their jobs. Not all, but she'd known plenty over the years. Maybe. Okay, maybe not plenty, but definitely a few. But still. "Yeah, well, you're the only patch-holder I know that has fucking coasters, so I guess we're both a goddamn mystery, huh?"

"*Former* patch-holder." He gripped her sides, picked her up and sat her on his desk. "Besides, I'm not that much of a mystery since you've obviously been snooping through my things."

"I was bored. You have photo albums." She tried to look innocent, but she doubted he'd fall for it. He pressed forward, and Rosie parted her legs, allowing him to slide between them.

"Now you need to be entertained?"

He smoothed his big palms up her thighs and around to her ass. Jeez, he felt good pressed against her, so good. Rosie circled his neck with her arms and held him just a little closer. "No, not exactly. But it's been hours. What are you doing in here anyway?"

"Work." He ran his hands up her sides.

Rosie let out a less-than-dignified snore. "Yes, work. Got that. What kind of work?"

"Digging up info on bad guys."

"Ah, bounty hunter work." She traced his hairline at the back of his neck.

He dipped his chin, tilting his head to the side. "How much snooping did you do exactly?"

"I didn't snoop that part." She rolled her eyes. "Evie told me you were a bounty hunter, but aside from that, don't worry. You're still a mystery."

"What about this." He nipped her bottom lip. "That a mystery?"

Rosie sucked in a breath as lust filled her belly. "Mmm. Nope. I got acquainted with that last night."

"Yeah? How about this?" Badger cupped her face in his palms, tilted her head to the side and met his lips with hers.

Rosie opened for him, and he slid his tongue inside her mouth. Hot, wet, and without mercy, he kissed her. She arched closer, sucking in air through her nose as he devoured her mouth like he was starving. When he finally pulled away, they were both breathing heavy. Rosie pressed her forehead to his. "Yeah, no. That's not a mystery, either, but I don't think I'm done exploring it."

Badger moved his hands up her shirt, thumbing her nipples. "How 'bout my cock. You done exploring that?"

Immediately her nipples hardened into tight points, and her pussy flooded with moisture. He sure did know how to ramp her up quick. "No way I'm done exploring that."

"Show me. On your knees, now." He stepped back from her and cupped the hard bulge in his jeans before popping the top button and sliding down the zipper.

Rosie licked her lips, hopped off the desk, and went straight to her knees. Anticipation burned through her like a wildfire, and she tilted her head back to gaze up at him. She wanted what he was about to give her. Bad enough, she'd beg if he told her to. Badger had made sure last night that she understood who was in charge. And who would be in charge going forward. He'd shown her this earlier that day as well.

Rosie had worried she might regret giving herself up in this way, and for a few minutes earlier in the day, she'd pushed back on him. No matter how much control she allowed him, Rosie still had a mind of her own *and* an opinion, most certainly an identity. Making sure Badger was clear on all of it was incredibly important to her. But aside from that, as far as the sex went, as far as what she knew he'd give her in exchange for her submission? She had no regrets or reservations.

Rosie wanted the freedom she felt last night when she surrendered her will to him. She was sure she could never do that with anyone else. But with Badger…it was different. He was different.

"Hands behind your back." After pushing his jeans and briefs down his hips, Badger pulled his hard cock free and fisted it. "You want this, baby?"

"Yes, sir. Very much."

"Good girl. Open for me." Badger inched forward and ran the head over her lips, coating them with the drop of pre-ejaculate that'd emerged from the tip. "Eyes on me."

Rosie kept her gaze locked with his as he teased her mouth with the swollen crown of his prick. Her breath sawed in and out of her as her arousal built, and she laced her fingers at her lower back and squeezed her hands together. She wanted to suck and lick, but he was making her wait.

She was so used to taking charge, deciding what she wanted and then just taking it, she struggled to control herself. But the desire to please him held her still.

Rosie knew he'd give her what she wanted…in time.

———

Badger stared down at the woman on her knees before him. God, the things he wanted to do to her. Fuck that, the things he *would* do to her. Because it appeared as though he didn't have to hold back. At all. Last night, he'd shown her how things would go—instructed her on his expectations. She'd agreed. Now here she was, a firm "yes, sir" from her, hands held willingly behind her back, eager mouth open as he gloried in the feel of her soft lips on the edge of his dick.

He told her he wasn't done fucking her, and that was the God's honest truth. But the way she made every inch of his skin get tight by just looking at her, at the same time making his cock go rock hard, Badger feared he might never be done fucking her.

With a tight grip on the shaft, he tapped the head on her warm and wet tongue, letting her have a taste of his come. She moaned, and his balls drew up tight, his prick so hard it throbbed in time with his pulse. "Keep your mouth open. Do not suck until I tell you to. Understand?"

"Yes, sir."

Fucking hell. Yeah, the things he was gonna do to her. With her mouth open wide, Badger shifted forward and slid the head deeper into her mouth. "Flatten out your tongue so I can glide over it. No sucking yet." She did as he asked, and, unable to help himself, he let out a groan.

Her hair was still piled on top of her head in a bun, and Badger grabbed hold of it and slid his cock to the back of her throat before retreating, only to do it again. She moaned and whimpered, shifting her hips in time with his movements. Using his hold on her hair, he pulled her back, freeing his dick from the haven of her mouth, and stroked his length in his fist. "You want to suck it, don't you, baby?"

"Yes, sir. Please. Please let me suck it."

"You make it impossible to deny you anything when you beg so sweetly." Badger bent and stole a quick kiss, tasting his salty flavor on her tongue, needing to give her more of it.

Leaving her lips, he leveled his dick with her mouth, and as she opened, he drove inside.

Rosie closed her lips around his shaft, whimpering as he controlled her movements. Slow and deep, clenching his teeth, biting back the urge to fuck her face hard and fast. The need was so great his skin itched with it. He wanted her mindless, moaning, gagging—complete with tears running down her cheeks as she sucked his dick until he shot his load down her throat.

As the heat of her mouth encompassed him and that heat spread out through his limbs, Badger couldn't take his gaze off her. She'd done good, keeping her hands locked behind her and her eyes open almost the whole time, gazing up at him as he took what he needed from her. "Faster, baby? You want it harder?"

She nodded, his cock buried deep in her mouth, and Badger lost his mind. His orgasm tingled at the base of his spine, radiating to his balls and up the shaft of his dick. Tightening his grip on her hair, he rocked his hips forward and back, pulling her head forward, fucking into her mouth.

Hard. Fast and filthy.

Perfect.

She gagged but kept going. Tears dripped as she blinked, moaning and sucking. Badger moved faster, thrusting to the back of her throat, ready to give her what she'd earned from him. Saliva dripped down her chin, and when he pulled back so only the head remained in her mouth, she slurped and sucked, rolling her tongue around the rim.

Better than perfect.

"Oh, fuck yes. It's yours!" Badger's climax blasted through him, his cock jerking in quick spasms as he spurted into her mouth. He pulled free and stroked his length, coating her lips, chin, and neck in creamy spurts of his semen. Again, his vision got a little blurry as he drew in needed air, and his dick softened in his grip. "You okay?"

She swiped her tongue over her bottom lip and smiled. "More than okay. My panties are soaked through, and I think I came, but I couldn't help it. So, if you have to punish me for it, I understand."

In an instant, his brows rose, and Badger's eyes went wide with shock…and something else he wasn't willing to examine. Instead of saying anything, he cupped her chin in his hand, crouched down in front of her and kissed her.

There was nothing in the world better than a wet, warm, and willing woman. But what was even better was a woman who just told you in so many words that she was also willing to be punished. He wasn't sure what he'd done to deserve the gift she'd just given him, and really, he couldn't care less.

The fact was, she'd given it…and he'd be a fool to turn it away.

CHAPTER SIXTEEN

Two DAYS LATER, Badger sat on the far end of the couch, one arm slung up on the back, the other on the armrest in Deuce's office at the club. It was time to let his boss know Rosie was going to be gone longer than a week. "She's got some shit going on and won't be back until I get it dealt with."

Deuce stroked over his long beard, concern and confusion alive in his eyes. "What? I thought her grandmother died. I take it that was all bullshit, then? Come on, Badger. Rosie has to come to work. We already took a hit without her here this weekend. Do you have any idea how much business has gone up since that little lady started dancing for us? Regulars already started whining they miss her."

"Yeah, boss. I get it. And I'm real sorry, but..." Badger leaned forward, propping his elbows on his knees. Over the past couple of days, he still hadn't settled on how much of Rosie's "shit" he should tell Deuce. But at the same time, the last thing he wanted was this mess spilling out all over the club in the form of Alvaro making his presence known. In an ugly way.

If Deuce knew, he'd be prepared, and Badger could be

sure to have extra eyes out on the floor keeping things cool. He'd already given his boys a picture of Alvaro when he got there that night, letting them know they needed to contact Badger right away if the guy showed up. So far, one of the bouncers remembered seeing Alvaro at least one time over the weekend. He hadn't made any trouble, but that didn't mean he'd keep behaving himself.

"But what? Please don't tell me she's all jacked on drugs. From what I've seen of that girl and what Evie tells me, she's clean. Doesn't mess with none of that shit. So, whatever this stuff is she's got going should be pretty simple, and I'm guessing you'll deal with it fast, but she has to come to work while you do that."

"She's not into drugs." Badger blew out a harsh breath and dragged his hand over his beard. "Look, just take my word that it's serious shit, Deuce. The kind of shit we don't need or want in the bar. She's not safe here. Actually, she's not safe anywhere until I get it handled."

"Well, what the fuck? You know Evie's gotten damn attached to that girl. That means she's gonna worry and then ask me a million fucking questions if she's not back in a week. One's I won't be able to answer. So spit it the fuck out, all right? What is it? She got a pissed-off boyfriend or, worse, a pimp?"

Badger shook his head and leaned back. No way Deuce was going to let it rest. "Fine. I hear you. But I'm telling you right now, no way in hell I'm gonna jeopardize the bar." Badger let out a growly sigh. "Here's the deal: due to her moron of a dead husband, she's now got a drug dealer after her from back east. He's looking for his money that her husband took from him and likely plans to put Rosie in a body bag like he did her husband. Fucker showed up here Friday night when she was on stage."

Deuce leaned back in his desk chair, linked his hands behind his head and stared up at the ceiling. "So that's why you took off, and she was nowhere to be found. Jesus. Fuck, that ain't good."

"Yeah, I know."

"How much money we talking?"

"She says she doesn't know." Badger rubbed the back of his neck.

"How does she not know? Little lady got a dealer after her for it, and she don't know?" Deuce shook his head and blew out an exasperated growl. "All right. Where's the money?"

Badger grunted. "She says she doesn't know that, either. Apparently, she went and looked where her husband said he hid it, but it wasn't there."

"You believe her?"

"I want to believe her. But I don't think she's being straight up." Badger crossed his arms. "If she's lying, I'm betting it's because she's scared. In her shoes, if I had the money, I don't know if I'd be so quick to just offer up where it was, either."

"This ain't good, Badger. Not good at all. No way this won't touch the club, but I got you. We'll handle it. You know that. We're family, and like I said, Evie's taken a liking to Rosie. That makes her family, too—" Deuce pressed his lips together, regarding Badger in a way that only years of knowing one another would allow, "—if I'm not mistaken, seems like you've taken a liking to her also."

There it was. For fuck's sake. Old-ass, tough-as-nails biker on the outside. All heart and hopeless romantic on the inside. Goddamn marshmallow puff. It's why Evie put up with his ornery-as-hell bulky ass. But at the same time, Deuce was good to his old lady. Plain and simple. And he never let her forget how much he loved her, how beautiful she was. He'd open a damn vein for that woman, and Evie knew it. It was admirable and not the kind of love most people ever got a chance at.

The boss had already grilled Badger during Turkey Day dinner about Rosie, and now he was gonna approach that particular road again. Badger didn't feel much like going there. But there wouldn't be much choice. Yeah, he'd taken a liking to Rosie. Fuck him, how could he not? She had a sweet ass and an even sweeter pussy. Nipples he'd dreamed of…but more than that, she was beautiful.

Different. Perfect.

But she was also drama and complication. He regarded his boss and long-time friend, determining how to respond. "Not sure we need to get into the details of that right now. But look, she's all heart, and she's in trouble. So yeah, I'm gonna help her. What happens after? I don't know. Just don't let Evie start planning a wedding or some crazy shit like that, we clear?" Deuce let out a loud chuckle, and Badger rolled his eyes. "No shit. Between the two of you? I swear, coupla hopeless romantics."

"All right, we're clear, my man." Deuce chuckled again but then sobered. "So, what's the plan? How you want to work it?"

"Still mapping that out. So far, all I know is the dude's out on bail, and he ain't skipped yet. Yet…" Badger leaned forward again. "I got feelers out. It could be months before he's scheduled in court. You know how that shit goes. I'm guessing he's got himself a good bloodsucker who'll get it postponed as long as possible. But you know as well as I do, if that fucker traveled clear across the country just to hunt down our girl, he ain't got no plans to stand before the judge."

"A dealer with a vendetta, facing a murder charge? Hell, that's the definition of dangerous."

Badger nodded. "Exactly. Which is why I'm still mapping shit out. It'd make it real easy if he'd already skipped. I could just take him in then."

"What if you just make an anonymous call to the law where she's from and get him taken in that way?"

"Rosie was dead set on me not calling the cops." Badger rubbed the back of his neck. "But even if I did, you know as well as I do, they ain't gonna just piss out a warrant for one murdering drug dealer who may or may not have left the state. The state of Connecticut likely has bigger fish to worry about until he *actually* misses his court date. I doubt the bondsman would jump at it, either."

"You're probably right." Deuce let out a sigh. "Brother, I gotta say, even if you send him back to jail, with the ego bruise he's carrying, he won't stop hunting her."

"Let's not go there yet." Badger sat back and pushed the underlying implications in the warning Deuce was giving him to the back of his mind. He was one hundred percent right, though. Alvaro wouldn't stop. Guys like that had no problem issuing a hit from behind bars.

"All right, fine. You gonna bring Wolf in?"

Badger shrugged. "Haven't decided."

"Telling you now, you need anything from the brothers, you let me know. I'll call 'em in. But I suggest you bring in Wolf now. My gut says you're gonna need him."

"Noted." Badger got to his feet. "I'll be here as much as possible, but I'm gonna need a little leeway from you on that, too."

"Do what you need to do." Deuce stood and extended his palm.

Badger linked forearms with his boss, and Deuce pulled him into an embrace. He clapped Badger on the back before pulling away. Badger cleared his throat at the unexpected emotion welling up inside him. "Thanks, boss. 'Preciate it. I'll check back in tomorrow."

Deuce nodded as he resumed his seat at his desk, and Badger stepped out of the office, closing the door behind him. He hated having to lay all that mess out to the old man. But it wasn't like he'd had much choice. Sure, Badger had a colorful past, which had likely earned him files in the many alphabet soup agency databases, and his bounty-hunting tactics teetered over the legal line on occasion, but he was still, for the most part, an honest man. Based on his biker lifestyle and his choice of work, some people might call bullshit on his claim of honor. But that didn't make them right.

Regardless, there was no way in hell he'd lie to Deuce. Badger had way too much respect for the man.

CHAPTER SEVENTEEN

Rosie looked up from the e-book she was reading when she heard the Harley pull into the driveway. Badger had left hours ago for the club, which was after she'd convinced him to let her borrow his tablet so she could download some books to read. He'd grumbled and growled the whole time, downloading the app for her, and continued after he'd handed over the device so she could log into her Amazon account and grab the unread books sitting in the cloud.

Rosie still didn't know how to read *him*, but tried her best not to let all his sound effects deter her. She'd fallen behind on her TBR list and, considering she was bored out of her friggin' skull and had been for the better part of the week being stuck in his house, this was about the best solution she could come up with. She looked to the kitchen, listening close for the sounds of the garage door opening, expecting to see him walk through the door at any moment.

After another minute, when he didn't appear, Rosie stood—

The doorbell rang. *Weird.* She headed for the front door. Unlocking it, she swung the door open. "What? Your garage door opener quit worki— Oh!" From what she could see through the metal security doorframe, the strange man standing there was tall, a little scary and very much a biker. But also very, *very* good-looking. Rosie swallowed her shock and got her mouth back online. "Umm. Can I help you?"

The guy pushed his clear night-riding shades up onto his head. "Who might you be?"

"Dude. Really? You're standing at *my* door. How 'bout you tell me who you are." Since she was behind the locked metal door, she figured she was relatively safe, though considering the guy's size, maybe not.

"Your door, huh?"

"Yeah. My door." She put her hand on her hip.

He cleared his throat as he pulled off his fingerless leather gloves. "Where's Badger?"

"And again, you're the one at the door. Who's asking?" Rosie crossed her arms and raised one eyebrow.

Mr. Scary smiled, exposing his perfectly straight white teeth before throwing his head back and bursting into a fit of laughter. The guy laughed so hard his whole body shook with it. It was a sight to behold, for sure.

Rosie pursed her lips and tilted her head to the side, watching him in a sort of twisted awe. Wonders never ceased. Biker dude just blew hot right off the Richter scale with his little display. Granted, Badger was still hotter, but this guy? He was an altogether different kind of good-looking.

Just as Rosie was about to ask him if he was done, Badger rolled up on his bike.

The dude stopped laughing and glanced over his shoulder. "Saved by the pipes, darlin'." He grinned and stepped away, presumably toward the driveway.

Oh, Christ. Rosie fumbled with the deadbolt, finally getting the damn thing unlocked and the door open by the time Badger parked his motorcycle, shut down the engine and got off. In a huff, she hurried her ass down the walk to the driveway but stopped short when she reached them.

"Glad you made it, brother." Badger eyed her as he clasped the other guy's forearm and pulled him into a biker bro-hug. "I see you met Rosie."

The stranger glanced over his shoulder at her before turning back to Badger. "We were working our way there. Bit of a feisty one you got on your hands."

Badger looked at her over the guy's shoulder, his gaze moving down her body before coming back to her face. "What'd you do now?"

"Now? What? Wait… He… Ugh! Whatever." Rosie threw her hands up in the air before crossing her arms in a huff. Agitation coursed through her blood with every beat of her heart. What had she done now? Not a fucking thing! Jesus, he was a dick. Apparently, they both were. And why the hell had Badger looked her up and down like that? Did he not approve of her outfit?

He had no issue with how she'd dressed any other time in the last six days. So she'd taken off her makeup and changed her clothes. Big deal. What was wrong with fitted black yoga pants and a tank top? Rosie was going for comfort, not sexy. Badger needed to get a damn grip if he thought she was going to just stay all made up twenty-four-seven, or worse, look like she did on stage. That just wasn't her. That was Arianna—her stage persona.

Rosie was just Rosie. Normal. Natural. Makeup-free and in fucking yoga pants!

———

Badger had to suppress a laugh at Rosie's reaction to his question. "Don't go gettin' yourself all in a lather. I was teasing, woman." He moved to the garage door keypad and punched in the code. "You want a beer, Wolf?"

"When don't I want a beer?"

"True story." Badger pushed his cycle into the garage, and

Wolf followed. After leaning the Dyna back on its kickstand, he glanced back to Rosie. She was still standing in the driveway. Arms crossed under her pert little tits. No bra under that fitted tank top either, and her nipples drawn into hard points —from either her agitation or the cool night air—poking through the thin fabric. Narrow hips shifted to one side.

For fuck's sake, those damn pants she had on were like a second skin, emphasizing her long legs and slender curves. His dick practically shot rod-hard as soon as he'd gotten a good look at her in the outdoor lights. Plus, her face was bare of all makeup, her hair piled high on top of her head.

The woman was straight-up killing him.

Her choice of attire, level of face paint, and hairstyle had varied all week. Some days, she'd done her hair all curly and full, makeup all done up to perfection and dressed as if she was heading out on a date. Other days, she'd come out, hair pulled up high, barely any makeup and clad in basic jeans and sneakers. She was beautiful. He liked seeing her all ways, especially naked ones, but the casual, no-makeup look got to him every time.

He liked it. A little too much.

Badger pulled his bandana off his head and let out a grumbly sigh. "You comin'?"

She dropped her arms and placed her hands on her hips. Then looked away from his gaze. All drama. He hadn't seen too much of it this week, but now it was in full swing. He waited, curious to see what she might do next. He heard Wolf's low chuckle behind him. Yeah, his best friend had gotten it right. She was definitely feisty. Badger liked that a little too much, too.

When she didn't move, Badger decided to give her a nudge—in the form of a one-word statement—to get her ass in gear. "Woman…"

She blew out a harsh breath, her chest rising and falling with it, before moving toward him. "Fine."

Drama still on high volume, Rosie brushed past him. Again, Badger had to suppress a laugh. For sure, after he was done briefing Wolf on their situation, he'd enjoy paddling her ass 'til it glowed pink for this little particular fit. "You get it all out your system?"

"Whatever. Leave me alone." She continued into the house.

"She like this all the time?" Wolf took off his leather jacket.

Badger followed suit, removing his leather as well. "Only been a week. Too soon to tell. Let's grab that beer. Got shit to tell you."

"Right behind you, brother."

After grabbing a couple bottles from the fridge, Badger settled on his back patio with Wolf and lit his first cigarette. Like earlier that week at the bar, he didn't want to involve anyone else in Rosie's mess, but his boss was right. Based on the intel he was digging up on Alvaro, he was going to need the backup. He'd be stupid not to let a trusted few in on what was going down. Deuce and Wolf were the only two men in that category.

Badger had a lot of acquaintances, some he might even refer to as friends...but few were actual, true friends. Deuce and Wolf were pretty much it. His relations with them dated back to his old MC days. Bonds were formed during those years between the three. Strong ones that would never be broken. Of that, Badger was certain.

"Planning on sittin' there all night, sucking on that cancer stick and barley and hops, or you gonna spit out what's going on?"

Badger chuckled before taking another swig of beer. "Yeah. Getting there."

"You in some sort of trouble?"

"Not sure. Might be." He glanced over his shoulder into the house through the sliding glass door. Rosie was on the couch, blanket on her lap, tablet on top of that. Christ, she was adorable. "She's got some shit swirling around her."

"Hold on a sec. You brought trouble into your world over some pussy? Brother, that ain't like you. The fuck is that about?"

A growl rumbled out of Badger, and he snapped his gaze back to Wolf. "Let's get something straight real fucking fast. I love you, you're my brother, but that woman in there, she ain't *just* pussy. So watch it."

Wolf raised his hands in defense. "Whoa, go easy. But hey, you know as well as I do, there's never been anything for you but 'just pussy,' so forgive my mistake. Then, if you don't mind, to ease my shock, what's so different about this one?"

"Fucking. Everything." He lit another cigarette. "Truth be told, I don't know what Rosie is yet, but she's definitely more than just pussy."

"All right then. How 'bout you tell me what you do know."

"I know she's full of drama and prone to little temper tantrums. I got my ways of handling that." Badger shook his head, pushing away the images of exactly how much he liked "handling" Rosie and how much she liked being "handled," and took a draw of his smoke. "I also know she's in a fuckton of trouble. And I'm gonna get her out of it."

"Define trouble?"

"There's a dealer from her past, more specific, her dead husband's past, in town looking to make an example of her by way of putting her in the morgue."

"No bueno."

"Exactly." Badger stared out into the dark expanse of his backyard. There was no other way to describe this sitch than to say it sucked. Plain and fucking simple.

As he laid everything out for Wolf, Badger knew his friend would have his back. Deuce would, too. Together, they'd get Rosie through the shit-storm that'd come calling. One way or another, Badger would make sure of it.

———

ROSIE'S ASS was planted on the couch, reading—or trying to read—while Badger kept his ass outside with that Wolf guy. On occasion, one of them would come in, grab another beer or hit the bathroom, only to disappear through the sliding glass door again. Both moved around her like she was invisible or something. She hated it. It was annoying beyond belief. And really, what kind of woman named their child "Wolf?"

"Same kind of woman who names their child Badger," she mumbled. "Weirdos."

They were likely just nicknames, ones they'd earned like real bikers in an MC often did, but it was still weird. Never mind the fact that Badger would probably never tell her his real name. It kind of sucked not knowing, but whatever. He didn't want her to know, so she wasn't going to ask again. With another huff, Rosie adjusted the blanket and focused on the screen of the tablet again. And read…the same line for about the fiftieth time. Ugh! So stupid. What the hell were they doing out there for so long? What on earth could they be talking about? Her? Her mess? A bolt of concern shot through her. Jesus, she hoped not. Rosie didn't know Wolf, but she sure didn't want him involved.

Badger was already at risk. She felt bad enough about that. And she knew he'd filled Deuce in, too. Guilt marked her insides like a black stain. God, the last thing she wanted was something to happen to Deuce and Evie. They were good people.

She stared out the glass door again, biting her nails. In an effort to distract herself, she focused on Wolf. His hair was blonde with highlights throughout, likely from the sun. And it was long. Really fucking long. He wore it pulled into a low ponytail at the nape of his neck, which hung all the way down to his lower back, touching his belt. There were black elastic hair ties every couple inches down the length of the tail to secure it.

Odd it wasn't braided, but then she remembered. No braid in long hair on a biker pretty much signified the dude was single. If Wolf had a woman, she'd have no doubt braided it for him. It served as a signal to all other chicks that a man was off limits. Surprising he didn't have a girlfriend, though. The guy was gorgeous in a totally anti-biker way and more of a rugged romance cover-model way. Big muscles, sparkling clear blue eyes (maybe that's where the name came from), and a long blonde goatee. The mustache part was grown in a Fu Manchu style, longer than the chin hairs.

Guys with long hair weren't her thing. Blondes weren't, either. But on Wolf, with the blue eyes and genuine smile, it was a lethal combo. Plus, he had two guns holstered and mounted upside down on his lower back. Rosie had never seen anything like it before. And he had a huge freaking knife in a leather sheath strapped to his right thigh. Because one weapon wasn't enough, apparently. Three were far better. Rosie snorted. Talk about a biker's version of the wild, wild west. Translation: The dude might be hot, but he also looked lethal as hell.

Rosie blinked, glancing away as both men were suddenly heading for the door. Badger had caught her staring at his friend. *Shit.* He was going to be so pissed. Except, what the fuck? It wasn't like they had some sort of commitment or something. They were fucking. That was it. And she was only looking. A girl could look at the menu as long as she didn't order off it.

They both moved past her toward the formal living room, and Badger clapped his friend on the back. "'Preciate you comin' by, brother."

"Anytime, man. You know that." Wolf looked back toward the couch, his gaze locked on Rosie. She bit her thumbnail and shifted under his penetrating gaze. "It was nice almost meeting you. Maybe we'll get to chat next time, darlin'." He smiled that killer smile of his before turning away, and Rosie felt her cheeks get warm.

For the love of all things! She fanned herself. He was steamy hot, but Badger was still hotter. Most definitely. Badger was breathtaking. And Badger was fan-fucking-tastic in bed. He was a grumpy asshole, too, but yeah. Whatever. So far, the sex rocked. Rosie closed her eyes and let her head fall back on the arm of the couch as she felt the rest of her body get warm. A craving for Badger she'd become accustomed to feeling swirled through her system.

As if on cue, reality plowed its way through her lust-filled desire, and she frowned. Her life was in danger, serious danger, and she was horny? How fucked up was that? Though it hadn't stopped her from shamelessly sucking his dick whenever he commanded her to or riding his face or cock into orgasm heaven at any time that week.

"Bed. Now."

Rosie opened her eyes to find Badger above her, his face upside down, staring down at her with an expression in his eyes she could not read. "Yes, sir."

He walked away, and she cringed as she got to her feet, totally unable to stop the sudden lust pulsing hot and fast through her veins, nor the automatic response to his command that'd flown out of her mouth. Rosie followed him to the bedroom. Praying as she navigated the hallway that if she was in trouble, it would be the kind that brought her to orgasm and not the kind that brought her to tears. Unless, of course, the orgasm was so good, she was in tears afterward. Which had already happened a couple of times that week.

Good grief, she was so screwed.

CHAPTER EIGHTEEN

Badger stalked into his bedroom and clicked on the bedside lamp. When he turned, Rosie was standing in the doorway, nibbling on her nails. He jerked his chin in her direction. "You hungry?"

She dropped her hands away from her mouth. "No. Why?"

He yanked the blankets to the foot of the bed. "The way you keep eating those nails of yours, I figured you might be."

"Very funny. I bite my nails. So what. Quit picking on me."

He smirked. "I can think of better uses for that mouth."

"Yeah, I bet you can. Can I bite that, too?" She crossed her arms.

Feisty. Mouthy. Fucking dramatic.

Pissed him off and made his dick hard at the same time. They'd been together several times already—he'd actually lost count, but Rosie knew what that attitude of hers would gain her. Unless…

Badger tilted his head to the side, dipping his chin as he looked her over. Unless she wanted to be punished. *That* he could do.

He unbuckled his belt and slid it free of the loops. "That attitude of yours needs some correcting. Also, don't think I didn't notice you looking Wolf up and down like he was something you wanted to make a meal of. Take off your clothes. Stand at the foot of the bed. Legs shoulder-width apart. Bend over and take ahold of the footboard."

Rosie's eyes went wide, and a little gasp escaped, but then she was moving. Doing as he'd ordered. Yeah, she wanted it. Likely needed it, too. She may not be a traditional sub, but with him, she was for sure his bottom. He had no problem whatsoever being her top.

She had a strong personality, though most all subs did, or should anyway. But Rosie was different. There was that word again. Every fucking thing about her was different for him. She wasn't his typical "pussy," as Wolf had pointed out earlier. But Badger suspected he wasn't her typical cock, either.

He didn't know shit about her relationship with her husband, and he didn't want to know. He was more interested in the here and now and the fact that this woman had gotten naked for him almost instantly and was currently bent over his bed, waiting for her punishment. His dick was rock solid simply because she'd obeyed his command. Far be it for him to keep either of them waiting any longer.

Badger took off his shirt and stepped behind her. "You were hoping for this, weren't you?"

"Yes, sir."

"You need it, Rosie?" He smoothed his palm down her lower back to the curve of her ass, loving how she trembled when he touched her.

"Never thought I'd say this, but yes, sir. I think I do."

"Good girl." He slid his fingers between the cleft of her ass. "Tell me, Rosie. You want Wolf's cock?"

She shook her head before glancing over at him. "No. No, sir. I swear I don't."

"Eyes forward." She quickly looked away, and he

continued stroking between her ass cheeks. "Saw you looking at him. Kinda looked like you wanted a taste. I gotta worry 'bout you stepping away from my cock for his?"

"No. Never, Badger. Never." She started to look at him again, but caught herself and stopped.

"Good to know." He slid his fingers between her legs and stroked over the mouth of her cunt. Badger knew she didn't really want Wolf. But she *had* been looking, and she needed to understand that Badger had seen it and didn't much care for it. He wasn't the jealous type at all. Never had been, anyway.

This wasn't about jealousy—at least, that's what he tried to tell himself. But then again, he didn't like watching her when she worked the floor at the club. Watching her eye Wolf struck a different and deeper chord in Badger. He and Wolf had shared a few chicks in the past. But this was different. This was Rosie, and Badger had no intention of sharing her with anyone. "Gonna use my belt on you tonight. Think you can handle it?"

Rosie moaned and arched against his touch. "I...I don't know."

"You can. But just in case, you remember the safe word?" He dipped his fingers into her hot core. Somehow he managed to stifle his groan, but his dick got twice as hard. She was dripping, and he hadn't even done a thing to her yet. Perfect.

"Oh God! *Yes...mmm...*" Rising to her tiptoes, she panted a breath. "I remember, sir."

Badger drew her wetness to her clit, spreading the slick juices around the tight nub. "Say it for me."

"Berry... Fuck that feels so good." She rocked her hips.

"Good girl. Look at you all slick and hot for me already." Badger pressed two fingers inside her pussy. "We'll see how wet you are when I get done making your ass candy-apple red."

She moaned, rolling her hips in time with his strokes. "Yes, sir."

Badger pulled away and stood behind, but just to her left. Once more, he smoothed his palm over one ass cheek and then the other. "We'll start slow and build it from there."

She nodded, but Badger let it go at that; he didn't need a response. With the belt looped in half and held tight in his right hand, he smoothed the curved end of it down her spine to the crack of her ass and over each mound of her buttocks. A visible shiver ran through her body, and she arched as he stroked between her thighs with the leather.

"Please..."

Badger's cock jerked, throbbing behind his zipper. Fuck, she was ready and begging for it, and she was going to love it. Somehow, knowing that she'd probably never done anything like this in her life amped his need for control up even higher. Yeah, he'd spanked plenty of ass with his hand or a belt, riding crop, flogger, you name it. But none of that other pussy compared to right now with Rosie. Not a single one of them.

Plus, the fact that he'd been the one to pop her Dom/sub-Top/bottom cherry had pushed things far over the edge of hot for him. It'd been like that all week. Hot, hard, and dominant. Each time, he'd taken her, and however he'd taken her. She'd wanted it and begged. It was fucking amazing.

He squared his shoulders, drew his arm back and, keeping his swing controlled, struck across Rosie's ass cheeks with the belt...and he knew it was a moment he'd never forget. The sound of the leather connecting with her fine skin echoed through the room, and she rose on tiptoe, her skin already turning pink as she let out a lust-filled moan so potent Badger thought he might come in his pants.

Different. So fucking different... He closed his eyes and drew in a slow breath before he struck again.

———

Rosie's ass stung like it'd been set on fire but in the most delicious kind of way. Badger had only struck her once, and she knew he hadn't hit her very hard, but she'd almost come instantly. Over the last few minutes leading up to that moment leather had connected with flesh, he'd been building her arousal. Even as he'd questioned her about her attraction to Wolf, her desire for Badger had only grown. Anticipation of what would come next, how high he would take her, raced through her veins as her heart thumped hard in her ears.

And then he struck her again, this time a little harder.

Rosie let out a guttural moan as she clenched her ass cheeks. She tried not to because holy God, it hurt, but it also felt so good. A literal contradiction of sensations tumbled through her body in an all-out war with each other. Both winning.

"Relax, baby. Breathe." Badger smoothed his palm over her hot skin.

She hissed at the new sensation his touch caused, but then his hand was gone. Rosie drew in a deep breath and let it out, forcing her body to relax. "Yes, sir."

He struck again. This time, a little lower on her bottom and harder. She moaned, long and low, her eyes rolling back in her head. Sweet Jesus. She had no idea it would be like this. And this was supposed to be a punishment for her mouthy attitude and checking out his best friend? Fucking hell, if this is what she got each time she shot him attitude, she planned on just being a bitch all the damn time. However, Rosie wasn't stupid. She'd for sure curb-check the ogling of his friends in his presence.

The belt smacked home again. The loud crack of leather connecting with skin rang out around her, and Rosie let out an even louder yelp followed by a moan. Holy fuck, she was going to come. The sound of the belt hitting her ass, combined with the sting of the leather against her skin, sent

Rosie's head spinning, and all she could think was more. *More…please.*

"Goddamn, that red glow is pretty." He smoothed his palm over her burning flesh before slipping between her legs to her core. "Oh yeah, baby. Love this sloppy and dripping wet cunt."

"Badger," she breathed, arching as he pressed two fingers inside her core. Her channel clenched down on the welcome intrusion, and her clit pulsed. Holding her orgasm back would be impossible if he kept this up. But he hadn't told her she could come yet. And as much as she wanted to obey him, disobeying him was becoming awfully appealing.

He bent close to her, his lips to her ear. "I feel you squeezing my fingers. You gonna come without my say so?" He placed the belt on the bed, reached around her front and rubbed her clit.

"Oh God! Badger! I'm trying…" Two fingers thrusting in her pussy, two fingers working her clit. Rosie gritted her teeth, moaning as she panted through the rising waves of her orgasm. It was on her, through her, taking her over.

Abruptly, he pulled free of her channel and cupped her mound in his palm. "Easy, now. Breathe through it. Hold it, Rosie. Not yet."

Somehow, God only knew how, she held her climax back. But not by much. She turned her head to the side as he let her go and gazed at him. The hard expression on his face shocked her. Was he not affected by any of this? Was this all her? She frowned as confusion and doubt boomeranged around her brain. "Badger?"

"Shhh." He tilted his head to the side as his expression turned soft. The feel of his palm smoothing over her heated ass cheeks and his fingers trailing up her spine made every inch of her skin tingle. And then he pressed a tender kiss to her temple. "Good girl. Such a good girl."

Picking up the belt again, Badger stepped back from her.

He was affected, at least based on the look she now recognized in his eyes and the way he touched her, he was. Warmth spread through Rosie, and she closed her eyes as she released her doubt and fell once again into her need for him.

"Not done making this ass shine yet. But when I am, I'm going to eat your pussy until you come on my face. Save your orgasms for then. We clear?"

She tightened her hold on the footboard of the bed. "Yes, sir."

"Go ahead and bend forward."

Grateful the frame was low enough, Rosie did as he said and laid her chest down on the bed. Her hard nipples pressed into the sheets, and she let out a moan at the contact. The hard wood of the frame met her right at the bend of her hip and thigh, giving her a whole other sensation to take in.

"God, you're fucking amazing." Badger smoothed his hand over her sensitive ass cheek again, and Rosie hissed. Heat radiated straight to her clit, and she knew in the next moment, she'd feel the slap of the belt.

THWAAP!

Oh God. Again. Again! Hard, fast and one after another.

Over and over until she thought she might scream. Rosie arched, raising her ass higher, writhing with each hit. Moaning, whimpering, and begging for more as tears dripped down her cheeks. She couldn't stop the need. Rosie's clit pulsed, and her skin tingled from the top of her head to the tip of her toes. She didn't want to stop it. The rush of adrenaline coursing through her system made her feel stoned, euphoric even.

And then he growled. The rumble of it vibrated through Rosie, arrowing straight to her core.

She needed to come. She needed to be fucked. She needed him.

———

BADGER DROPPED the belt and fell to his knees behind Rosie. Between the bright red shade, he'd turned her ass and the guttural moans and pleas coming out of her while he made it that way, he'd lost his mind. He was nothing more than all primal male. Two thoughts raced through his mind: Taste her and mark her—in every way possible.

With his dick throbbing behind his zipper, Badger placed his palms on her heated ass cheeks and spread them apart, baring her to him. "So fucking wet for me. Dripping down your thighs, woman." She moaned, and Badger backed away from her, spun, and lay down on the floor. "Come here, baby. Want you on my face."

Taking hold of her calves, he inched her backward a few steps and pulled her down. Her moves shaky, Rosie straddled him, her knees landing on the carpet on either side of his head. Badger wrapped his arms around her thighs to hold her in place and licked through the folds of her pussy.

She jerked above him, and her hands landed on his head. "Fuck!"

"Oh, yeah. Right on the edge. Give it to me." Badger sucked her clit between his lips, working the tight nub with his tongue.

Rosie rolled her hips, grinding down on his mouth. "Yes. Oh God, yes."

He worked her as she squirmed above him, riding his face. With her fingers digging into his scalp, she begged through moans and whimpers until, finally, her orgasm broke free, and she seized above him. Badger didn't let up, sucking harder on her clit until her body broke into a fit of tremors, her sweeter-than-candy juices coating his tongue.

"Badger!" Gasping, she raised up, pulling her cunt away from his mouth. "I can't...it's too much."

"Far from done with you yet." Badger urged her off him to his side, and when he got to his feet, he picked her up and carried her to the bed. Once he'd laid her on the sheets, he removed his jeans and grabbed a condom from the night table drawer.

Rosie lay with her knees pulled to her chest, watching him, her feet crossed at the ankle. The sated and dazed expression on her face sent a bolt of satisfaction through him. He'd given her that look, and he wanted to keep it there.

Her eyes dipped down to his dick as he sheathed himself in latex. She licked her lips. "I want that, please."

He smirked and climbed onto the bed and knelt in front of her. Taking her by the ankles, Badger spread her legs apart and groaned when he caught sight of her swollen and glistening pussy. "So fucking sexy."

Badger framed her small waist with his palms and smoothed them up her skin until he found her breasts. Massaging them, he squeezed the small mounds before tugging her hard nipples. Unable to deny himself, he bent over her and sucked one solid peak into his mouth as he rolled the other between his finger and thumb. Almost immediately, her hands were on the back of his head, gripping him tight and holding him to her as she arched against him.

Releasing her sweet nipples, he moved to her mouth and kissed her. There was just no getting enough of her. He kissed her until they were both gasping for air, devouring her tongue and lips with almost a desperate need. He'd never needed someone so much in his life.

Rosie reached between them and gripped his shaft, positioning him at her opening. He pulled from her lips and gazed down at her. "You ready?"

She nodded. "Yes, sir."

In one thrust, he penetrated her tight core. Badger gritted his teeth as her cunt clenched in little spasms around his shaft. With his gaze locked on hers, he pulled back and then slid deep again. "Fucking hell, this pussy. So slick and hot."

She raised her knees higher and tilted her pelvis forward. "You make it that way."

The need to pound into her, take her hard and fast, beat through him, but instead, Badger settled his whole body on top of hers, bracing himself on his forearms. Her hard nipples pressed into his chest as he rolled his hips, thrusting forward, keeping his pelvis tight to hers and his dick buried deep in tightness. "Milking my cock. Can't get enough."

"Badger…" Rosie undulated beneath him, grinding her clit against him as he thrust into her.

With each push of his hips, she whimpered, and he drove her harder. Fucking hell, the way she moved with him. The way she felt. Like some sort of orchestrated dance, they were in perfect sync. Badger buried his hands in her long hair, tilted her head back and licked down her neck. "Want to feel you without a barrier between us."

"I want that, too. Fuck, Badger, I need to come. Please, tell me I can come for you?" Rosie ran her hands down his back to his ass. Gripping hard, she pulled him against her.

"Fuck yes. Give it to me. Let me feel your tight cunt squeezing my dick." The tingles of his own orgasm climbed up his spine. "Ah, Christ!"

Rosie writhed beneath him, gripping his sides as her moans got louder. Her climax rolled through her, and her sweet pussy gripped, milking his shaft. Heat radiated through his limbs, and he moved faster, thrusting harder, deeper. Their slick bodies slid against each other. Her hard nipples dragged against his chest. The heels of her feet dug into his lower back.

With every gasp from her lips and each touch from her body, he died a thousand blissful deaths. He knew in the span of a nanosecond, he'd never get enough of this—of her. Badger stilled, buried deep inside her and focused on her face. She was caught in the whirlwind of her orgasm…and she was the most beautiful thing he'd ever seen.

As endless waves rocked through her core, her pussy stroked his shaft, clenching him like a fist, and he tumbled headlong, right over the edge with her. His orgasm rolled up his body with a force he'd never felt before. Badger dipped his head and covered her mouth with his lips, seeking her tongue.

His cock jerked inside her core, over and over, spurting his release into the condom. Rosie moaned into his mouth, rocking against him as they both rode out the aftershocks of their shared climax.

When he broke from her lips, his head was spinning, and he could barely catch his breath. He pressed his face to her neck, and unable to stop himself, Badger mumbled the only complete thought he was capable of at that moment. "Mine…" He pressed a soft kiss behind her ear. "Mine."

CHAPTER NINETEEN

Badger woke to warm, soft woman pressed against his side. She had one arm slung over his stomach and her head on his chest. He was not a man who liked to cuddle. Ever. Hell, he never really even slept next to a woman. Not for the whole night, anyway. Fuck them, minus the intimacy, and send them on their way. Less complication that way.

But with Rosie, ever since he'd had her beside him beneath the blankets, he couldn't seem to let her go. He didn't even want to think about what that meant. He also didn't want to think about how epic the sex with her had been, either. Or how she'd taken so nicely to his belt across her ass. Didn't even want to get into how snug her cunt was around his cock…

Fucking hell, speaking of cock—his jumped to life at the very thought of getting back inside her. He smoothed his palm along his beard and let out a sigh. Contrary to what his dick wanted, Badger needed to shelf that little idea and get his ass out of bed. There was work to be done. He needed to check in with the boys at the cabaret and see if Alvaro had shown his face.

With any luck, the asshole had come back into the club,

though with Rosie nowhere to be found, maybe he'd given up. Yeah right. Badger shook his head. Lady Luck had never been on his side before; it was highly unlikely the old bitch would show up for this particular situation.

He pressed a soft kiss to the top of Rosie's head before he slid from beneath her and got to his feet. Before heading to the bathroom, he turned and made sure the covers were tucked around her. Why he cared whether or not she was all snuggled and warm in the bed, he had no clue, but it was another thing to add to the steadily growing list of shit he didn't want to think about regarding Rosie.

With one last glance at her, he made his way to the shower. Somewhere between the shampoo and bar of soap, the memory came back to him. *"Mine."*

Holy shit. He'd said that out loud to her. *Mine…* Fucking hell, he'd said it out loud twice!

Badger let the hot water beat on the back of his neck. If he was being honest, he'd really said it three times because the first night he'd fucked her, that shit came out of his mouth too. Although he'd meant it as claiming her pussy as his. Not that *she* was *actually* his.

Badger tried to add it to the list but failed. Instead, the damn "list" tumbled like an avalanche in his brain, blanketing everything and leaving him no choice but to survey the wreckage. He was catching feelings for her. Fuck catching… No, he'd caught feelings for her. But why? How?

Yeah, so the sex was incredible. Sex could be that way, especially when the people having it happened to be really fucking compatible with each other. Badger and Rosie happened to be way compatible in bed. In ways he hadn't anticipated, but it was more than that. It wasn't just the sex. Granted, they hadn't been together long. Not according to the calendar, anyway.

After turning off the water, Badger reached for a towel and dried off. A week wasn't long enough to have feelings for someone, or was it? He supposed it could be. But technically, it'd been much longer than a week. It'd been just about five months.

He wrapped the towel around his waist and approached the mirror. Five months of watching Rosie on that stage. Avoiding her, but always somehow managing to find her at the right time in the hallway, so when he passed her—refusing to even look at her—he could catch a scent of her perfume.

The way her eyes always found his when she was onstage or suspended from the pole—when she thought he wouldn't notice. She knew he watched her. She had to know. He loaded up his toothbrush and stuck it in his mouth. But she never called him out on his watching. She stayed quiet, except, hell, on Halloween night, she'd acted all shocked when he helped her out with all the money she made. Like she didn't understand why he was doing it. Then, on Thanksgiving, she said that she didn't know how to read him and that she got that he didn't like her, but didn't know why. Fuck, her eyes had been so sad when those words came out of her mouth. It damn near broke his heart. But she had to have known, right?

Badger spit a mouthful of toothpaste foam into the sink and wiped off the steamy mirror. God, he was stupid. Just because they'd been staring at each other for months didn't mean she'd known. Looking back, he was certain he hadn't known, either. Except…

Jesus fucking Christ! Talk about a V8 moment. Badger may as well go ahead and slap his forehead. "Hi, my name is Badger, and I am a dumbass!" He shook his head and laughed. He and Rosie had been having a relationship…of sorts for months, and neither one of them had even realized it. That was why emotions had reared their heads so fast. He'd already been feeling for her, and now that he was up close and becoming real damn personal, there was no holding those feelings back anymore.

Popping the toothbrush back in his mouth, Badger

finished the scrub job. That list he was so adamant about making in order to avoid the stuff he was feeling suddenly didn't seem so necessary. The fact that he'd claimed her, called her "mine," felt right. It felt true. Not that he knew what the hell to do now that he'd had this little revelation.

Fuck it. He was too old to let this chance slip through his fingers. He'd make a new list, one that was all about determining where they went from there and hoping like hell she was up for figuring it out with him. Plus, that whole keeping-her-safe thing. That was top on the list. Since, now Badger knew for sure he wanted her in his life for a *very* long time.

ROSIE WOKE with the covers wrapped tightly around her. Blinking the sleep from her eyes, she looked toward Badger's side of the bed. Empty. Not that it was a shock. She often woke up after he did. Rolling over, she drew in a breath and listened for any sounds in the house. The running water coming from the bathroom clued her in that he hadn't gotten far. Probably hadn't made coffee yet, either.

Unwrapping herself from the blankets, Rosie pressed her feet to the carpeted floor and stood—and holy shit, did her body retaliate with a vengeance. Wow! Rosie walked with slow, measured steps to the dresser and pulled out one of his T-shirts and a pair of boxer briefs. Good God, she was sore from head to toe, but in the best possible way. She smiled and pulled her long hair from the neck of the shirt.

Rosie managed to suppress a giggle, but only barely, as she made her way to the kitchen. A couple of Advil and coffee. Maybe some toast, too. Badger never ate breakfast, but he did like his coffee. Considering she was on an extended vacation and living in his house rent-free, the least she could do is help out: take care of the man.

Lord knew he'd been taking care of her in the most delicious ways. This time, when the giggle rose inside her, Rosie let it out as she got the coffee pot ready to brew. Carnal ways. Dirty ways… Heat swirled in Rosie's tummy, and she groaned. Ways that made her sore and left her wanting more.

"What's all this giggling and groaning about?"

Rosie looked to her right to see him standing there. Fresh from the shower, smelling all yummy and clad in a black T-shirt and blue jeans. His feet were still bare, and he held his socks and boots in one hand. Jesus, he was breathtaking. She dipped her chin and felt her cheeks get warm.

"Now she's blushing. Woman, what on earth?" He strode to her, hooked her around her waist and pulled her against him.

"I'm not blushing." She suppressed a smile by pursing her lips, but she knew it wasn't working.

"Uh-huh. Kinda looks that way to me." He nuzzled her neck.

"Okay, fine. Yes, blushing, but can you blame me? I mean, seriously, you come out here looking all too beautiful for words. Every time I see you, you take my breath away, and I just…" He pulled away and stared down at her—a blank expression on his face. Oh shit, she'd said too much. She'd…*crap.* "Um…" She bit her bottom lip.

He furrowed his brow. "You think I'm beautiful, Rosie?"

"Well, yeah." Unable to meet his gaze, she traced the edge of his T-shirt sleeve stretched tight across his bicep. "I mean, is that okay? I don't want to freak you out or anything." She shrugged.

Badger placed his finger below her chin and raised her eyes to his. "Never been told that before. Sweetest thing anyone's ever said to me, baby."

Melt.

Swoon.

Putty.

Seriously? Oh God. Warmth spread from Rosie's cheeks

down her chest, and her throat got tight. How come no one had ever told him he…she frowned. "Really?"

"Yeah, really." His tone was soft, and then his lips curled into a meek smile.

How in the *hell* a biker could look meek baffled her, but there he was, gazing down at her, looking all humbled. And beautiful. Damn, she was in trouble. "Badg—"

He bent his head and kissed her. And oh man, she hadn't brushed her teeth yet…but wow. He didn't seem to care because his tongue was in her mouth, taking what he wanted from her, as was his way. Rosie went with it and wrapped her arms around his neck, pressing against his big body.

Jeez, he tasted good, and the scent of clean soap and everything Badger weaved its way into her senses. Before Rosie knew it, her head was spinning. He smoothed his hands down her back to her ass, and she yelped into his mouth.

He jerked back. "Aw, hell, baby!" He cupped her ass cheeks with gentle pressure. "Sore today, huh? I'm sorry. Let me get you some ibu's."

"Sorry?" She held him so he wouldn't step away. "Badger, don't ever be sorry for that. I loved every minute of what you did to me last night."

"I should've gone a bit easier on you."

"No. Listen, please?" He tried to avoid her gaze, and she touched his face. "I loved it. Fucking loved it. And yeah, I'm sore, but I'm digging the sore. I'm betting you marked me. I'm digging that a whole lot, too." The corner of his lip twitched, so she went on. "If it makes a difference, that's what I was giggling and groaning about when you came in."

"Groaning because you're sore."

"No, honey. Groaning because I want more."

He'd moved to step away, but her words stopped him, and instead, he straightened and placed his hands on her hips. He stared down at her for a long time, so long she started to wonder what on earth was rolling around his mind, until finally he spoke. "Rosie?"

"Yeah?"

"You're mine."

Oh. Wow. *Wow.*

Melt.

Swoon.

Complete and total putty.

And once again, Rosie blushed.

CHAPTER TWENTY

BADGER PULLED his cycle into the parking lot of the assisted living facility his grandmother lived in. She was going to tear into him for not showing up this whole week. But in his defense, he'd been just a little busy. As she always did, she'd say her piece and then move on from it.

After heading through the main entrance, he walked down the long corridor which led to her unit. The place was nice, looked like a damn resort. Cost about as much, too. Badger hadn't ever wanted her to be in one of these places, but she'd been set on it. Being the kind of man he was, only the best would do for her.

He owed her that much. The woman had taken care of him nearly his entire life, and now he was giving that back to her. He navigated another short hall and arrived at her door. Badger smiled as he gave the door three raps with his knuckles and then took a step back. She had one of those old-fashioned plastic Christmas wreaths hanging on the door. It was the same one Badger had grown up seeing every year on the front door of her house.

The same house Badger now owned.

"I'm coming! Hold your horses!"

Badger chuckled. She always yelled like that to whoever was there, as if they were outside banging like a lunatic. The door swung open, and, as always, he was greeted with a scowl until she saw that it was him, and her face softened in a sweet smile. "Well, now! Been wondering where you got off to, young man. Get in here and give me some love."

Badger stepped forward and bent low for a hug and a kiss on his cheek. "Hi, Nana. Sorry, been real busy this week."

She pulled away and looked up at him. "All right, come inside and tell me all about it." He followed her inside her one-bedroom unit and closed the door behind them. "Always so busy. Catching bad guys, I'm guessing?" With the use of her cane, she moved into the small kitchen, pulled down a plate from the cabinet, and loaded it up with five chocolate chip cookies. "Can't wait to hear all about it. Sit." She pointed toward the stools situated on the other side of the countertop breakfast bar.

Without question, he took off his leather jacket, pulled off his bandana, and, after setting them on the arm of the recliner, did as he was told. By the time he'd planted his ass on the stool, she'd poured him a glass of milk. It was her way and their thing. She'd put out too many cookies and a full glass of milk for him and listened intently as he told her the edited versions of whatever bounty hunter adventure he'd been on.

In reality, most hunts were boring as hell, and the majority of his time was spent tracking the skip. Following leads. Staking out apartment complexes or neighborhoods. Of course, all that work came to fruition when he finally got the skip and got paid. That part was exciting, but could also be dangerous. She didn't need to know those parts, so Badger dressed up the stories, made them less boring and less dangerous, and she ate it up while he ate the cookies.

Badger picked up the first cookie as she came around the

counter, her cane in hand, and took the stool beside him. "Growing that beard in pretty good. It needs a trim." She tickled beneath his chin with a bright smile, arching her lips.

"Yes, ma'am." He took a sip of the milk. "Tell me how you been?"

She waved her hand at him. "Shoo. Nothing exciting here. Just the same old bridge games and *Judge Judy* on television. She's a feisty one. Oh, except that Marilyn Sanchez down the hall." She gestured over her shoulder with her thumb. "Her great-grandkids were here all week. You can't even imagine the noise. Word in the dining hall is her granddaughter is getting a divorce. Poor thing." She inched the plate closer to him. Her way of urging him to eat more. "Anyway. I got my hair colored on Monday. What do you think?" Without pausing for him to answer, she went on. "Oh, and since you hadn't been by and I didn't know when you were coming, yesterday I convinced one of the volunteers to help me get the decorations out. I got it all set up last night."

This time, she did pause, and Badger had to stifle a laugh. "Definitely nothing exciting. Pretty boring stuff, Nana."

"Oh, you. Don't be sassy." She swatted his arm with a laugh. "Well? How's it look?"

Badger twisted on his stool and looked around her living room. She'd set up the small artificial tree he'd bought her a couple of years ago and had it decorated with all her favorite ornaments. The nativity scene was displayed on one of the end tables, and the coffee table had the decades-old poinsettia print table runner on it with her holiday snow globe collection placed atop it. He'd moved her into the home three years ago, but once the first Christmas rolled around, he'd brought her back to her house—which had since become his—so she could go through all her decorations.

Many of the items needed to be thrown out. Too worn from the heat of the Arizona summers or lack of use over the years. Nana hadn't been real happy to part with any of it, but like the trooper she was, she'd picked out all her favorite things. The items that remained he stored back in the garage. Seeing as though he'd grown up with all of it, he was happy to keep it all close.

Badger looked back to her. "It looks as beautiful as always, Nana. Sorry, I wasn't here to help."

She gave him a soft smile. "It's okay. Tell me all about what's been happening."

He took another bite of cookie, stalling as he contemplated what to tell her. Obviously, it hadn't been the skip work that'd kept him away. He'd been with Rosie and dealing with her mess—and pretty much falling head over heels for the woman. But that was beside the point. Or was it?

From the moment Badger had decided he was coming to see his grandmother that day, he'd wanted to tell her about Rosie. He knew Nana would love her. Rosie would probably love his grandmother right back. How could she not? His Nana was awesome.

She touched his arm. "What's the matter, Drew? You look like you got something on your mind. Is everything okay?"

He shifted so he could face her. "Yes, and no. Everything's okay, so don't worry, but I haven't been busy on a job." He blew out a breath at her concerned look. "I met someone, and she's in a little bit of trouble. I've been helping her."

Her eyes went wide. "She?"

He chuckled. "Yes, Nana. Her name is Rosie."

"What kind of trouble is she in?"

"I don't want you to worry about that. But rest assured, I'm making it so she gets through it."

"Is it legal trouble?"

"Not at all. She's a good girl, Nana."

"That's good. Real good." Nana broke a piece off one of the cookies and ate it. When she was done chewing, she continued. "Aside from this trouble you're helping her with, is there more to it? I raised you to be an honorable man, so you helping someone who needs it doesn't surprise me, but do you also care for her?"

Badger's insides went soft just thinking about his grandmother's question. There hadn't been a woman in his life that he'd ever deemed worthy of telling his Nana about before now. Let alone introducing them. The woman might be eighty-eight years old, but she was still sharp as a tack and didn't miss much. Badger took a sip of milk, then cleared his throat. "Yeah, I guess you could say I do."

"Wow." The word came out as a half-breath, half-whisper. "Oh, my…" She turned her head and tapped her nails on the counter.

"Nana?" She looked back at him, and there were tears in her eyes. Panic raced through him, and he cupped her elbow. "Holy sh—crap. Are you crying? What's wrong?"

She sniffled. "I never thought it would happen. You've never talked about women. I may be old, but I'm not stupid, Drew." She gave him a sideways grin and wiped beneath one eye. "Good-looking boy like you? I knew there had to be one or two at some point—maybe more. But you've never mentioned anyone. Ever."

Relief washed through him. Those tears were happy ones, thank fuck. He could live with that. "I know. But there hasn't been anyone worth mentioning."

She cupped her hands over her mouth and let out a little giggle before pulling them away. "Well, now I want to know all about her!"

Badger couldn't hold back a chuckle at her enthusiasm. He hadn't seen his Nana this excited in so long that he couldn't help but feel just as excited. "Rosie's different, Nana. I don't know if I can explain the whys of it. I just know she's special for sure. I know you'd like her."

"When do I get to meet her? Why isn't she here now?"

"Well, I wasn't just gonna show up at your door with a woman. You raised me better than that." He bit into a cookie.

"Phooey! The minute I knew she was someone dear to you, I would've forgiven the surprise!"

"All right, well?" He laughed. "I gotta see to her trouble, and once that's all taken care of, I'll come get you, and we'll go out to a nice dinner. How's that sound?"

"Sounds like you better hurry because I'm not going to wait long. Wait. Are you planning on having her over for Christmas?"

Holy shit, Christmas. Considering he had no idea how long things with Alvaro would take, Rosie would likely still be living with him once Christmas arrived. But to be honest, he hadn't even given the fact that Christmas was right around the corner much thought. "Definitely. I guess, if I haven't cleared up her troubles before then, that's when you'll get to meet her. Think you can wait that long?"

"I'll manage." She beamed. "Eat your cookies, and tell me more."

He laughed. "What else do you want to know?"

"You're such a man!" She swatted his arm again. "What does she look like? Do you have a picture? No wait. Don't show me. Describe her to me instead! I want to paint a picture in my mind, and then you can show me the photo."

"Nana, you're kinda cracking me up right now."

"Laugh it up all you want. Just give me the details." She grinned.

Badger took another bite of cookie and proceeded to describe his Rosie to his Nana. As he explained each detail of his woman, from her long hair to her long legs, as well as Rosie's quick-witted personality, his Nana listened intently, eyes wide, taking it all in. Occasionally, she'd ask for more detail, and he'd try again.

When he was done, and so were the cookies and milk, he

showed her a picture of Rosie on his phone. She'd gasped and covered her mouth with her hands again before declaring how perfectly he'd described her and how beautiful she thought Rosie was.

His Nana was right. Badger couldn't help but agree. Rosie was beautiful. Inside and out.

CHAPTER TWENTY-ONE

BADGER SAT BACK from the desk in the office at the club and stared at the screen of his cell phone. After two weeks, the answer he'd been waiting on finally arrived. Alvaro's court date wasn't for another seven months. Knowing how the justice game was played, the dealer's attorney would probably file one continuance after another, and it'd take even longer for him to land on the skip list.

No one had to tell Badger that Alvaro had no intention of standing trial. Any idiot with half a brain could figure that shit out. The dealer hadn't come this far, hunting Rosie down to get his money and prove a point, just to go back and appear before a jury of his peers. As far as the dude being out of the state when he wasn't supposed to be—well, there wasn't anyone checking up on the scumbag, and since Badger wasn't calling that into the law, it didn't matter.

He shot a text to Wolf, letting him know the sitch. Badger needed to figure out their next move. No way Rosie was going to just sit tight, all nice and quiet, holed up in his house for the next seven fucking months. It had only been two weeks, and she was already getting restless. Maybe they could go away together. Head down to Mexico or something... *Shit.*

Badger ran his palm along his beard. Rosie *might* be game for that, but he'd have to leave his grandmother, never mind also work. Deuce would tell him to take her and go, keep her safe, but it wasn't that simple. Badger had an obligation to the woman who practically raised him, to Deuce and Evie, and to the boys who worked the floor in the club.

The bounty-hunting gig was another sort of obligation. He was the one who handled all the really dangerous skips because no one else wanted to get their hands dirty. There had to be a way to stay in Phoenix and keep her safe at the same time. His phone buzzed with a text, and Badger swiped the screen to read it.

Wolf Hendricks: I'll catch you back at your place tonight after 10. We'll discuss plan B.

Badger: Sounds good.

Badger pushed away from the desk and got to his feet. After sticking his gun in the cabinet, he shoved his phone in his back pocket and made his way down the hall to the bar. The plan was to hang out for a few hours tonight, like he'd done on and off since this all started. Alvaro had been quiet, and every time Badger was in house, the bastard hadn't shown his face. Maybe tonight he'd show. Maybe.

He exited the long corridor, and the familiar sights, sounds, and scents of Deuce's Cabaret wrapped around him. Booze, perfume, and cologne filled his system. Two strippers were on the main stage, the small birdcage stage empty, off the docket due to it being a weeknight.

Sabrina, or Sage, rather, was one of the girls dancing. Rosie and her had gotten to be friends. In order to keep them both safe, he hadn't allowed Rosie to contact her. Rosie'd been real pissed at him about it, too. Threw one hell of a drama fit. He understood why, but until Badger knew more about Alvaro and what the guy was capable of, he couldn't risk it.

He glanced around. Rig was at the door, and Jayson and Charlie had the floor. Sadie was on the bar, and Badger headed that way.

As he stepped in front of her, she looked up from wiping the bar top. "Hey, Badger. Didn't think you were coming in tonight. You want the usual?"

"Yes, ma'am. Coffee, please. Go ahead and make a second pot. I plan on staying for the duration." He nodded at her and made his way to Rig.

"Hey, boss. How's it hanging?" Rig gave him one of his full-of-sunshine smiles.

Chuckling, Badger shook his head. Damn kid was always so cheerful. A smile on his face, no matter what was going on. Badger had no clue why he was bouncing instead of working at a grocery store or some sort of customer-friendly atmosphere type of business. Hell, even bartending or serving food would suit him better. "A little to the left, kid. Thanks for asking. You good?"

"Hell yeah. Definitely good. Been a quiet night, a lot slower since Rosie's been gone." Rig shoved his hands in his pockets. "You heard from her? Everyone's real worried about her. I guess her grandma died or something."

"Here you go, Badger." He glanced away to see Sadie set his cup of coffee on the end of the bar. He thanked her and turned back to Rig. "Yeah, I heard that, too. Hopefully, she'll be back soon." Badger cringed and stepped away to grab his beverage of choice. He hated lying to the kid, but he had no choice. He sipped the hot brew and waved Rig over. "You seen that guy I asked you all to keep a lookout for?"

"Nah. I don't think he's been back in the last few days. But we're all still keeping our eyes peeled."

"That's good. Real good." He nodded and took another sip. "You let me know ASAP if he shows."

"You got it, boss." Rig shot him another bright-ass smile and moved back to his post at the door.

Badger looked out over the floor as the first beats of Halestorm's "Unapologetic" rang out through the club's sound system. Sage was still on stage, so this must've come from her. But all Badger could think about was that this was the very first song he'd seen Rosie dance to. The spell she'd cast on him that morning when she'd come in looking for a job had kicked into high gear as he watched her on that stage.

He'd been lost to her completely and totally, though, at the time, he hadn't known it. But thinking back, he sure as hell knew it now. Badger focused on the stage, almost able to see her there. He missed it. Her shows, the way she moved and performed, holding the crowd in the palm of her hand.

Shit, she'd wrapped Badger right around her little pinky finger in a matter of one song. Damn, if he didn't wish she were there with him right then. He'd give anything to see her on that stage. A year ago, if anyone had told him he'd be head over heels for a stripper, he'd have told them they were out of their damn mind. Yet here he was…totally head over heels. Crazy how shit happened sometimes.

With a shake of his head, Badger took his coffee, got off his ass and headed for the front door. It was time for some nicotine. Hopefully, the night wouldn't drag too much. Since Rosie wasn't able to be here with him, he was eager to get home to her. She'd make him watch some pay-per-view movie with him—some silly chick flick, he was sure. But he didn't care. If that's what she wanted, he'd give it to her.

At that point, Badger would pretty much give his Rosie anything she wanted.

CHAPTER TWENTY-TWO

Badger stepped outside into the cool desert air and glanced around. Pulling in a deep breath, he moved a few feet down the sidewalk and planted his back against the brick wall. He tucked a cigarette between his lips and raised his lighter to scorch the tip. Drawing on the filter, he sucked in a deep drag. As he exhaled, Badger caught some movement to his right.

Check that out... The infamous Alvaro Balzan was approaching the entrance door, complete with two goons trailing a few feet behind him.

"Hey, man." Badger stepped toward him. Alvaro glanced up as he opened the door and attempted to move inside, but Badger got there before he made it and pushed it closed again.

"Problem, my friend?"

"Need a word with you." Badger tilted his head to the side and took in the alleged murderer standing before him. Thick, black hair, slicked back. Dark eyes. Narrow nose. Deep lines marked his forehead and between his brows, making him look a hell of a lot older than his forty-one years. A long scar from the corner of his mouth that arced up his cheek gave away the fact that he hadn't lived those years easy.

Alvaro looked over his shoulder to his men. "Easy, gentlemen." He turned back to Badger as he stepped a few feet away from the door and did his own sizing up before a slow smile spread across his full lips. "What can I help you with? I'm all ears, my friend."

Badger eyed the bodyguards as he took a final drag of his smoke and flicked it to the ground. "Hear you been in a couple of times asking about one of the girls."

The man shrugged, an unconcerned expression on his face as he tugged the collar of his jacket higher. "Not seeing that as your concern."

Alvaro moved toward the door again, and Badger put his hand on the man's chest, stopping him. They were almost the same height, though Badger had him by at least an inch and probably fifty pounds. "My club. My girls. My concern."

Alvaro looked down at Badger's hand, then back to his eyes. "May I suggest you take your hand off my body, my friend." The words Alvaro used may have been polite. The tone, however, was not.

The threat was clear. Any other guy might've backed off. Badger wasn't any other guy, and that meant it was time to cut through the niceties and make his point. "Suggest all you like. But I'll give you one right back. This club?" Badger stepped up to Alvaro. Close enough that their noses almost touched. "This is a no-stupid zone. The way I see it, *you* are being stupid, Alvaro. So I suggest you take your ass back east where it belongs. The girl? Gone. Guaranteed, you won't find her, either. Cut your losses and move the fuck on."

Alvaro didn't move, didn't break Badger's stare, either. A few beats passed before he sighed through his nose and finally answered. "I see."

Badger stepped back. He didn't have his gun on him. Never carried while in the club. If this turned ugly, he'd have to rely on brute force. Not the first time he'd been outnumbered, sure as hell wouldn't be the last. He could handle it, but he wasn't about to court it further. "See all you want. Just take your boys and do it elsewhere."

Alvaro brushed down the front of his overcoat and sniffed the air. "You know, my friend. I hear you. I really do." He sucked his teeth and then pursed his lips. "But I got a little thing I need to discuss with *your* girl. Until I do that—" he nodded, "—I'm not going any-fucking-where."

"Do what you gotta do. Bring your best, because you'll be dealing with me. But you won't step foot in this club again."

"You the one hiding her?"

Badger stood stock still, schooling his expression. No way he'd give this douche any opportunity to interpret an answer he wanted to see. Though Badger knew the guy already had his answer.

Alvaro looked away and gave an exaggerated shake of his body. "Brr. Chilly here at night. Didn't expect that. Deserts are supposed to be hot, aren't they?" He turned, giving Badger his back.

Again, Badger said nothing but was well aware of the game. Alvaro had a point to make. He'd make it, and when he was done, he'd walk away. In his mind, he'd see it as depriving Badger of an opportunity to walk him away. It just so happened Badger's ego wasn't the size of the building, so he didn't give a fuck how the asshole walked away, just as long as he did and stayed gone.

"Even so, the desert appeals to me still. It's nice here. Sunsets are beautiful." Alvaro glanced over his shoulder before he turned and faced Badger once more. "You tell her I want my money." He reached in his coat pocket.

Badger braced his legs, prepared to charge him. "Don't you fu—"

Alvaro pulled his hand out, holding a white card between his fore and middle fingers, and extended it to Badger with a sharp chuckle. "Easy, my friend. Just my card."

Badger contemplated his opponent and the obviously loyal

soldiers behind him. The two guys hadn't moved a muscle, even when Badger got in their boss's face. Alvaro might be a grade-A scumbag, but he wasn't a stupid one, at least not in the traditional sense. He knew what he was doing, and he also knew Badger was protecting Rosie. "I'll take your card, but like I said—"

"Right. I'll be dealing with you. With pleasure, my friend." With that, cool as can be, he turned and walked away—his boys following behind him.

Badger flicked the edge of the card as he watched the men make their way down the sidewalk and disappear around the corner into the parking lot. A few minutes later, a black 7-series BMW pulled out of the lot and cruised nice and slowly past the front of the club. Rear window down, Alvaro nodded at Badger before the car sped away.

Badger stared down at the embossed lettering on the card. All it had was the guy's name and phone number printed on it in bold, black font. He blew out a breath and ran his palm over his beard. Alvaro may not be coming back to the club, but he was nowhere near done with his quest.

Between the news of how long the trial would take and the exciting face-to-face encounter with the man and crew, Badger needed to get home and have a conversation with his woman. He blew out a breath. Without a doubt, the confrontation he'd just had with Alvaro would be the easy part of the night. They might live in the hottest place in the U.S., but telling Rosie she was going to have to stay hidden for another seven months or more was going to be pure hell on earth.

There was also the fact that Badger had been holding out hope that she'd come clean with him about the money. He wanted to believe her, but his gut knew better and wouldn't stop nagging him. Maybe she finally trusted him enough to tell him the truth? Regardless, confronting her about the money and talking through the rest of the mess was the last thing he wanted to do tonight.

His phone chimed with a text. Badger pulled it out and read the message from Wolf, letting him know he'd be late. An idea struck, and Badger leaned against the wall and lit another cigarette. He typed a message back to Wolf.

> Badger: Let's do it tomorrow night. I need a favor, though.

> Wolf Hendricks: Name it.

> Badger: I need to borrow your car tonight.

> Wolf Hendricks: No problem.

Badger put his phone away and drew on his smoke. The talk with Rosie was necessary for sure, but it didn't have to happen that night. He just wanted a little more time, maybe even to pretend for a little longer that they were a normal couple. He couldn't take her on a regular date, but he could do *something* for her.

He could take her somewhere, ensuring she was still safe, and at the same time give her something they hadn't yet had together.

A date.

CHAPTER TWENTY-THREE

ROSIE PACED from the kitchen to the den…around the couch, and back through the kitchen. She was antsy. Restless. And damn irritable. She'd been cooped up in his place for what felt like months, though it'd only been two weeks. Badger hadn't allowed her to leave the house, or go to work, or any-fucking-thing. Not even go to the grocery store, for fuck's sake.

Christmas shopping was completely out of the question—which she thought was totally unfair. Although earlier, she'd been online window shopping and, through a series of bored searches, stumbled on an adult store out of Connecticut. Irony was amusing, but Pandora's Parlour had all sorts of fun items for sale. And when she'd gone into their "kink" section, she'd found a few items Badger might want to use on her. At least Rosie thought she might (for sure, definitely, most likely, really) *want* him to use on her. She'd made a point to bookmark the dotcom to show him later. After finding that, she'd been beyond amped up…needing him.

An orgasm might help. She'd had plenty of those with him, but they weren't fully taking the edge off anymore. Make no mistake, the sex was good. Like mind-blowingly good. Best of her life, hard and dirty—every night. Sometimes, a few times a night, but it wasn't solving her issue.

Rosie needed to—of all things—dance. Or go work out. Just…something. Back in Waterbury, she'd taken that pole-dancing exercise class. It kept her skills in check, but more than that, it helped her get her constant need to move, expel the ever-present energy within her in a way that not even sex could. Rosie ran her fingers through her hair as energy bounced through her like a ping-pong ball, ricocheting through her mind and body. She swore it helped keep her sane. And right now, she was jumpy and felt utterly *insane*.

He'd called earlier, promising to take her out for a drive just as soon as he got back from Deuce's. It was already after midnight, but regardless, what the fuck good would a drive do her? Not much. Rosie twisted her fingers in a knot. But it was better than nothing. She made another round, chewing her nails down to nothing. Not like there was much to chew, but whatever. Anything to distract her.

"You 'bout ready?"

Rosie spun to find Badger standing just inside the kitchen doorway. She hadn't even heard the garage door. Jesus, she was distracted. The noise in her mind drowning out every-thing else. She dropped her hands to her sides and then clasped them behind her back. "I've been ready."

His gaze roamed up and down her body from head to toe and back again. "That what you're wearing?"

"You don't like it?" Rosie smoothed her hands over her tank top and stared down at her red, petticoat-style short skirt to her painted toes in her high-heeled strappy sandals. She guessed she did look a bit like she was dressed for a dance club, but fucking hell, she was bored. Antsy. Restless… Ugh! She just needed to do something!

"Didn't say that. It's cold out. Grab a jacket. Let's go, woman. Move your cute ass."

Crap. Rosie grabbed her little black jacket from behind

the laundry room door and followed Badger out through the garage. She hadn't thought about it, and hadn't said anything but hoped like hell they were going out in the truck. The skirt and heels weren't exactly the best choice for the Harley. When she stepped into the garage, she glanced toward the driveway and— "Oh wow! Whose is that?"

"Borrowed it from Wolf. Figured we'd go up to one of my favorite mountain spots and check out the view."

Holy wow, this was Wolf's car? Jeez, that guy had sides to him, Rosie was sure she didn't need to be curious about. Shoving the thought aside, Rosie whistled low, raised both eyebrows, and dipped her chin. "You planning on making out with me in that rockin'-hot car?"

The corner of Badger's lips quirked in a slight grin. "Woman, as good as you look tonight? I'd say it's a definite."

Rosie moved toward the restored-to-perfection, tricked-out, white convertible. "I may just let you get to first base." Badger opened the passenger door for her, and she slid onto the soft leather seat. She glanced up at him as he closed her in. "Wow! Red interior? I match!" She giggled. "Okay, that just landed you at second base for sure."

"Damn, what's it gonna take for me to slide into home?" He chuckled as he walked around the car and slid behind the wheel. "Ready?"

"Yes! And, you keep playing your cards right, I'm sure you'll figure it out." Excitement pulsed through Rosie in time with her heartbeat. He was a rough biker, dominant as hell with her—and not just in bed. But he also had this surprisingly romantic side. Probably why she found his bossy side so appealing, even though, at times, it could be annoying.

When you combined everything that was Badger, it made her heart melt into a pool of decadent swoon—which was almost too much to take. He'd already told her earlier that morning she was his, as in *his*. Rosie's insides had turned into complete putty.

She was still trying to sort that gooey mess out inside her brain. In an effort to distract herself, she gazed up at the dark sky. "I assume the top's staying down, so say bye-bye to the curls I took an hour to get into my hair tonight."

Badger leaned over, ran his fingers up the back of her scalp and gripped her hair tight. "Curls are hot, baby. But windblown curls'll be hotter."

He gave her a quick kiss, delving his tongue into her mouth and making her moan and swoon just a bit more than she already was. Jesus...*he's killing me.* Badger released her, leaving her breathless, and started the vehicle. Rosie licked her lips as the rumble of the engine and exhaust sent another bolt of excitement through her. The car oozed cool, but so did the man sitting next to her. Okay, enough already. She was starting to annoy herself with all the lash-batting, swoon-filled thoughts. "What kind of car is this?"

Badger looked over his shoulder as he backed out of the driveway. "Sixty-six GTO. A complete customized restore from top to bottom. Including the interior."

"I don't know anything about cars, except that some are beautiful and some are just cars, you know?" She shrugged as she pushed a lock of hair away from her face.

"Wanna know what I think?"

"Of course." Rosie gathered up her hair, holding it from going wild as they picked up speed getting out of his neighborhood.

"Yeah, sure, the car's pretty. You in that little skirt, those heels, looking perfect as hell, sitting in that red leather seat? Yeah, that makes it beautiful."

Fucking hell, that was a direct hit! Sheesh. Rosie gasped, but thank God the noise from the wind and the rumble of the car's engine drowned it out. Someone somewhere should've screamed, *"Incoming!"* to give a girl a little warning to take cover.

If Badger was aiming to sweep her off her feet and make

her fall in love with him, he was winning. After his declaration that morning, plus the lines he was running on her now, she didn't have a shot in hell of resisting. With him doing this sort of stuff, saying these kinds of things to her? Rosie would definitely lose the battle of keeping her heart off limits. Though, really, why bother trying? "Wow, Badger."

"Wow, what?" He glanced at her before making a left onto the freeway.

She shook her head but gave him a smile. "Just…wow."

Yeah, he was doing a number on her heart, body, *and* mind, and Rosie knew, without a doubt, she was defenseless. She would tumble ass over teakettle for him.

Truth was, she probably already had.

———

BADGER DROVE AS FAR up the mountain as he could and parked in the dirt lot in front of what he considered to be the best view in the valley. However, the scenery sitting next to him was even better. Rosie had been getting damn snippy with him—her drama mama was definitely front and center as of late, but really, he couldn't blame her.

She liked to read, but how much could a woman read in the span of two weeks? He'd been busy and, as a result, had to leave her alone a lot more than he'd intended. Bills had to be paid, his and hers. That meant, even though he'd cut back, he still ran security at Deuce's, so he had to put time in there and also had skips to hunt down, too. In his spare time, he was putting feelers out, trying to find out where Alvaro had set up house.

The guy had been quiet…that was until the fucker had shown his face earlier at Deuce's. Badger had hoped, even though it was stupid, that the guy had headed back to CT. Deep down inside, Badger's experience knew better. No way in hell a sociopath like that was going to stand trial for murder.

Also, no way in hell the dude would swallow the hit to his ego without making someone pay…and that someone was Rosie.

Badger frowned, staring out at the lights of the city.

"Soooo…you're awfully quiet sitting over there."

He glanced over at Rosie. Lips drawn in a small smile, her windblown hair framing her face. She looked like an angel. "Sorry. Lot on my mind." He took her hand in his, raised it to his lips and kissed her fingers.

She glanced away from his gaze and looked toward the skyline. "Sure is a pretty view."

As it always was with her, Badger couldn't take his eyes from her. So different. So…everything. Jesus, she'd become so precious to him. "Agreed."

"Ooh! I love this song." She smiled and turned up the radio. "Haven't heard it in forever."

Badger listened for a moment as the beat of the music echoed around them. "Who is this? Eminem?"

"Yep. 'Lose Yourself' from that movie he did, *Eight Mile*. Remember?" She popped her shoulders in time with the beat.

"Yeah." He grinned, watching her. "I remember."

"God, I need to dance, Badger. I'm so full of energy."

Badger turned on the headlights. "Go for it. Get out and dance, baby."

She laughed, her hypnotizing smile gracing her face. "Yeah? Right here?"

"Right here." He nodded with a smile. Christ, he smiled all the time now, it seemed. How could he not, especially with the beautiful expression she had on her face at that moment?

"All right." She turned the music up a little louder. In the next moment, she slipped her heels off before climbing over the center console and straddling his lap.

Badger gazed up at her as she cupped his face in her hands, slanted her head and laid a kiss on him, hot and wet enough to make his fucking body light up in flames. After she pulled away from his lips—a devilish little glint in her eyes—

she rocked her hips once, then rose up, twisted her body and planted a foot on the doorframe, climbing over the driver's door and onto the hood of the GTO.

Oh, shit…

Rosie stood on the hood of the car and began to move her body. She rocked her hips from side to side, spun, and slapped her hands down on her fine ass, popping her hips back. She was teasing, tempting…dancing just for him. Badger grabbed the steering wheel and watched, unable to tear his gaze away.

The music built. Eminem's rap and the hard beat of the song rolled through Badger as he watched his woman move her body in perfect time. Off went the shirt, the chill in the desert air hardening her nipples to tight points. Badger licked his lips, wanting those sweet berries in his mouth more than he wanted to breathe. But no way in hell he was going to move. His woman needed to dance, and Badger needed to watch her. He'd missed this, knew that, but hadn't realized how much until just that moment.

She wasn't *just* a stripper or a pole jockey, as he often called them. Rosie wasn't *just* a dancer, either. She was an entertainer—and she was fucking amazing at it.

With her hands cupping her breasts, she pinched her nipples, tugging on them before she spun, rotating her hips. Rosie bent forward and, reaching beneath that little skirt, tugged down her panties. Bent in half as she was, he got a full view of her ass and bare pussy lips, already glistening from her juices.

Clenching his teeth, he let out a groan and ran his palm along the side of his beard. He had no idea what she was going to do next, but his dick was rock hard in his jeans, and whenever she got done giving him the show, he'd be fucking her over the same hood she was standing on.

Rosie spun again, facing him. The music built…and she stepped closer to the windshield, rubbing her hands up her inner thighs to her pussy, pulling her skirt up as she stroked her skin. Bending her knees, she rocked her hips side to side as she teased her clit and dipped her fingers inside her tight cunt.

Badger popped the top button on his jeans, reached inside and straightened his cock. She was killing him. His dick throbbed, aching to be inside that sweet heaven she was playing with in front of him.

She moved again, and Badger's eyes went wide. Rosie gripped the top of the windshield, spread her knees wide, dropped down into a squat and pressed her pussy right against the glass.

Holy fuck! *Fuuuuuck!* "Rosie. *Holyyysheeit.*" Badger shook his head with a growl. The woman was limber—real fucking limber. The beat hit harder, and she thrust her hips up and down in time with it, rubbing her clit against the glass. Not wanting to look away from the gorgeous view of her pussy, Badger forced himself to glance up at her face. Her eyes were locked on him, her bottom lip caught in her teeth. "Goddamn. Show me, baby. Come all over that glass."

Tugging down his zipper, he gripped his cock, stroking as he focused on her wet pussy. Her juices smeared on the glass as she moved faster and faster, working herself up. She was so fucking hot, so fucking dirty.

As if he needed more proof, Badger was beyond convinced she now owned him. Completely spun on an East Coast girl, with complicated baggage for days, enough drama to fill a football stadium, a body to die for, along with multiple layers of heart he could get lost in for days. Rosie owned *him* from head to toe.

"Badger…" She moaned, moving faster.

His balls drew up tight, arousal coating the head of his prick. "Show me that sloppy wet cunt. Come for me, baby."

"Oh God! Baby… *Yesssss!*" Rosie threw her head back, arching her back as she came. The mouth of her cunt spasmed, clenching right before his eyes as her wetness smeared all over the glass. She kept moving, a little slower, rubbing that tight clit against the windshield as her orgasm settled and the song faded to an end.

Unable to hold back any longer, Badger threw open the door and came to the side of the car. "Off now. I want you bent over the fender. Need inside you."

"Yes, sir," she breathed as she let go of the windshield and climbed off the car.

He grabbed her, slammed his lips down on hers and drove his tongue into her mouth. Fuck's sake, he was so hot for her. Lost. Spun. Insane… No way he'd ever get enough. No fucking way. Yanking from her lips, he gripped her long hair, spun her, and pushed her down onto the hood of the car. Badger tugged her skirt up over her hips and smoothed his palm over her heated skin, then slipped his fingers between the cleft of her ass to her pussy. "You're drenched. Look how wet you made that glass. All that sweet honey."

She moaned and turned her head toward the windshield. "Need you."

"Yeah? Baby, got news for you. I fucking need you, too." Badger pulled a condom from his wallet and sheathed his dick. "Spread wider, show me that sweet cunt." She did as instructed, and in one thrust, Badger drove his prick into her heaven.

"Fuck. Yes. Harder. Please, Badger. Fuck me harder."

He bent over her and grabbed a fist full of her hair. Badger yanked her head back and nipped her earlobe. "You need it harder, baby? Harder than I already give it to you?" He thrust deep, his hips slapping against her ass.

"Yes, sir." She let out a feral moan.

"Fuck, such a dirty good girl—" *SLAM!* "—hard enough now? Or you need more?"

"More, sir."

Badger gritted his teeth and drove into her harder. "I want to hear you scream it, Rosie. Beg me."

"Please, sir! *Oh God, yes*! Please fuck me harder, sir!"

Fucking hell, he was going to lose his mind. Rosie was giving him so much more than he ever thought he'd get from a woman. It was everything he never allowed himself to wish for, let alone dream of. But at that moment, up on the side of a mountain, with nothing but the light from the moon shining down on them, Badger knew he'd give his life to keep her.

Because he'd already given her his heart.

Rosie's head spun, and she laid her cheek down on the hood of the car. Her nipples were drawn into hard points as her body slid back and forth over the cool metal of the hood. Badger was driving his cock deep into her core, his hips banging against her ass, and she wanted more. Rosie *needed* more. "Badg—"

Without warning, he pulled free of her channel. Rosie let out a gasp as she was yanked away from the car and spun to face him. "I need more from you, too, baby."

In the next second, he'd lifted her, and her ass hit the cool metal of the hood. With a tight grip on the back of her thighs, he spread them apart and slid his cock deep. Rosie screamed, and Badger covered her mouth with his, stealing her breath. When he broke from her lips, Badger pressed his forehead against hers, panting as he thrust into her. "Rub your clit. But don't you dare fucking come until I say."

She nodded, slid one hand between them and rubbed the tight bundle of nerves. "*Ffffuuuucckkk!*"

He slowed his pace. "Oh yeah. That's it. I can feel your cunt milking my cock. Look at all your honey coating my prick, baby."

Rosie focused as best she could between their bodies. Shifting her hand, she spread her fingers around his shaft and pressed her palm against her clit. Her orgasm was rushing fast to the surface, the pressure inside her building, and she knew holding it at bay would be impossible. "Badger…"

"You need my cock, Rosie?"

"Yes."

"Love my cock?"

"Oh God, yes!" Each time he thrust into her, Rosie tilted her hips just enough so her palm rubbed her clit.

He grunted, pulled out to the head and drove back in. "Is it yours?"

"Yes." Rosie gasped as the first ripples of her climax rolled through her. "I'm gonna come...I can't..."

"Is this hot cunt mine?"

Holy God, Rosie was going to explode. Every inch of her skin tingled, and her channel clenched in little spasms. He was driving her hard, with his gorgeous cock, yes, but also with his words.

Claiming her and giving himself in exchange. She wanted that. She needed it.

Badger gripped her by the jaw and stared into her eyes. "Say it's mine, baby, and then give me your sweet orgasm."

"It's yours," she panted and then gave him more. "Been yours since the first day I laid eyes on you."

"You're goddamn right it was." Badger pulled her to his lips, thrust his tongue into her mouth as he fucked into her cunt. Hard. Fast. Dominating her body, her soul, as he drove her over the edge.

Rosie's orgasm hit, erupting through her body like a hot lava explosion, and her channel clenched over and over again around his shaft, her clit tingling with little spasms. She moaned into his mouth, riding the wave, letting it drown her.

He growled as he broke the kiss. With one final thrust, he slammed into her and came too. His dick jerked deep inside her core, pulsing as he spurted inside the condom. "Mine." Gasping for air, he drew her tight to his chest. "Mine..."

Rosie collapsed against him and buried her face in his neck. His cologne mixed with his sweat was an intoxicating comfort she'd grown attached to. His big arms around her as he held her against his hard body, something else she'd grown attached to.

She was his.

She'd never belonged to someone before—had never wanted to. He'd said it many times over the past two weeks, and Rosie didn't take it lightly. It wasn't just a word thrown around in the heat of passion. Badger didn't play games like that. Rosie knew, with every fiber of her being, that he meant it.

She was his.

CHAPTER TWENTY-FOUR

BADGER OPENED the door leading from the garage into the laundry room and poked his head inside. "Rosie!"

She popped her head up from the couch. "Jesus! You scared me. Why are you yelling?"

"Come here, woman!" He jerked his chin at her before stepping away from the door. Letting it close behind him, Badger moved to his truck and dropped the tailgate, stood to the side, and waited.

No more than ten seconds passed before she appeared. "What on earth are you doing, Badger?" When she got closer, she stopped short. "Oh, my! Wow. Is that—" with eyes wide as saucers, she cupped her hands over her mouth and bounced on her toes, "—is that a Christmas tree?"

"Sure is." Badger grinned as pride washed through him like a summer storm. He'd just made his woman's day. Nothing better than that. Nothing at all.

Rosie launched herself at him, and Badger caught her, pulling her tight to his body. She pressed a hard kiss to his lips. "Thank you! Thank you." She giggled. "Thank you! Wow, I don't even know what else to say!" She gave him another kiss and then moved her lips to his cheek and chin before traveling back to his mouth and kissing him a little longer that time. "This is…wow."

Badger set her down on her feet, and she cupped his cheek in her palm, gazing up at him as if she was seeing the moon and stars. Yeah, nothing better than what he'd just given her. "Guess this means you like it?"

She giggled again. "Yep."

"Perfect." He bent his head and stroked his lips over hers. "Let's get it inside."

Rosie let out a squeal filled with excitement, clapping her hands together as Badger yanked the tree from the back of the bed. He hoisted the seven-foot Douglas fir onto his shoulder. "Grab the door, baby."

She was already moving when she called a "yes, sir" over her shoulder. Goddamn, she had him wrapped pretty damn tight. When she was sweet and giggly like this with him, Badger could barely think straight.

All he could see was her. All he *wanted* to see was Rosie.

After muscling the tree inside and through the house, he laid it down on the floor in front of the big picture window in the formal living room. He turned, and she was right beside him, big smile still firmly in place, excitement stamped all over her face. Everything about her was so damn intoxicating he couldn't help but smile back.

"So, what now?"

"Back to the garage. Need to pull out the Christmas stuff, find the stand."

"Yay! Let's go." Rosie turned, and Badger caught her arm before she got too far away. "Hey, now!" She laughed.

He pulled her back to him and took her mouth in a deep kiss. Her hand found the back of his neck as she pressed her body against his with a moan. Badger stroked his tongue over hers, savoring her sweet taste. So good, so different. A groan came out of him, and his dick got in the game. Fucking hell, he wanted her. As she started rubbing against his erection,

Badger broke the kiss. "Gonna wrap you in tinsel and fuck you on the floor next to this tree once we get it decorated."

She stroked her thumb over his bottom lip. "I'm so absolutely on board with that."

"Good."

Taking her hand in his, they made their way to the garage. After pulling down the ten or so boxes labeled "XMAS" from the shelves in the far corner, Badger brought them inside. Rosie carried a few, but her curiosity got the better of her and had opened three of them and was digging through a fourth before Badger had set the last one down. He chuckled. "You find the stand yet?"

"Nope. But I found this!" She raised a hand-painted snowman made from hard Styrofoam balls. "Looks like it was made by a child. Maybe a school project, perhaps?" She smiled, both eyebrows raised. "Was it you?"

"I cannot confirm or deny that accusation." He chuckled and opened the short, wide box he knew had the stand in it. "Got the stand."

"Yeah, totally was you. So cute! But you know? I'm having a hard time picturing you as a little boy. For some reason, all I see in my head is a third grader wearing a biker leather and sporting a full beard."

Okay, shit. Now, *that* was damn funny. A laugh burst out of Badger before he managed to get the stand set down on the floor in front of the window. "Rosie, the stuff you say. Jesus, woman..." He laughed a little more before finally getting himself under control. After a few minutes, he looked up from his task to find she was quietly watching him, smile still in place from ear to ear. "What are you grinning about now?"

Her expression softened. "I like that I make you laugh."

"I like that you make me laugh, too."

The silent moment stretched between them. Not an uncomfortable silence; a happy one. A peaceful one. The only other time Badger felt that kind of peace was when he was a child with his Nana. He opened his heart and welcomed the feeling at that moment with Rosie, knowing it was safe to do so.

Knowing he was right where he was supposed to be—no matter how he got there—with her at that moment.

AFTER HELPING him mount the tree in the stand, Rosie went back to unpacking boxes, and Badger went to make them some hot cocoa—with a little kick of peppermint Schnapps. She was utterly amazed at the different kinds of decorations she'd pulled out. Who'd have thought a scary badass biker would have anything more than a bunch of red, gold, green, and blue balls? Rosie snorted a laugh at the joke she'd unintentionally made.

"What's funny?"

She glanced up as Badger walked toward her, a mug in each hand. She took hers from him. "Thank you. Just laughing at a thought I had."

"Gonna share it?"

She shrugged as she took a sip of the spiked hot cocoa. "Mmm. Yummy!" She licked her lip. "So, where'd you get all this stuff? Not the typical guy kind of decorations."

He set his mug down on one of the end tables and squatted in front of a box. "My grandmother—Nana."

"Your *Nana*?"

"Yeah, babe. My Nana." He reached in one of the boxes and pulled out the angel for the top. "What? Bikers can't have Nanas?"

"Of course they can."

"Then what's with the tone?"

"No tone." She set her mug beside his. "You just never stop surprising me, is all."

"Back at ya." He moved to the tree and placed the angel on top. "How's it look? Is it straight?"

She stepped back. "It's perfect, just…perfect." And so was he. For the love of all things holy, he called his grandmother "Nana."

"Will you tell me about her?"

"Sure, but she'll be here for Christmas with us, so you'll get a lot of time to get to know her."

Rosie was really glad she wasn't taking a sip of her cocoa right then. She'd just assumed the woman had passed. And wait, what? "I will?"

"Of course." He glanced to her as if she'd just said something ridiculous, and returned his focus back to the tree. "It's settling nice, don't you think? Gonna have to make sure we keep it watered constantly. Live trees dry out real quick in the desert if we don't."

Holy shit…he'd just laid that on her and moved right along to the business of the tree. Rosie was still stuck on the fact that she'd be meeting his Nana in a matter of a few weeks. Obviously, he intended to still have her in his life. Which was good, but Rosie hadn't thought much past where they'd be once the situation with Alvaro was handled.

And now, maybe she needed to. She watched him as he played with some of the branches. Curiosity blazed through her like a wildfire. There was so much she didn't know about him, and so much she wanted to know. "Can you tell me about her now, anyway?"

"Yeah, babe." He blew out a loud sigh and, took a seat on the sofa, and patted the spot next to him. "Sit."

"I'm not trying to be a pest, just curious, is all." She handed him his cocoa.

"What the hell made you think I thought you were being a pest?"

She raised her mug to her lips. "The loud sigh gave it away."

Badger chuckled. "Haven't you figured out that half the time, my noises are just that, noises?"

"Well, the other half of the time, they're an indication of your mood, so no. I guess I haven't."

"Touché." He leaned over and placed a kiss to her forehead. "Don't worry. You will."

Rosie all but sighed at the intimacy of the forehead kiss. That shit was a big deal. Yeah, definitely needed to consider what the future was going to look like. She placed her palm on top of Badger's hand and laced her fingers with his. "Okay then. So…Nana?"

"Right, Nana. Well, she raised me. She's about that tall—" he lifted his free hand, not very far in the air, to indicate her size. "She's full of spit and vinegar but a whole ton of sugar, too."

"Where does she live?"

"She used to live here. This was her home. I bought it from her when she'd decided it was time for her to be in assisted living."

"*She* decided that?" Rosie sipped her cocoa. "Wow."

"Told you, spit and vinegar. She decided it, and I made sure it happened." He scratched his chin through his scruff.

"So, is she well? I mean, how old is she?"

"Quite. She's eighty-eight, and her mind is solid as a rock." He shook his head and lifted his mug to his lips.

Rosie smiled. "Wow. God bless her."

He cleared his throat. "I went and saw her last week. Told her about you."

Cue the swoon! Warmth spread through Rosie like warm molasses. She was almost afraid to ask, but *had* to. "Um… What did you tell her?"

Badger looked at her. "I told her how special you are to me."

And cue another swoon—this one the size of a tidal wave. Rosie swallowed a gasp as the warm molasses turned to hot lust.

Did this man know how *amazing* he was?

Did he have *any* idea how he affected her?

Did he have *any clue at all* that he'd somehow reached inside her soul and held her heart in his hand?

Lord help her, she hoped so. Because it was his.

And as scary as that thought was, it was the best feeling in the freaking world.

"Do you miss him?"

The question jerked her from the pink cloud she was floating on. Where had that come from? "What?"

"Your husband...do you miss him? Do you think about him?" Badger shifted his hand and turned his palm over so they could link hands properly.

Rosie stared at him a few moments, contemplating how best to answer him. Coming up with nothing, she decided going with the truth was probably best. "He's dead, and I can't bring him back. But I do miss him, yes. And I do think about him. Every day."

Badger blew out a breath, one that sounded far too much like the wind had been knocked out of him rather than one of relief. "Okay. Then I—"

"But..." she squeezed his hand. "I hadn't been in love with him for a long time. I loved him. We'd been together since we were barely out of high school. He was my best friend. He was a big pain in my ass. And I stayed far longer than I should have. But I also stayed because he needed me."

In an instant, his expression changed, and he blew out another breath. This one sounding a whole lot more like relief. Rosie leaned forward and pressed a soft kiss to his mouth.

"Rosie?" he mumbled against her lips.

"Yes?" she breathed.

"You're mine, baby."

"Yes, honey. I am."

CHAPTER TWENTY-FIVE

Rosie heard Badger call her name just as she finished curling her hair in the bathroom. She'd woken that morning to an empty bed, which was totally normal during the week, but on Sunday? Not so much. She'd texted him a few times and gotten no answer, either. If she wasn't worried, she'd have been pissed. Finally, he gave her a call, letting her know he'd been running a few errands and was coming home in the next two hours…with a guest. "I'm in the bathroom. Be out in a minute."

After setting the curling iron down on the vanity top, she unplugged it. Rosie had no idea who he was bringing over, but she figured it wasn't Wolf. He'd have said so. She ran her fingers through the bouncy curls and added a light layer of hairspray. One thing was for sure: Arizona had been amazing for her long, straight hair. The lack of humidity made it possible to do just about anything to it and have it stay. Discovering she could have curls for days was flipping awesome. One last check of her makeup, and she headed out and down the hall.

"Badger?" Rosie peeked into the formal living room and froze. *Whoa!*

"Hey, baby." Badger rushed toward her, a big smile on his face. "Someone I want you to meet."

Rosie's eyes went wide as the elderly woman got to her feet with the help of a cane. Rosie swallowed past the large lump that'd lodged in her throat and glanced up at Badger. "Is that…?"

"Yeah." He pressed a kiss to her forehead and turned away from her. "Nana, this is Rosie." He glanced back at Rosie after taking his grandmother's hand when she neared them. "Rosie, this is Patricia."

"Oh my. Drew, she's beautiful! Just like her pictures, but even better." Patricia nudged Badger in the ribs with her elbow before extending her hand to Rosie.

Rosie forced the lump back down her throat because… *Drew? His name was Drew? And, wow, pictures?* Getting her racing thoughts in line, she forced a smile and clasped his grand-mother's palm. "Nice to meet you, Patricia. And thank you. You're quite beautiful, too."

"Charming, as well." She smiled as she slipped her hand from Rosie's. "Better hold on to this one; she's a catch."

Badger laughed. "Duly noted, Nana. I'm going to go put some coffee on. Why don't you two have a seat and, I don't know, do that girl thing."

"What thing is that, *Drew?*" Rosie smiled and crossed her arms.

"Talk about me, of course." He tossed her a grin as he stepped away, chuckling.

Oh, Lord. Rosie rolled her eyes and laughed as he made his way out of the room. How interesting was this? Badger, or wait… Drew—yes, *Drewww* appeared to be a little…giddy? Before that moment, she'd been pretty damn sure such a thing wasn't possible. Yet Rosie had seen it with her own eyes. Scary badass biker was also a giddy one. Kind of an oxymoron in her book, but she wouldn't trade it. She looked back at his grandmother and gestured to the sectional. "So, shall we sit?"

"Yes, but let's not talk about him. I'd rather hear all about you." Patricia smiled and resumed her seat on the couch.

And the lump was back in Rosie's throat as a beat of fear drummed through her. "Maybe I should go check on Badger…he sometimes—"

His grandmother patted the space next to her. "Come on, dear. I don't bite. At least not right away." She smiled, her soft eyes smiling, too.

Rosie chewed her thumbnail and took the offered seat. She had no idea what to say to the woman or what Badger had told Patricia about her. Did she know she was a stripper? Rosie cringed and smoothed her hands down her thighs. Did she know there was a drug dealer on the hunt for Rosie's head? Good God, she was sweating.

Patricia covered Rosie's hand with her own, patting it. "He told me you were in some trouble, but he wouldn't tell me what. I imagine you're not inclined to share, either, so don't worry, Rosie, we don't have to talk about that."

Relief washed through Rosie like a cool splash of water. At least that took one unsavory topic off the table. "Thank you. I appreciate that."

"He said you moved here recently. Where from?"

"Connecticut. Waterbury. Do you know the area?"

"I'm familiar, yes. Though I haven't been on that side of the country in a good sixty years at least."

Rosie's jaw dropped open, though she tried to stop it. "Sixty years? That's a really long time."

"It is, yes. I imagine it's changed a bit since then." Patricia giggled.

Good grief, how old was she? On the verge of asking the question—as polite as she could—Rosie remembered that Badger had already told her his nana's age when they'd decorated the tree a couple of days ago. But seeing her in person, Rosie never would've guessed she was eighty-eight. Seventy maybe. Close to the top end of it, even, but not on the top end of eighty. Her short hair was colored a chestnut brown and curled to perfection around her head. She wore lipstick in the sweetest shade of pink and definitely blush. The woman was put together more than some younger people Rosie knew. "I bet it has. It was probably a lot nicer when you saw it last."

"Is that where you grew up?"

Rosie shifted on the couch so she could face her and smiled. "Born and raised."

"Aw, I bet you miss it, dear. Is your family still there?"

Rosie ran her fingers through the ends of her hair. "No, ma'am. It's just me." She glanced away from Patricia's gaze. It wasn't exactly true that she had no family, but mostly. Even so, guilt bounced around Rosie's brain like a rubber ball anyway. She looked back at Badger's Nana. "I have some cousins in New York, my father's side. But I haven't had any contact with them in something like thirty years." Rosie shrugged.

"You'd have been pretty little at that time, right?"

"Around seven." Rosie chewed on a cuticle as she shrugged.

With brows pulled together in a frown, Patricia let out three tsk's as she shook her head. "Families can be full of assholes sometimes."

Whaaaat? A laugh burst out of her at what'd just come out of Badger's grandmother. There was no stopping it. By the time Rosie drew in her first breath, Badger was heading toward them, a big ass grin on his beautiful face. Rosie covered her mouth, trying for all it was worth to stem her fit of giggles, but…no way that was happening.

"She got you, didn't she?" He bent and kissed Rosie's cheek.

All Rosie could do was nod as she continued to laugh. Talk about an icebreaker of epic proportions. With every chuckle, the tension just eased right out of her limbs.

"Got her how?" Patricia winked at him.

"Yeah, you know exactly how. So, I got coffee and some fresh cinnamon buns out on the table. Who's game?"

"Hot dog! Don't have to tell me twice." Patricia was up and out of her seat before Rosie even realized it.

Rosie stood, and Badger pulled her into his arms as his grandmother made her way toward the kitchen. "Knew she'd like you."

She stared up at him and smoothed her palm along his beard. "I like her, too. Thanks, honey." She rose on tiptoe and pressed a soft kiss to his lips.

He'd brought her an incredible gift that morning. Given her something special. Seeing that deeply into his life meant a lot to her. Knowing that it was a place he likely hadn't shared with many made it all the more significant. It made her feel special. It made her feel wanted and not just someone he was trying to rescue. And that meant the world.

She'd never forget it.

AFTER GETTING his Nana back to her little assisted living apartment, Badger walked through the kitchen and den in search of Rosie. He peeked in the living room, and when he didn't find her there, he turned to head down the hall. He found her just as she was coming out of the bedroom.

"Oh, hey. You're back." She smiled and brushed her hair off her shoulder. "You okay?"

Badger nodded as he hooked her around the waist, pulled her to his body and then backed her against the wall. She let out a gasp and stared up at him.

There was nothing to say. Words wouldn't be enough.

Instead, he let his gaze roam over her face before settling on her lips. Badger had one thing on his mind since spending time with her and the only other woman who'd been important in his life, and that was showing Rosie where she stood in his world. So, instead of talking, he just acted.

Badger brushed his lips over hers, once, twice…teasing before finally covering her mouth with his own. The kiss was powerful, fueled by passion. The kind of kiss where neither moved and just stayed locked to each other, savoring the moment as the heat built. He moved his hands to her face, cupping her jaw in his palms, unwilling to let her go.

Their breath quickened, and Rosie moaned and ran her hands up his back. Shifting, he broke the hard press of his lips and delved his tongue inside her mouth. Her sweet taste hit him like a tidal wave, and Badger's knees went weak. Jesus, he was lost to her. At some point, she'd become heaven for him, and he never wanted to go back.

Badger smoothed his palms down her neck to her shoulders and lower to her sides. Tugging up her shirt, he skated his hands over her soft skin until he found her hard nipples. She rarely wore a bra, didn't need one, and he was just fine with that. Breaking from her mouth, he pulled back and gazed down at her as he pinched and tugged on the tight peaks.

Rosie gasped and bit her bottom lip. Badger groaned and tugged a little harder. She let out a little squeak, and his dick jerked behind his zipper, growing harder than it already was.

"Badger…"

He dropped to his knees and cupped her petite breasts in his palms, massaging them before leaning in and wrapping his lips around one hard berry. Rosie circled her arms around his neck and arched against him. Badger sucked and nibbled her perfect nipple before moving to the other and giving it the same treatment. He couldn't get enough of this woman. Her scent, her taste, the little sounds she made when he touched her body. Fucking hell, he'd never been so greedy in his life for a woman.

She moaned, gripping his T-shirt, holding him close. She loved her tits played with. Loved it when he pinched, bit and sucked her nipples. Badger gave Rosie what she wanted and gave it to her hard.

She took it all from him and begged for more.

The unbelievable connection between them in perfect sync. Always. But right then, he wasn't being as rough as he usually was, and she didn't seem to mind that, either.

Popping the top button on her jeans and sliding the zipper down, Badger grabbed hold of the sides and peeled the tight denim down her hips. After helping Rosie step out of her pants, Badger pulled the thin strip of her panties to the side and slid two fingers through her folds.

She thrust her hips forward, and with a groan, he drove his fingers into the tight mouth of her cunt. "Always so wet for me."

"Mmhmm." Rosie panted and grabbed his shoulders harder as she rode his fingers.

Badger leaned forward and licked over her clit, and Rosie cried out, jerking against him. "Easy, baby. I got you." He urged one leg over his shoulder and bent close again. She tilted her pelvis forward, and Badger sucked the tight bud between his lips as he worked her channel with his fingers.

Rosie grew wetter, hotter the longer he worked her. Whimpering with each stroke of his tongue and slide of his fingers, her juices dripped down his hand. She'd come for him like she always did, and he'd soak up every second of it. Her grip tightened, and Badger sucked harder, driving into her core a little faster.

"Badger! I need…oh God!"

Not wanting to pull his mouth away, he nodded enough so she'd feel it and kept at her. He wanted it. Needed her orgasm like he needed the air to breathe. Rosie arched, rolling her hips as her orgasm hit, and she gripped his head, grinding her pussy against his mouth. Badger growled, excitement at her pleasure racing through him as his dick throbbed, aching to be inside her.

Easing back as her climax settled, Badger got to his feet and picked Rosie up. He walked them into the bedroom and laid her down on the bed. "Now, I need inside you."

"Yes, honey." Rosie pulled her shirt over her head and tossed it aside.

Badger did the same and then shed his jeans. As he opened the night table drawer to retrieve a condom, Rosie moved to the edge of the bed and sucked his cock between her lips. He paused, losing track of what he was doing for a moment as the heat of her wet mouth encompassed his shaft. Staring down at her, he stroked his fingers through her hair and let her take him how she wanted.

After a few moments, she pulled him from her mouth with a smile and stroked his length. "You were dripping. I needed to take care of that." She held out her hand for the condom. "May I, sir?"

Fucking hell, she was perfect. He bent and stole a quick kiss and handed her the small square. "You may."

Rosie pulled the latex from the wrapper and sheathed his prick, then bent and licked over his sac, suckling each globe before pulling away with another smile. "All ready."

A bolt of lust shot down his spine, and Badger growled as she moved away from him and lay down on the bed. He climbed between her spread legs and settled on top of her, resting his weight on one forearm. As always, he was overcome by how beautiful she was in his eyes. He could stare at her all day. Hell, he had for months, and he still wasn't done. Badger traced her jawline with his fingertip, then trailed it down her chin to her throat and beyond to between her cleavage.

Rosie shivered beneath his touch, and Badger felt her body's response deep in his bones. She felt like a warm spring breeze within his soul. She'd given him peace, quieting the noise that'd always been present in his mind. Rosie brought a softness out of Badger he'd never known he was capable of possessing. "Who do you belong to?"

"You."

"Yes." He continued his exploration of her soft skin down to her stomach, circling her belly button. "Who do I belong to?"

When she didn't answer, Badger glanced up at her. The expression in her eyes was one of tenderness, but he could see the underlying fear of whether or not she should answer. He'd told her a few times already that she was his. She'd accepted his claim. But he'd yet to actually say the words and offer himself in return, thinking she'd just know that she owned him.

He realized in that moment she didn't know.

———

ROSIE STARED into Badger's eyes as a plethora of emotions rolled through her. He was being so different with her. Softer, so much softer than he'd ever been. There was a tenderness in his touch that he'd never shown her before.

It was wonderful and sweet and almost confusing.

But then he'd asked her that question. Who *did* he belong to? Was it her? Was that what he was saying? Rosie bit her lip, afraid to answer…afraid that she might be misinterpreting what he was asking or, more importantly, what he was saying with the question. She was his. He'd claimed her. Had made it clear she belonged to him and only him. But he'd never—

"Rosie?" He cupped her cheek.

She blew out a shaky breath but couldn't bring herself to answer. What if she was wrong…what if she said her? That he belonged to her? And he said no. That he didn't belong to anyone. Rosie had already fallen hard for him— *Oh God.* She glanced away from his intense gaze. Yeah, she'd fallen totally and completely in love. And she wasn't ready to feel the pain and embarrassment of her ass crash landing on the floor.

He stroked his thumb over her cheek. "Baby, look at me."

She did, trying her best to keep the tears she felt pricking her eyes at bay. Badger's gaze roamed over her face, and instead of forcing her to answer, he closed the distance between them and kissed her. Soft. Tender. Sweet… At the same time, she felt the blunt head of his cock press against the mouth of her sex, and, ever so slowly, he entered her.

As she was filled with his thickness, Badger stroked his tongue over hers, teasing and tasting, hypnotizing her soul and taking her deeper. When he broke the kiss and pressed his forehead to hers, he moved within her, thrusting his pelvis forward and rubbing against her clit. Tingles spread over every inch of Rosie's skin, and she raised her knees higher and dug her heels into the mattress so she could rock her hips in opposition to his. He kept his pace even and consistent, concentrated. Building it inside her—building it between them.

Rosie ran her palms down his back to his ass and grabbed hold, feeling the tightness of the muscles as he thrust into her. "Badger…"

He buried his hands in her hair and kissed her again, stealing her breath before pulling away. "Is my kiss yours, baby?"

Rosie let out a moan and pressed her lips to his throat. "Yes."

"That's right." He drew his cock out and then slid deep. "Is my body, my dick yours, baby?"

God, he was killing her. Every move he made and each word he said was filled with intense passion laced within his gravely tone, and it just kept increasing. She was drowning in it and in him. He pulled out and drove in again. Rosie arched, her orgasm climbing to the surface. "Yes."

With a growl, Badger ground against her clit, thrusting

faster. With his fingers tangled in her hair, he tugged her head back and ran his tongue up the side of her neck to her ear. "Who has my heart? Who do I belong to?"

His whispered question took her under the waves of emotion swirling around her, and everything became clear. Clearer than they'd already been. Life had shown her that not everyone got the chance to feel what it was like to be rocked to the core with just a look or a whisper of a touch. Not everyone got to meet someone, totally out of the blue or accidentally, who for sure wasn't what they were looking for or maybe was nothing like them…but was completely and wholly their other half.

But once in a blue moon, a lifetime, maybe even a hundred lifetimes, a person got to find their match. They got to be whole. They got their chance. And this was Rosie's chance. She wasn't about to let it go.

There was no going back for her. Rosie's old life was gone, and she never wanted it back. All she wanted was Badger. He was it for her. From that moment going forward, he always would be.

The weight of his body on top of hers was a welcome comfort in such a raw moment as he made love to her for the very first time. Rosie moved her hands to the sides of his head and urged him up to look at her. "You belong to me, Badger. And I belong to you."

He closed his eyes. "Say it again."

Rosie cupped his face in her palms, losing her breath at the sight of his beautiful face. "You belong to me, and I belong to you."

After opening his eyes and focusing on her, Badger let out a sigh and brushed his lips over hers. "Always."

"Yes, honey." The climax that'd been building within her surfaced, poised to break free as Badger moved within her, their bodies in perfect sync.

"I feel you. So sweet and warm. So different. So perfect." Badger moved faster, his thrusts more frantic.

Rosie let him take her higher until she couldn't hold it back any longer. Her cunt clenched, her clit spasming as her climax blasted through her. She gasped and let out a whimper before biting down on his shoulder, her whole body going tight as she came for him.

Breathing heavy, Badger drew out and drilled back into her with long, hard strokes. "Mine, Rosie. This cunt, this body…you. You're mine, always!"

After one final, hard thrust, Badger came. With a loud growl, his body seized above her. His cock, buried deep inside her, pulsed as he spurted his climax into the condom. Rosie ached to feel that hot fluid coating her channel. She wanted all of Badger. Nothing could change that now.

In that moment—body, heart and soul—every part of Rosie burned for him.

CHAPTER TWENTY-SIX

ROSIE SET a fresh cup of coffee down on Badger's desk. "Here you go, honey." She bent and kissed his cheek.

"Hey, thanks. How'd you know I needed that?" He smiled and took a sip.

"Wild guess." With a grin, she rested her bottom against the desk. "Least I can do, you know, since I'm like June Cleaver or some shit—minus the kids, of course."

"What?"

"June Cleaver. I know you're old enough to know who I'm talking about. Or would you prefer Susie Homemaker? Maybe that's a better reference." She snorted a laugh and picked at a piece of skin on her cuticle. "Speaking of...you know what? I don't think I even know how old you are."

Badger leaned back in his seat and clasped his hands over his stomach. More like washboard abs, but anyway. "I'm still cracking up at the labels you've assigned yourself. Just remember, you said it, not me." He winked. "And yes, my little drama queen, I know who June Cleaver is. As far as my age goes, how old do you think I am?"

"Drama queen, huh? Don't know what you're talking about." Rosie tried like hell to hide her smirk but failed miserably. "And fine, let's play the 'guess your age' game. How old do you think *I* am?"

Badger caught her wrist and tugged her onto his lap. She landed, an *oomph* coming out of her, and he grinned and smoothed his palm up her thigh. "I asked you first."

Rosie bit her bottom lip and smoothed her palm along his beard, and then traced the fine lines around his eyes. He was so beautiful, in a very rugged and masculine way. She could add romantic to the list of things about him she adored. And when he smiled, it almost hurt to look at him, but Rosie would take the pain any day and any time because it was the sweetest ache she'd ever felt. "I'd say late thirties."

A grin tugged at the corners of his lips, and he touched the tip of her nose. "Ah, no. But nice try."

"Was I close? Shit. Are you younger?" She frowned.

Badger chuckled. "Yes and no. I'm forty-two."

"Hmm, really? Well, for a biker, who used to run with an MC, you look pretty damn good to me." Rosie leaned up and rubbed the tip of her nose over his. "Your turn."

With his lips pursed, he tilted his head to the side and slid his palm around to her ass. "You are thirty-six years young."

Rosie's jaw dropped, and she let out a gasp in mock astonishment. "Years young, huh? Are you trying to get in my pants with flattery?"

Badger jerked his head back and tilted his chin up as he smirked. "Woman, as if I need to try?"

"True. Very true." She pressed a soft kiss to his lips. "This could be kind of fun, actually. How about we play twenty questions?"

"Twenty questions, huh? All right, I'm game." He brushed her hair over her shoulder. "Ladies first."

Rosie nibbled on her thumbnail as curiosity pulsed through her. There were so many things she could ask, so much she wanted to know. Decision made, she started with the easiest. "What's your full name?"

His gaze roamed over her face. "Drew."

"Yes, I know it's Drew. Thanks to your Nana. Tell me your whole name."

He raised his brows. "Does that count as two questions?"

"No. Your answer was incomplete." She smiled.

He laughed, and Rosie's whole body went warm. "Fair enough. It's Drew Baxter."

"Drew Baxter. I like it. But…hmm." She giggled. "Is your middle name Badger?"

"Now you're cheating." He tickled her side, and Rosie squirmed, giggling as she tried to pull his hand away. Tried being the operative word. With a grin in place, he stopped the tickling and traced a line down her thigh with his fingertip. "It's my turn now. You'll have to ask that question again when I let you have another turn. Now tell me, what's *your full* name…first, middle, and last?"

She smiled and raised one eyebrow. "All righty there, Mr. Thorough. It's Rose Marie Santini."

"Confession: I knew that already. I just wanted to hear you say it." He grinned.

"Figures!" She laughed and swatted his arm. "Checking up on me with those bounty hunter skills."

His expression softened. "Yeah, well. It's pretty. Like you."

Rosie's cheeks got warm right along with her insides. Though since the other night, after she'd met his Nana and he'd taken her to his bed, she hadn't stopped feeling warm. "Thanks. It's a family name. I was named after my Noni."

"Even better. Plus, Noni? Nana? Almost the same. That's pretty cool." He touched her cheek and brushed his lips over hers. "Your turn."

Rosie sighed at the soft contact but forced her expression into a serious one. "It is pretty cool. Okay! What's your middle name?"

Badger rolled his eyes and let out a snore. "Knew that was coming. It's Lawrence."

"I love it!" She smiled, laughing as she clapped her hands together. "Okay, you go."

"Hmm." He glanced around the room, then back to her. "Let's see. How 'bout, what did you want to be when you were a little girl?"

"A nurse."

"Wow. I can totally see that." He grinned, a devilish glint in his eyes.

"Nuh-uh." Rosie laughed and poked her fingertip in his chest. "You're just picturing me in a naughty nurse costume. I can totally tell by that look you have in your eyes."

He laughed with her as he bent and nipped the side of her neck. "Maybe."

"Mmm. Yeah, maybe for your birthday." She smoothed her hand up his bicep. "Ooh! When's your birthday?"

"The twentieth of February."

"Mine's April seventh. You probably knew that already." She traced his bottom lip with her fingertip.

"Guilty." He winked.

"My mother was hoping I'd be born on April Fools. But I was late."

He frowned but chuckled and shook his head. "That's funny. In a twisted sort of way."

"My mother was funny *and* twisted, so it fits." She shrugged and glanced away. Her mother was definitely not a topic she wanted to get into.

Badger pinched her chin between his thumb and forefinger and tilted her face back in his direction. "Sounds like there's a story there."

"Another time. Plus, it's my turn." She gave him a small smile. She was enjoying what had unexpectedly turned into a very intimate time with him. The last thing she wanted was to put a downer on the mood. "Do you have any siblings?"

"Actually, it was my turn, but because I like you so much, I'll let you slide. Only child."

In an instant, Rosie's mood bounced right back to the top of the happy chart. "So generous of you." She couldn't help but smile. "This is where I pretend you didn't already know that I'm an only child, too. Kinda cool we have that in common, huh?"

"Yeah, baby. It is." Badger cupped her cheek in his palm, stroking his thumb along her chin before sliding his hand behind her neck and threading his fingers into her hair.

She raised a brow. "The cool part or the generous part?"

"Both." Badger's gaze roamed over her face again, and she felt it just the same as the touch of his hand on her skin. He focused on her eyes, and they stayed that way for what felt like an endless amount of time. She let out a sigh as a silence stretched between them, but it wasn't an uncomfortable one. On the contrary, it was easy and peaceful.

Rosie sank deeper into his light brown eyes. And for the first time, felt something flow through her that could only be described as contentment. This was where she was meant to be. She'd known it the other night, even said it to herself.

Badger was where she belonged. Always and forever. For as long as he'd have her.

BADGER STARED into a pair of eyes so beautiful and alive with layers of softness, he could hardly believe they'd ever reflected sadness in them. He never wanted to see her eyes haunted in that way again. Badger had gotten himself in deep with her— hadn't planned it, but it'd happened just the same. He'd welcomed it and tried to show her that the other night when he'd made love to her.

A lump rose in his throat, and he swallowed past it. God, what if he lost her? For the first time in a very long time, Badger felt fear. What if he'd not gone looking for her the night Alvaro showed up at the club? Fuck, what if he hadn't been working that night? She'd have left town…and Badger would have never known what he was missing.

He would've been missing a world he swore he never wanted or needed or ever dared to dream for. He was grateful to God and anything else he could pray to, that he hadn't missed it. Minutes passed, but time stood still in the space between them as Badger let himself sink into the depths of her gaze.

He'd drown in her undertow if he could.

"You okay, honey?" Her brow furrowed into a slight frown, and she touched her fingertips to his cheek.

Badger closed his eyes long enough to draw in a deep breath. It was time to let her in on what was going on regarding Alvaro, and also ask her about the money again. Putting it off any longer wasn't an option. He focused on her once more, pulled her close and pressed a soft kiss to her lips. After he pulled back, he patted her hip. "Let's go out back so I can smoke. We need to have a talk."

She frowned and slid off his lap. "*Ooohkay*. That doesn't sound good."

"Stop. It'll be fine. Come on." Badger took her by the hand and led her through the house to the back door.

Rosie tugged from his hold. "Hang on. Let me grab my sweatshirt, your coffee, and one for me. I'll meet you out there."

Badger nodded and slid open the glass door. Once outside, he took a seat on the wooden bench and lit a smoke.

Rosie came through the door he'd left open for her, a mug of coffee in each hand. "Still amazes me you can just leave the door open like this, and there's no bugs swarming to get in the house. If this was Connecticut, we'd be dealing with any number of flying pests."

"We got plenty of bugs in the Valley of the Sun. Have you seen a flying cockroach yet?" He took his coffee from her and sipped it.

"A flying—wait. Did you say cockroach? Please…no. Don't. I can't even." She covered her mouth and sat next to him. "Really? Flying? What the fuck?"

"Damn straight. Fuckers are almost two inches long." He indicated with his fingers. "Grossest things on the planet as far as I'm concerned. I just as soon shoot one than deal with it."

She raised her hand, letting him know he needed to shut his trap, and glanced around the backyard. "Stop. That's just hideous. But you don't have them in your house, right? I mean…I've never seen one before, so no, right?"

He took a drag and blew the smoke away from her. "I don't have them, no. But they do come up through the drains on occasion."

"Badger, you're fucking with me, right?"

"Nope. Being totally straight with you. It's rare, but it happens." He nudged her arm. "Don't stress. If one crawls out, just stand back, and I'll shoot it before it takes flight." He laughed.

"That's not funny!" Despite her declaration, she laughed, too, and then took a sip of her coffee. "I can't even. Just…no." She shivered.

"Cold, baby?" He chuckled.

"No. I'm fucking grossed out. And totally paranoid now."

Badger laughed harder, slipping his arm around her waist. Jesus, he really *did not* want to ruin the night they were enjoying by having the doom and gloom convo, but… "Not that I really want to, but we need to talk about Alvaro."

Rosie snapped her head in his direction. "Oh shit. Did you find something out?"

"He showed at the Cabaret the other night. We had a little chat."

"Oh my God! What did he say? What happened? What did you say?"

"Go easy, woman. Take a breath, and let me get it out." She rolled her eyes, and he continued. He wanted to try and keep this as light as possible, but that was pretty fucking stupid considering there was nothing light about the news. "He made his intentions known." He drew on his cigarette. "He intends to have a little chat with you. But that ain't gonna happen."

Rosie blew out an exasperated breath and got to her feet. Gnawing on her fingernails, she paced in front of him. "I don't know what the hell he wants to chat about. There's nothing to chat about."

Badger looked down into his coffee cup. "He wants his money, baby."

"I don't have his fucking money, Badger. I already told you that."

He glanced up at her. She'd stopped her pacing and was standing with her hands on her hips. All drama. All complication. Damn, he loved that about her. What he didn't love was that she still wasn't being straight with him. Disappointment pulsed through Badger in time with his heartbeat, and he took another drag of his smoke before stubbing it out in the ashtray. "All right, Rosie. Fine, you don't have the money."

"You don't believe me, do you?"

"It doesn't matter what I believe." Badger looked up at her. "Here's the deal. His trial isn't scheduled for another seven months, maybe more if his attorney decides to file postponements—which, I'm sure, he'll do."

"Fuck me. Seven months?" She plopped down beside him again.

"Yeah. So that means you need to stay hidden. I'm sorry, but he's not going away, and if he gets his way, his little chat with you will include way more than a conversation."

"I can't stay hidden for that long. No way. It's been almost three weeks, and I'm already losing my mind. For fuck's sake, you won't even let me go Christmas shopping." She crossed her arms and frowned. "And no, I don't want to shop online. That just sucks the Christmas right the hell out of the whole thing!"

"Look. I get it, okay? Just stop with the drama and listen." He ran his hand over his short hair. "I know you're frustrated. What if we get out of here? Go on a few vacations or something. See the country, or maybe even another country."

"A vacation? Wow, you know what? That sounds great, honey!" A smile spread across her mouth that smacked of the unspoken words of "fuck him and the horse he rode in on" before she frowned, glaring at him. "In case you missed the sarcasm, let me translate for you. *I don't think it's great at all.* And what? You're just gonna pack up to run around the globe with me and leave your grandmother here to fend for herself? Did you even think about that? I mean, what is this? Drew Baxter's witness protection program?"

The point about leaving his grandmother hit Badger right between the eyes, and he tried to suppress the growl that boiled to the surface as a result, but failed. "You let me worry about my grandmother, all right? This is the best option, and you know it. That man wants his money. He believes you have it. Whether you do or not doesn't really matter. He *will* kill you, Rosie."

"This is fucking stupid!" She stood in a huff and paced again. "And selfish!"

"Woman, you better get that mouth of yours in check." Badger let out another growl, barely able to comprehend all the emotions flying around his brain like a boomerang. The fact that she continued to think of others was something he definitely admired about her. She'd worried about Deuce and Evie being involved, as well as Wolf. But now she'd just added his grandmother to the mix. Jesus, his heart was in deep with her. But he was still pissed.

She continued to pace, glaring at him as she did. "Whatever!"

"Whatever, my ass. Might be stupid, Rosie, but no way in hell I'm losing you. Not now. Not after—"

Halting her movement, she looked at him. "Not after what?"

Frustration beat through him like a hammer, making him want to put his fist through the wall. Instead, Badger pressed his lips together and sighed through his nose. He didn't even want to examine what had almost come out of his mouth. Not the right time for that. He wasn't going to tell the woman all he felt—for the first time—while having an argument.

Instead, he got to his feet. "It doesn't matter. Bottom line: I'm not fucking losing you. We clear? You let me worry about the details. Eventually, he'll skip bail, and once he does, I can take him down. Until then, or until he's back in jail? Consider your ass the first customer of the Drew Baxter witness protection program and a frequent online shopper. You're just gonna have to fucking deal with it."

"No." Rosie crossed her arms and jutted out her chin— defiance and drama oozing from her expression.

"No?"

"You heard me."

Badger shook his head and headed toward the back door. Enough of this. She wasn't going to let it go, which was going to make the next several months hell. Not how he wanted things, but he'd deal. Dramatic temper tantrums and probably lots of slamming of cabinet doors would become the norm. Awesome. Just the perfect way to start out a relationship.

But it was better than the alternative—which was no relationship at all. No, Rosie making the world a prettier place.

No Rosie.

No Ro—Badger's stomach rolled into a tight ball, and a low growl rumbled from his chest. He couldn't imagine his world without her in it. It wasn't possible. This woman had embedded herself into his life, marking Badger as hers. That fact had been set in stone the other night.

There was no fucking way in hell he'd let her fuck that up for both of them.

CHAPTER TWENTY-SEVEN

ROSIE TURNED off the television and got to her feet. It was almost five p.m., and she was getting hungry. God only knew where Badger was or when he'd be home. Not that she cared. She was still pissed at him. It'd been three days since their fight on the back patio, and Rosie hadn't spoken a word to him since. And she didn't plan on breaking her silence any time soon.

They hadn't even had sex, which was really starting to wear her down. And regardless of the fact that she'd made an art of ignoring him, the bastard still held her tight to his body every single night when they slept.

Between the scent of him invading her senses and his dick pressed against her ass while he was spooned up behind her, Rosie was pretty much a walking horn dog with a libido that just wouldn't quit. Last night, she woke to find that she'd been rubbing against him in her sleep. She must've been dreaming, so it was *totally not* her fault. But of course, his cock had gone rock hard as a result, and before she knew it, his hands were traveling over her body from breasts to pussy and back again.

Rosie's stomach got tight at the memory, and her clit throbbed. Jesus, she'd wanted to fuck him so bad. But she hadn't. She'd held her ground and kept her wet pussy under wraps—by pretending she was asleep. Of course, in the morning, when he'd left for work or whatever else he was doing, she'd gotten herself off three times in the shower. Rosie groaned and closed her eyes. If she didn't stop thinking about it, she was going to end up getting herself off again. She could already feel her wetness coating her panties. Maybe she could fuck him when he got home and still maintain the silent treatment? *Ugh.* Yeah, right.

With a hard mental shove, Rosie banished the thoughts and put a lid on her arousal. Remembering she was hungry, she moved into the kitchen and opened the refrigerator doors. There wasn't much left in there that appealed to her. Maybe she should order a pizza. Or maybe some Chinese. Rosie opened the kitchen drawer that had some take-out menus in it. She sifted through the pile, searching for the menu for the Chinese place around the corner. They had really good kung pao chicken… "For fuck's sake. Where the hell is it?"

She slid the drawer closed and nibbled her thumbnail, trying to recall the last time she'd seen it. *Oh, yeah.* Pivoting, she headed through the den and down the hall to Badger's office. They'd ordered from the place a little over a week ago, and the menu was probably still on his desk.

After picking up a few pieces of paper and moving a couple of notebooks, Rosie finally located the menu. She took a seat and grabbed the cordless phone from its base and dialed the number. As the phone rang in her ear, Rosie sat back and glanced over his things. The edge of a white business card tucked inside a notebook she'd moved caught her attention. Curious, Rosie slid it from its place, and her eyes went wide—

"Mandarin Wok, how can I help you?"

"Uh…sorry. I'm gonna have to call you back." Rosie pulled the phone from her ear and pressed the "off" button. She stared down at the card with Alvaro's name and phone number on it. When the fuck had he… Shit, Badger probably got this the night he had his little talk with the dealer.

Rosie set the card down on the desk and stared at it. What if she just…

Raising her fingers to her mouth, she chewed the edge of a nail. The idea racing through her mind was crazy. Pure insanity. She knew it, but the train had already left the station. And at that moment, Rosie was powerless to stop it.

This madness needed to end, and she could end it. She needed to get on with her life. Badger did, too. Rosie picked up the phone and dialed the first nine digits of the number on the card. With her finger hovering over the tenth digit, she paused. Clicking the "off" button, she drew in a deep breath. She could do this. She had to. Resigned, she drew on any courage she could find within and punched all the numbers into the keypad. She put the phone to her ear as the call connected and began to ring. Her hands shook, and her heart pounded while Rosie waited for him to answer. "Come on, pick up."

"My friend. So good to hear from you."

My friend? What the fuck was that about? Rosie cleared her throat. "I want you to leave me alone."

"Ah, Mrs. Santini. What a nice surprise."

His deep voice crawled over Rosie's skin, and bile rose in the back of her throat. She swallowed it down and did her best to keep calm. "Did you hear me? I want you to leave me alone."

"And I want my money."

"I don't have your money."

He tsk'd her before continuing, "Dishonesty doesn't become you."

"I'll call the police. This is harassment."

"Now, now, Mrs. Santini. Do you take me for a fool? If you were going to do that, you would've already done so. We both know that."

She blew out a breath, unsure of what to do next. But she already jumped into the deep end; she'd have to figure out how to swim. "What my late husband did has nothing to do with me."

"Come now, we should discuss this in person. Bring me the money, and I will leave you alone. You have my word."

She laughed. "Your word? Excuse me, but your word means nothing to me. You murdered my husband."

"This is true. But I am still a man of my word."

Could what he say actually hold true? Wasn't there supposed to be some sort of code among drug dealers, or was that just the mafia? Rosie shook her head in annoyance. She was not this naïve, though she was seriously starting to question her soundness of mind. Calling him was crazy, and she was even crazier for considering going to meet with him.

But she was also desperate. Rosie wanted her life back, or at least to resume the new life she'd begun in Arizona. And she wanted to see if that life included Badger. "Fine, I'll come meet you. Scottsdale Fashion Square. By the waterfall. Tomorrow at noon."

"Planning on a little shopping?"

"Fuck you." Rosie disconnected before he could say anything else to her. She drew in a deep breath and dropped the phone on the desk.

"Who were you talking to?"

Rosie jumped as a scream punched out of her. She clutched her chest. "Jesus Christ, Badger. You scared me."

He crossed his arms and leaned against the doorframe. "Who were you talking to?"

"Good grief! I wasn't talking to anyone. I was cursing at the phone." As discreetly as she could, she shoved the business card under the other papers littering the desk as she picked up the take-out menu. "I was trying to order some take-out, but their line is busy. How is that even possible with call waiting?" She stood and moved to him. "Maybe something's wrong with your phone. Why don't you try from your cell?" He took the menu from her as he eyed her up and down. She could tell by his expression that he didn't believe her, but whatever. It didn't matter. "I'm craving some—"

"I know what you want." He drew his phone from his pocket.

"Great." She forced a smile and pushed past him. "Grabbing a beer. I'll take one out for you, too."

Considering she was about to do something really stupid in hopes of convincing a maniac to leave her alone, Rosie figured it was time to put an end to the silent scorn she'd been tossing Badger's way the last few days. Besides, it was really hard to stay mad at the guy when he knew, without even having to think about it, what her favorite foods were. Never mind the fact that Christmas was a week away. She wanted this done and over with. If things went well tomorrow with Alvaro, this whole nightmare would be over, and she'd be home before Badger ever knew she was gone.

And if they didn't…well, at least she'd have made the most of her last night with Badger.

Badger came out to the den after placing their order for take-out. Rosie was slumped down on the couch, television on, her feet up on the table. He paused a moment, taking in her profile as she lifted the bottle of Bud to her lips and took a sip. Her makeup was done, but only lightly and her hair was pulled up on the sides, leaving the length to drape over her shoulders. She wore a bright pink T-shirt—no bra, of course —with little rainbow-colored butterflies all over it and faded Levi's that clung to her body like a second skin.

As always… Beautiful. Different. Perfect.

"You okay?"

"Yeah." He moved into the room. "You?"

"I'm good, honey. Beer's on the counter for you." She smiled, all bright and pretty.

"Thanks." Badger walked to the kitchen to grab the beer. He couldn't shake the bad feeling that'd taken up residence in his gut like a lead weight since he'd found her in his office. There was something she wasn't telling him. At least she was finally speaking to him again—which was partly why he was leery.

The woman had gone seventy-two hours without so much as muttering a single word to him, and suddenly, she was acting like nothing had happened. They may not have been together very long, but they had been living together the *entire* time. Talk about getting up close and personal with someone real damn quick. Rosie'd already shown him she was stubborn as hell and knew exactly how to make a point, but the flip-on-a-dime demeanor wasn't like her.

Badger picked up the bottle and took a long gulp. Actually, he was damn lucky they got along as well as they did, considering they'd skipped the whole dating and getting-to-know-each-other phase, and went straight to being a cohabitating couple in two-point-two milliseconds. Casting off his feeling of unease, or trying to anyway, he moved to the den. "Not complaining, but I'm curious. What's changed?"

She looked up at him. "What do you mean?"

Badger took a seat on the couch beside her. "I've had nothing but dead air out of you for three days."

She shrugged. "Guess I got over it."

He grunted. "What if I'm not?"

Rosie leaned forward, placed her beer on the coffee table. "Hmm." Shifting, she rose to her knees on the couch, slid a leg over his thighs and straddled his lap. "Then, I guess I'll have to get you there."

Badger growled. Fucking hell, this woman! He *was* over it. Had been the minute it'd started. He'd given her the space she needed anyway. But he hadn't liked it. Not one damn bit. He'd missed the hell out of her, even though she had been there the whole time. He'd missed kissing her. Laughing with her. Touching her. Fucking her—good Christ, he'd missed fucking her.

The only thing that'd kept him sane had been that he'd held onto her when they were in bed sleeping. She'd allowed it, but she hadn't been happy about it. "Too bad," had been his reply to her when she'd tried to pull away the first night. Rosie hadn't liked that, either. But again, too bad. Badger gazed up into her brown eyes, wanting nothing more than to pull her down for a kiss. "How do you plan on doing that?"

With a slight shift of her hips, she tilted her head to the side, pursed her fine lips, quirked one eyebrow and gave him a lust-filled look. "Oh, I have my ways."

"I bet you do." Badger's eyes went to her mouth before focusing on her gaze again. Between the pressure of her sweet pussy against his zipper and the sexy expression on her face, blood started flowing fast and hot to his dick.

Rosie smoothed her palms down his chest and bent close, her lips hovering a bare breath above his. "May I kiss you, sir?"

Oh, goddamn. Lust hit him like a punch in the gut. Yeah, she sure as hell had her ways. She knew exactly what to do and say. He'd fucking taught her well. What he wanted to do was grab all that long hair of hers in his fist, force her to her knees and fuck that hot mouth of hers. More curious to see what she'd do next, he held himself still. "You may."

Rosie closed the small distance between their lips and covered his mouth with hers. She slipped her tongue into his mouth, stroking it over his, and Badger fisted his hands at his sides. He wanted to see how far she'd go, how she'd take him where she wanted him to go. But goddamn if she didn't taste like heaven. The finest sugar he'd ever had on his tongue flowed through his system, making his cock solid as steel while he let her control the kiss.

He swallowed her moan as she slid her hands beneath his shirt, kneading his muscled stomach and chest with her fingers and rolling her hips, grinding against his erection. As the kiss grew hotter and wetter, Badger's control slipped. Fuck, she was so fine…so hot. Breaking from her mouth, he gripped her hips and held her tight to his pelvis. "Missed this. Fucking missed you, Rosie."

"I know, honey. I missed you, too." Her head fell back as Badger kissed down her jaw to her throat. "I couldn't hold out any longer."

"That so?" He tugged the neck of her shirt aside and nipped at her collarbone. "Missing my cock?"

"Yes." Her voice was a breathless whisper as she arched, pressing her fine tits and hard nipples against his chest.

Badger's dick ached behind his zipper. He needed her naked. He needed her on his cock. He needed those hard berries in his mouth. He just fucking needed her… Fisting her hair in his palm, he shoved her off his lap. "On your knees. Take me between your lips now."

"Yes, sir."

He tore his jeans open and pushed them down his hips just enough to free his prick. "Take your shirt off and then hands behind your back."

She did as he directed, but before he let her have his cock, Badger needed some of her. Leaning forward, he rolled each tight nipple between his fingers, then tugged them hard, not letting go. Rosie moaned and whimpered, panting for breath as he gave her that sting of pain he knew she'd come to crave from him. "More?"

"Fuck, yes. Please, sir. More."

Badger tugged harder, pulling on the dark points. Jesus, he loved her nipples. Perfect for sucking and biting. "I'm going to buy you nipple clamps. Make you wear them for hours. How about that?"

"Badger—" she let out a hiss, "—oh God, yes, please? I want that."

"Yeah, that's my baby. Knew you would. Now, suck the cock you own." He fell back, relaxing against the cushions of the couch.

Rosie leaned forward, circling her tongue around the rim. Taking her by the back of the hair, he gripped the soft strands and thrust hard between her lips. He bumped the back of her throat, and she moaned. Badger gritted his teeth. "You got about five minutes to make me come down your throat before the food gets here. Show me how much you love my cock."

Rosie nodded, hands behind her back, sliding her mouth up and down his prick. He kept hold of her hair, guiding her, urging her, controlling how deep she took him. She was good. So fucking good at sucking his cock, he knew he'd come for her in less than the five-minute time limit he'd given her. With each thrust, she took him to the back of her throat, her saliva making his shaft slicker with each pass.

Moaning, she looked up at him, a dazed expression in her eyes. Badger's orgasm crawled up his spine at the sight of her lips stretched tightly around his shaft, her cheeks hollowed as she sucked, and he drove in and out of her mouth. "God-damn. Building it for you, baby. Draw it out of me. You're going to swallow every drop, aren't you?"

She nodded, and he drove hard and fast into her mouth, pressing her down on his cock. Badger could feel her throat contracting around the head as he held her there. She took it, all he gave her, and kept her hands behind her back the whole time. Jesus, she never ceased to blow his mind. "Fuck! That's my woman. Your cunt is soaked right now, isn't it? You love when I gag you on my dick. So fucking hot. I love it." Badger sucked in a strangled breath as his balls drew up tight, his orgasm rushing up on him. He pulled her back, sliding his shaft all the way out so only the head remained between her swollen lips, and he gripped his length with his free hand. "Suck it. Hard."

She gazed at him, her eyes filled with tears from each time she gagged a little on his prick and did exactly what he demanded. She sucked. Hard. Perfect.

Fucking hell, he loved her—

With his grip tight on his shaft, Badger's orgasm exploded out of him, and he straightened from his slouch on the sofa. Waves of his climax rippled through him, his shaft pulsing hard as he filled her mouth, spurting down her throat. She swallowed, whimpering as she sucked, shifting her hips. With his grip still tight in her hair, he pulled her off his cock-head.

She let out a loud moan, and he stroked his length, spurting down her chin and throat, as his come dripped from her lips. "Oh yeah, baby. All for you."

Badger released her, barely able to catch his breath, and collapsed against the back of the couch. Rosie bent forward and licked up the shaft, cleaning the remains of his climax. When she was done, she rested her cheek on his hip, and he smoothed his hand over the top of her head.

The doorbell rang, and Rosie let out a little giggle. "Guess I made it."

"I didn't doubt you would. Mouth like you got? Baby, you know just how to work me." He smiled down at her. "Best go clean up. I'll grab the door."

"Yes, sir." She shifted to the side.

Badger stood and helped her to her feet. After giving her a soft kiss on the lips and then the forehead, he tucked himself back in his jeans and headed for the door. Take-out, beer, and a movie beside his woman. Nothing better. With a smile, Badger pulled his wallet from his back pocket and opened the door.

The woman he just told himself he loved. *Wow…*

CHAPTER TWENTY-EIGHT

BADGER WAS RUNNING LATE GETTING out of the bar. Some asshole had started a fight. One of his bouncers got his nose busted in the scuffle…shit had been a mess. He pulled his gun from the filing cabinet and slid the holster on his belt. It was already after five p.m., and he'd promised Rosie that he'd be home by four.

She'd sent him off that morning with a long-as-hell grocery list, which included everything they were out of, plus some additional things she wanted to cook. The woman was going to be pissed as hell, and considering they'd just made up, he was not looking forward to the fit he knew he'd have to deal with.

He'd tried to call the house line just after four to let her know he'd be awhile, but she hadn't answered. Probably in the shower or working out on the back patio, earbuds stuck in her ears. After one last look around the office, Badger made his way out the door and the back exit.

When he'd finished at the grocery store, he tried the house line again and again and got no answer. Okay, so maybe she was more pissed than he'd figured. Dammit. Badger headed for home, grumbling to himself the whole drive.

Once there, he backed the truck in the driveway and hit the garage door opener. Christ, she hadn't even turned on the exterior lights for him. Pissed might be an understatement. He should've gotten her some flowers. Drawing in a deep breath in preparation for the coming drama-filled display, Badger propped open the laundry room door, flipped on the light switch and called her name.

Not waiting for her to answer, he headed back to the truck to grab an armload of grocery bags. When he returned and walked through the laundry room, he stepped into a dark kitchen. "Rosie?"

Where the hell was she? Badger flipped on the kitchen light with his elbow and placed the bags on the counter. He glanced into the den, noticing the lights were off in there, too. Shit, maybe she was asleep in the bedroom, but she usually left the end table light on. If she was sleeping, maybe he had a shot at not having to do battle with her and instead get some quality time in.

With his fingers crossed, Badger headed back out to the truck and grabbed the remaining bags. After muscling them into the house, he set them next to the others and began the unpacking and putting away routine. He'd let her sleep. Safer that way and the best way to increase his odds of a drama-free night.

When he got everything sorted and in its place, he pulled a beer from the fridge and headed for their bedroom. *Their bedroom*…he hadn't thought about it that way before. For over three weeks, she'd been in his home—his bed. For over three weeks, she'd been part of his daily life, night and day. Rosie had given him a taste of something he hadn't even known he was missing: A real relationship. Plus, she'd fulfilled every sexual fantasy he ever had.

Yeah, it was their bed. It was their bedroom. It was their home.

Badger kept his steps light as he walked into the room. It

was dark, and rather than turn on the light, he slipped onto the bed. "Rosie?" he whispered and reached for her.

But she wasn't there.

What the fuck? Badger rolled over and turned on the bedside lamp. He glanced around, not quite understanding what was going on. He stepped out of the room and systematically checked the spare bedroom and his office.

Nothing.

He continued down the hall, calling her name and getting no response. Shit, he hadn't thought about it, but maybe she'd fallen asleep in the formal living room on the couch. She'd taken to sitting in there, with only the lights from the Christmas tree illuminating the room. Badger ran into the dark room. The Christmas tree wasn't lit, and there was no Rosie, either.

Baffled, he stood for a moment, hands propped on his hips. Had she left him? No way she'd just leave him. Not with the threat of Alva— Oh God!

Panic lanced Badger's veins like an ice pick as he stared at the empty couch. He was not a man who overreacted or jumped to conclusions. Ever. But in that moment, his brain was doing a figure eight on the assumption and conclusion track, rounding each corner at breakneck speed.

He needed to calm down. He needed to think rationally… he needed to see if her things were still there. Pivoting, he walked, at an overly swift pace, to the bathroom. After flipping on the light, Badger pulled open the top drawer where she stored her makeup. It was all there. Thank fuck…she hadn't left him.

Women didn't just up and leave without their makeup, right? Clothes, maybe, but not their facial essentials. Even *his* woman, who didn't pack on the face paint. He blew out a relieved breath as he braced his hands on the counter and closed his eyes.

When he opened them, he spotted a folded note taped to

the mirror. As if everything had gone into slow motion, Badger reached forward and peeled the piece of yellow notebook paper from the glass. Backing up, his boots hit the side of the bathtub, and he sat his ass down on the edge and read.

> Badger,
> I know you're going to be mad. But please don't be. If you're reading this, then that means you either got home earlier than expected and I'm not back yet, or you're home when you're supposed to be, and likely, he didn't keep his word, and obviously, I failed to convince him that I didn't have his money and that he should leave me alone. By him, I mean Alvaro.

HOLY SHIT! Was she fucking insane? Badger got to his feet and stormed to the kitchen as equal parts fear and anger pulsed through him, making his heart race.

> You're mad. I know it. Please, don't be mad. Please, honey? I needed to do this, and I knew there was no way you'd let me. But the thing is, I didn't keep my word to him, either. He told me to bring the money, and I didn't. Fuck him. No way in hell I'd let that bastard have the money back.
> This is when I have to come clean and apologize. I'm sorry I lied to you. Obviously, you now know that I did have the money. I've had it the whole time.

. . .

THE WOMAN WAS KILLING HIM. Badger stood in the kitchen and ran his palm over his short hair. He'd known she was lying about the money, but he sure as fuck hadn't figured on her confessing like this.

I don't know why I lied exactly, which sounds pretty lame now that I'm writing it, but it's the truth. I know you're probably thinking you have no reason to believe anything I ever tell you again, but please know that's the only thing I ever lied to you about.

I took the money right when I was heading out of town. I don't know why I did that, either, except that maybe now I've realized that I didn't want anyone to have it.

It's dirty money. But not only that, it's also blood money. Which is a trillion times worse, in my opinion. And, as stupid as Joey was, my husband lost his life over it.

You might be surprised to know I never spent a dime. But if you know me as well as I think you do, maybe not. I don't know. Doesn't matter, I guess. But I just hid it when I got here and went on with my life. That's why I went back to stripping. The trip out from CT plus setting up home here broke my small savings, and when you weren't hiring for the bar or waiting tables, I went back to the stage. I don't know why I'm telling you all of this now...I guess in some way, I'm hoping, in case you don't get it, it'll help you understand me better.

From the first day that I met you, you took my breath

away. But on that first day, when I'd told you I'd go for the stage, I saw the look in your eyes change from a gaze I felt on my skin as if you were touching me to one of shame. Well, I have to tell you, honey, I was ashamed of myself, too. The last thing I ever wanted was to be back up on that damn stage.

And yeah, maybe I could've walked out of Deuce's that day and found another bar that would've hired me as a bartender rather than making the choice I did. At the time, I should have.

But if I had done that, I never would've gotten to have you.

I love you, Drew. Have fallen, completely and totally, madly in love with you. And I wish I'd been able to tell you that in person and not in this letter. But there it is. And it doesn't even matter if you feel the same. You gave me something I'd never had with anyone. Not even Joey.

You let me be a queen (even a drama one) because you are my true and one and only king.

You let me be strong by being my rock. You were my lighthouse in the storm, my guide that I could count on. A solid foundation of strength so that when I needed to be weak, I could be.

Please know there aren't enough words to express how grateful I am to have had that. You made it possible to breathe easy for the first time in my life. Even with the threat of Alvaro constantly looming.

All I can say is thank you.

With all my heart,

Your Rosie.

. . .

Ps: The money is located in Glendale Discount Storage, unit 1325. The key is taped to the bottom of my makeup drawer. Take the money—do something good with it. Maybe it'll somehow make all of this right.
I love you.

As soon as Badger stepped onto the back patio, he lit a cigarette. Tossing the pack down on the table, he pulled his phone from his pocket and called up Alvaro's contact info. After hitting "Call Contact" on the screen, he pressed the phone to his ear.

"My friend. I was beginning to think I wouldn't hear from you."

Alvaro's condescending tone of voice set Badger's blood boiling hotter than fresh lava. "Put her on the phone. Now."

"As you wish."

Badger took a drag from his smoke as he waited. The guy could take his high and mighty and go get himself fucked in hell. Badger was all too willing to show him the way.

"Ouch! That fucking hurt!" Rosie yelled.

Badger gritted his teeth at the sound of her voice in the background. He wanted to scream her name, but knew Alvaro would only get off on it. Badger wasn't about to give the bastard the satisfaction of knowing he had a full gamut of emotions flying through his mind, making him physically shake.

"Mrs. Santini, behave, please. Else, I will be forced to make you tolerable once again if you continue to conduct yourself in this manner. Now...there is someone who wishes to speak with you."

A growl escaped, and Badger cleared his throat to stifle it. "Just hand her the phone, asshole."

"Yes, yes. Patience, Mr. Baxter."

"Yeah, ye—"

"Badger!"

"I'm here. You okay?"

"More or less."

Less? "Yeah. Okay. Got it." Hell fucking no. Another growl surfaced, and Badger took a drag from his smoke. "Don't worry, we clear? I'll handle it."

She let out a sigh. "Yeah, we'r— Hey! I wasn't done! Damn you!"

Obviously, Alvaro had taken the phone back from her. Badger could hear her voice growing distant as the asshole was probably walking away from her. Motherfucking-sono-fabitch! Badger was so going to make the bastard suffer for this. "If you harm even one hair on her head—"

"She does have such pretty hair." Alvaro tsk'd at him. "Would be a shame…but…in order to avoid harm to all those nice dark locks, I do believe a negotiation is in order. Wouldn't you agree?"

"Name the terms, asshole. I got shit to do." Badger's skin itched to beat Alvaro until he choked on his own blood. Badger would play the game for now and set the stage.

Rosie would be coming home to Badger, breathing and in one perfect piece—although when he was done tanning her ass for making such a stupid mistake, she wouldn't be able to sit down for a week, maybe more.

In the end, there would be no fucking negotiation with Alvaro—not once all was said and done. What there would be was one dead drug-dealing scumbag and his disposable sidekicks.

CHAPTER TWENTY-NINE

Rosie shifted her weight as best she could to one hip. Her ass had gone numb hours ago, but it was starting to hurt again. Her arms tingled from being bound behind her back, and her head ached like there was a small marching band inside it. Likely from the goose egg on the back of her skull that she'd earned when Alvaro forced her inside his car, and she wasn't cooperating.

Jesus, she'd fucked up. Maybe the blow had knocked some sense back into her because it was quite clear to her now that going to see a man she knew was a lunatic in hopes of convincing him to leave her alone had landed at the top of her "bright idea" list.

At least he hadn't taped her mouth shut again. It was the little things that got a person by sometimes…

Rosie craned her neck to the side and peered through the doorway, listening for his voice, trying to get a bead on where Alvaro had gone. After he'd placed the phone to her ear and she got to hear the greatest sound in the world—Badger's voice—he pulled it away and walked off to finish his conversation in some unknown corner of the abandoned building they were in.

His two guards had gone off somewhere, too. Those two assholes had been a surprise she hadn't expected, which was another tribute to her stupid and rash decision-making skills. It wasn't like she had a lot of experience with drug dealers, but she should've figured he'd have goons with him. She wondered if Badger knew they existed. Taking advantage of being left alone, she strained against the duct tape wrapped tightly around her wrists as she glanced around what must've at one time been an office, searching for anything she might be able to use as a weapon. There were two gray metal desks set off to one side, a couple of other chairs and a shit-ton of old papers and garbage strewn about the space.

Someone had graffitied "The End is Near" with black spray paint on the wall opposite her. Yeah right. It sure as hell wasn't her end that was near. As far as Alvaro and his boys' future? Well, that was debatable. Badger would come for her. He'd come, probably with his own crew, and then this would all be over.

If only she could... Ugh! Blowing out a breath fueled by annoyance, Rosie twisted her wrists, straining against the binding, trying to get the tape to give. Even just a little. "Okay, Rosie. Buck up and just wait it out. Your inability to make sane choices got you into this mess...better put your big girl panties on and get yourself right back out of it." She craned her neck to the side, as far as she could, trying to see how much tape he'd used on her ankles. The fucker had taped her to the legs of the chair, rendering her pretty much immobile.

His laugh caught her attention, and she jerked her head up. Alvaro straightened from his lean against the doorframe and stepped inside the space. "Please, go on. I find your little self-pep-talk quite entertaining."

"Go fuck yourself. Better yet, go fuck your little minions. I bet they like it when you're nice and rough. How's that for an entertaining pep talk?"

With his lips pulled into a sneer, he tilted his head to the side. "I find you interesting. Very feisty. Though you could use some training. I can see why Mr. Baxter has become your savior. He's definitely a better match for you than your spineless husband was." He linked his hands behind his back and began pacing in front of her. "Honestly, I find Mr. Baxter interesting as well. In another life, I've no doubt we'd all have been friends."

"Not likely. I don't care for the company of liars or drug dealers, or murderers, for that matter. And neither does he. As far as my husband goes, you better pray to whatever God you believe in that you don't end up like you left Joey when Badger is done with you."

He laughed. "I'm the only God I believe in. I am no liar; I have kept my word, unlike you. That's a bit like the pot calling the kettle black, wouldn't you say?"

Fuck him for bringing up her husband. And fuck him and his money. She'd shove it down his throat and watch as he choked on it if she could. "I don't have your money, you sick motherfucker!"

With slow, calculated steps, he approached Rosie. As he got closer, she tilted her head back to keep her gaze locked with his. There was nothing but a cold darkness in his expression, as if he was dead inside. He likely was. The man showed no remorse for what he'd done to her husband. In fact, he gloated. It was disgusting. Psychopath was the only word that came to mind to describe him.

His face hovered no more than half a foot from hers. Rosie blinked once, and Alvaro's nostrils flared…but neither of them made a sound. Before Rosie realized what was happening, he'd raised his hand and slapped her across the face. Rosie's head snapped to the right as light exploded behind her eyes, and the coppery taste of blood filled her mouth. The hot sting was instantaneous, and so was the high-pitched groan that erupted from her throat.

In the next moment, Alvaro gripped her jaw, dug in with

his fingertips and forced her head back to look at him again. "Poor thing. But this is just what you need, isn't it?" Bending closer to her, he smoothed the hair away from her face and tsk'd at her. "Did that hurt?"

Rosie spit a mouthful of blood in his face. "Fuck you."

And then he slapped her again.

CHAPTER THIRTY

BADGER TURNED THE KEY, unlocking the heavy padlock on the small storage unit Rosie had directed him to in her letter. After removing it from the latch, he raised the door and peered inside the dimly lit five-by-five concrete space. On the floor, in the center, was a black leather duffel bag.

Typical of Alvaro that it was leather. Beyond arrogant, really. With a grunt, Badger moved inside the unit and crouched down in front of the bag. After unzipping it, he pulled the top apart and found exactly what she'd said would be there. The fucking money. He shook his head and straightened, pulling the bag up off the floor with him.

On the drive home, he placed a call to Deuce and then to Wolf. They'd both agreed to meet at his house within thirty minutes.

Once Badger arrived home, he set the bag down on the dining room table and started pulling out the money. It was time to count exactly how much money Alvaro had taken a life over. One by one, he stacked the wrapped thousand-dollar bundles of cash on the surface of the table. Just as he finished laying them out, both Deuce and Wolf walked in from the garage.

"Holy shit, that's a pile of money." Deuce smoothed his palm down his long beard.

Wolf stepped up beside Deuce. "Holy shit is right. How much?"

Badger set his hands on his hips and glanced over the table. "Looks like a decent amount, but haven't counted up yet."

"I'll grab us some beers," Deuce said and made his way back to the kitchen.

Wolf clapped his hands together. "Let's do it then."

Badger slid several stacks Wolf's way and began counting off his share. When he was done, he glanced over at Wolf. "Nineteen K. You?"

"Shush. Don't make me lose my place. Twenty-two, twenty-three, four, five…" Wolf moved over to the next pile. "Six, seven, eight…" Wolf glanced up. "Wow."

"Wow, what? How much?" Badger crossed his arms, growing impatient because he needed a damn cigarette, but needed to know how much money was there more.

"Thirty-one K on this end. You said nineteen, right?"

"That's only—" Badger double checked the math in his head a couple of times, "—fifty K? Right?"

"Yep. Fifty K. Unless you want to count it again?"

"There has to be more than fifty-large, Wolf. Count up again."

Deuce returned, two beers in one hand, a third in the other. "How much?"

"Shh. One sec," Badger said and continued counting his stack again while Wolf did his. "Yeah. Nineteen."

Wolf stood back. "Thirty-one, brother."

"Oh, hell fucking no. Serious?"

"Serious."

"Only fifty K? What the fuck." Deuce handed a bottle to Wolf. "That's just stupid."

Badger threw his hands up in the air and then headed for

the back door, grabbing his bottle from Deuce on his way past. "I *cannot fucking* believe this."

He hadn't even lit the cigarette before both guys were out there with him. Wolf stood off to the side of them, quiet as a mouse, and Deuce took a seat next to Badger.

Badger lit his smoke and inhaled a deep drag, exhaled, and drew in another. "I just…" He took another drag, then a swig of beer. "This motherfucker is crazy. Crazier than I already knew he had to be." Badger turned and faced his friends. "A man who's facing a murder charge goes after a measly fifty-thousand dollars? What kind of man does that?"

Wolf crossed his arms. "You said it already, brother. A crazy one."

"Nah, I'm thinking this is more than just your average crazy." Deuce rubbed his palm down his belly.

Badger smoothed his palm over his beard. "Her husband made a fool of him in the game. So Alvaro made his point by taking the guy's life. I get that. Even coming after Rosie, with intent to take her life and further make his point, plus get his dollars back…" Badger threw a hand out in front of him. "Shit, that's still a stretch because there ain't no honor in coming for a family member but considering an ego that big is at play, I get that, too. I even get he probably doesn't give one fuck about the murder charge, but I figured it had to mean he was coming after a few hundred thousand. Not a piddly fifty large." Badger looked at Wolf. "This isn't crazy, this is psychotic. This is…real deal personality disorder, narcissistic, egomaniac shit."

"Sociopath." Deuce took a swig of beer.

Wolf stepped closer. "No guilt. No conscience. And a vendetta. Bad, bad combo."

"Dangerous, too." Deuce looked Badger's way. "You remember what we talked about weeks ago when you first brought this to me?"

Badger blew out a harsh breath. He remembered exactly

what he and Deuce had discussed or what Deuce had implied anyway. That little convo had been stored in the back of his mind in the "just in case" folder. Badger needed to put Alvaro down like a rabid dog. End of discussion.

The man was fucking nuts. Most big drug dealers were, but from everything Badger had found out about the guy, he wasn't a big-time trafficker. For fuck's sake, Alvaro only had a small Puerto Rican operation. Definitely no Mexican Mafia by any stretch, but still big enough to employ a crew, line his pockets, and live like a wannabe high-roller.

Considering how high the stakes had gone, Badger had clearly underestimated how nuts the guy really was. Alvaro took crazy to a supreme level. Whacked in the head enough to ignore a murder charge and instead track a woman clear across the fucking country only to double up on that murder charge.

The fact that the guy was chasing a measly fifty thousand dollars, hell-bent on gaining his vengeance, only reinforced Deuce's original point.

There was no way in hell Alvaro would ever stop coming for Rosie.

Once he was done with her, the dealer would likely leave the country and set up shop wherever he landed. He'd use the fifty-K for that. Badger had no choice but to take him out. But he had to do it in such a way that he walked away clean.

No blowback to his brothers, the Cabaret and especially to Rosie.

BADGER PACKED the money back in the bag. "He said even trade. The money for Rosie. But we all know that's a load of bullshit."

Wolf looked up from loading bullets into his clip. "Betting he's planning on taking you out, too."

"Right, but he's gotta figure I'm coming prepared. Or at

least that I won't go down without a fight. He might be batshit, but he's not stupid." Badger zipped the bag closed.

Deuce leaned back in the kitchen chair, balancing it on two legs. "Don't count on it. Vengeance has a way of making men stupid. Wars have been fought for less than the vendetta he's got, especially on our modern-day streets. Hell, at one time, with a patch on each of our backs, we fought plenty of wars over something as stupid as turf. City streets we had no right to claim, for fuck's sake. If that ain't stupid, I don't know what is."

"Come on now, what we did was to keep our presence solid." Wolf shrugged and took a swig of his beer.

Badger shook his head. "Qualifying it now don't make it right. I gotta agree with Deuce on this one. It didn't seem stupid at the time. But in hindsight, it's pretty fucking stupid."

"Maybe." Wolf set his beer down on the table and started loading another clip.

Badger put his hands on his hips. "I'm going in alone. If it gets messy, it's on me."

Wolf's head jerked up. "Nope. No fucking way I'm letting you do that. We already know he's got two babysitters with him, who knows if he's got more. Plus, the minute you step foot in that door, he's going to disarm you."

"No *way* we're letting you do that." Deuce placed his hands behind his head. "No doubt this *will* get messy, and we're gonna make sure the mess is all on him *and* his boys."

"Deuce, look, brother—" Badger blew out a sigh, followed by a grunt. He needed to make himself clear. "—I appreciate it. But I never should've involved you to begin with. Had I known then what I know now, I never would've. Only way to make that right is to make sure you don't get touched. You got Evie and the bar to think about. I'd never forgive myself if any of this blew back on you."

Deuce let the chair fall forward, and the legs hit the floor with a loud thud. "Now, listen to me. No way in—"

"He's right, Deuce. Don't argue it." Wolf got to his feet and gripped Badger's shoulder. "As far as me? Blowback doesn't apply. I'm going in with you. No question."

Badger stared at Wolf as Deuce grumbled in the background. Wolf had his back always, Deuce had also. The fact that they no longer wore a patch to drive that bond home didn't matter. They were brothers, forever. "Meet me halfway, Wolf. I'm planning on giving him one chance to stay by his word. If he doesn't, which we both know he won't, and shit gets messy, then you'll know."

Wolf stared at him for what felt like forever. Badger waited, practically able to see the wheels turning behind Wolf's eyes as he tried to sort out what Badger wanted. But there was no way Badger was going to give in on this one. The situation was just too critical; Alvaro was too unpredictable. Considering the odds were in the dealer's favor, Badger wasn't sure if he and Rosie would make it out of this alive, and bringing Wolf down with them wasn't an option.

"New proposition: I am going in with you, but I'll do it through another entrance—back door or something. No way I'm waiting outside for shit to go south only to get to you too late. You're going to need the backup firepower, and you're going to need it up close and personal."

"Fuck this. If he gets to go inside, then I'm coming too— Goddammit! Don't either of you look at me like that!" Deuce glared at the two of them. "I'll wait outside, and *when*, not *if*, shit gets messy, I'll call the PD." Deuce ran his palm over the top of his head. "Can't believe I'm even saying that, but yeah. I'll call the law. You just make sure it looks like self-defense."

Badger shook his head, knowing full well that his two best friends weren't going to back down. They were right, he knew it, and he hated it. "Fine. Jesus fucking Christ, you two are a pain in my ass. Fine."

"Fine." Wolf clapped him on the shoulder and moved back to his seat. "What's the plan?"

Anticipation thrummed through Badger in time with his heart. The plan? How about kill the motherfuckers and bring his woman back home? Easy enough. But that was all much easier said than done. "I need to show my face by ten p.m. That gives us a little over an hour. But look, Rosie doesn't want him to have this money. She doesn't want anyone to have it. Honestly? I don't, either. So, I can either show up with a bag stuffed with cash or newspaper. Makes no difference to me. Like I said before, no way he's gonna stand by his word, so I'll do what needs doing."

"All right, you decide how that plays. I'll find an entrance, when I do, I text you. You head in the front and do what you gotta do to negotiate." Wolf slid a fully loaded clip into his .45. "Betting he's got her secluded somewhere in that warehouse. I'll search her out while you make small talk with Alvaro."

Deuce nodded. "He's probably got one of his henchmen guarding her. You'll need to take him out nice and quiet, then bring her out to me."

"I don't think that's smart. I'm staying inside. I'll make sure she's safe before I go find Badger to finish the job."

"No, Wolf. Too dangerous. I can handle Alvaro and whatever he brings to the party. Especially if you take one babysitter out of the game for me. Just get Rosie out of the building. Deuce, the minute you have her, I want you to get ghost," Badger said.

Deuce shot up in his seat. "No way. I'm not leaving the scene. What if yo—"

"Enough! I'll fucking handle it!" Badger's words came out on a growl. "Listen, I want her safe. That's the most important thing to me. Which means if Wolf gets Rosie out, which he will, then I want her as far away from there as possible."

Deuce stared at him for a long moment before his lips curled into a grin. "You love her."

"For fuck's sake, *do not* start your romantic bullshit with me right now."

"You do. It's good, brother. All good. You deserve it." Deuce's grin spread into a full smile. "We're clear. I'll keep her safe. You have my word."

"Thank you." Badger stood and looked at Wolf. "You good?"

"Yeah. All good." Wolf didn't meet his eyes; just continued wiping residual oil off the slide of one of his guns.

Badger let out a grunt and made his way out back again. Regardless of what Badger had just instructed, Wolf would do what he thought was right once the heat got turned up. That's just the kind of man he was. Unpredictable but in a save-his-partner's-ass sort of way.

When Badger got outside, he lit a smoke and stared up at the sky. The plan was set, the deal done. Mostly. He needed to decide if he was taking the money along or not—but regardless, none of what was happening was right. All of it was wrong. Rosie losing her husband, even though it'd led her to Badger, was wrong. Her having to get back on that stage… fucking wrong. Hiding out in order to save her life also wrong. Right up to Badger having to go to any length, no matter that he was willing, was totally, fucking, undeniably wrong.

The only thing that felt right in the whole twisted situation was how he felt about Rosie. And that was the key to all of it. Deuce was right. Badger loved her. That love was what was driving him now, and would continue to drive him while he did what he needed to do to make sure she was safe. He'd never loved a woman before. He'd never wanted to.

But all he wanted now, more than anything, was to love Rosie. Forever and always.

CHAPTER THIRTY-ONE

BADGER APPROACHED the side door of the old warehouse on Lower Buckeye Road with the leather duffel hanging from his grip. He had his 9mm on his hip and his .22 Smith and Wesson at his ankle. But neither mattered, because they'd for sure be relieving him of weapons as soon as he crossed the threshold. Unless he got lucky and no one was there to greet him, which wasn't likely.

Deuce was parked down the street in his truck, engine running and Wolf had headed to the service dock around the back, seeking an alternative way inside. He was supposed to text Badger when he'd gained entry to the building, but Badger had yet to hear from him.

Badger's skin itched in anticipation of the confrontation ahead as he took a final drag of his cigarette before dropping it to the sidewalk and smashing it beneath his boot. Waiting... Waiting. He blew out an exasperated breath and stretched his neck from side to side, trying to relieve some of the tension in it. Normally, he was good at waiting. The many stakeouts he'd been on as a bounty hunter had taught him patience. But in this case? The wait was about to make him lose his ever-loving mind.

His woman was in there, goddammit.

Three minutes—which felt like three hours—later, his phone vibrated in his pocket. Grabbing the device, he checked the screen. The little "thumbs up" emoticon made him shake his head. Wolf was inside. Badger drew in a deep breath and let it out. It was time to crash the party.

Badger pulled open the front door and stepped inside the dark, wide-open space to the welcoming committee.

"Ah, my friend. You're a few minutes late." Alvaro stood with his arms crossed in front of him, and to his right was one of his boys, 9mm tight in the dude's grip and right where Badger could see it. Alvaro tipped his head toward the bodyguard. "Luis just wagered that you weren't coming. I won."

Fuuuuck! Badger cleared his throat and braced himself.

———

ROSIE SWALLOWED, still trying to gain her bearings. With a groan, she snaked out her tongue and licked over the open cut on her bottom lip. She winced at the sting. The sonofabitch had hit her hard and way too many times. Her ears were still ringing, and her cheek throbbed in time with her heart.

After he'd got done working her over, likely because she probably tired him out since she hadn't shut her mouth, he stalked out of the room—one of his little bitches in tow. Good. Fuck him. Apparently, he hadn't expected her to be so resilient. Maybe his Puerto Rican ass hadn't gone head to head with a half-Italian, half-Puerto Rican girl before. He could mark that off his bucket list and maybe learn a lesson from it.

Nothing and no one shut Rosie up. Not when she had a point to make. There hadn't been anyone strong enough, and Alvaro was no exception.

Except Badger—he'd been the exception to every rule in her world.

Fuck, she'd give anything to see him one more time. Or maybe not be so stupid and run off to try and reason with a crazy motherfucker? Yeah, that might've been a good option. She needed a do-over—a reset button. Either would be fan-fucking-tastic. Rosie groaned, pulling against the tape around her wrists again, but no closer to loosening it.

She glanced over to the doorway. Alvaro's other bitch was still there, all calm, cool and collected. Standing at attention, clad in a black suit, white shirt, and black tie. The other jackoff was dressed the same. A matching set. How very *Men in Black* of them.

Rosie laughed, uncaring if the asshole heard her. She was quite possibly losing her mind, or maybe Alvaro had knocked a screw loose because there was nothing funny about this situation. Then again, she always did resort to sarcastic humor in major times of stress. She'd had to; it was what made life bearable.

He watched her in silence. Rosie tilted her head to the side and cracked her neck, and repeated the motion in the other direction. "I need to pee."

No answer.

She didn't have to, really. She was just hoping that maybe he'd take mercy on her and give her an opportunity to get away. "Okay then. So should I just go in my pants?"

Still, nothing. And his stare didn't waver, either.

Rosie frowned, but then, appearing out of nowhere, Wolf was there, right behind her babysitter. She blinked, unsure if she was hallucinating…that was until Wolf cracked the guy on the back of the head with something, and he went down like a sack of potatoes. Rosie opened her mouth to say something and Wolf placed his fingertip to his lips in signal for her to be quiet. She nodded, and Wolf stepped over the knocked-out Alvaro wannabe and straight to her.

Sweet Jesus, she'd never been so happy to see someone in her entire freaking life! In spite of her excitement, she managed to lower her voice. "That was fucking awesome. What did you hit him with?"

Wolf pinched her chin between his finger and thumb and looked over her face. "Badger is going to flip the fuck out when he sees you. Fucking hell, are you okay?" he whispered.

"Yeah, sort of. Just hurry and get me untaped."

"You got it." Wolf moved behind her and cut the tape off her wrists, and then came back around to her front.

Finally free, Rosie flexed her hands and rolled her wrists, trying to get the feeling to come back in them. She bent down to one leg and started on the tape there as Wolf cut the tape off the other.

A flash of movement from the corner of her eye caught Rosie's attention, and she glanced up to find the goon had regained consciousness and had a gun pointed in their direction. "Wolf! Look out!"

As the fucker pulled the trigger, and the loud pop echoed through the room, everything went into slow motion. Rosie was shoved backward, toppling to her side. Eyes wide, she watched as Wolf fired off two shots as he attempted to rise to his full height, and the bullet that'd been meant for her hit him. He stumbled backward but held his footing until his feet tangled on a broken chair and he tipped backward, landing on his back on the floor, his head cracking hard on the concrete.

With his eyes closed, arms splayed out at his sides, he was not moving.

This wasn't happening.

This *could not* be happening.

Panic climbed up Rosie's throat and belted out of her in the form of one word. "*Wolffff!*"

CHAPTER THIRTY-TWO

Badger had been completely disarmed when the shots rang out, and the sound of Rosie screaming Wolf's name echoed from somewhere in the building. Alvaro's eyes went wide, and he immediately turned and ran, yelling over his shoulder to his man, Luis, to take care of Badger.

With less than a second to move before the bodyguard turned from where he'd been securing Badger's weapons to draw his own gun and come at him, Badger didn't waste time thinking. He just acted. He dropped the bag and launched into a full run at the guy. Luis raised his weapon to Badger's face, and Badger gripped the man's wrist, shoving his hand to the side just as he pulled the trigger.

The loud blast so close to Badger's ear set a piercing ringing off in his head. Ignoring it, Badger continued forward, struggling to hold the man's arm above his head to keep the weapon away until their combined weight and Badger's momentum took them both to the ground.

As they slammed hard onto the concrete, the wind was knocked out of Badger, and he let out a loud groan. Luis's gun skittered away from them. Just what Badger had been hoping for. Doing his best to shake off the ringing in his ears and the pain in his ribs, Badger rolled to his feet, prepared to do what he had to in order to take this fucker down and find Rosie.

Badger turned and—*Fuck!*—ducked as the guard swung a metal pipe at his head. Badger came up with a hard punch to the guy's midsection and followed with one to his face. Luis stumbled backward, and Badger followed, tackling him to the ground again. As they rolled, the guy ended up on top, straddling Badger and then landed a hard fist into Badger's cheek. Badger's head jerked to the side as the pain from the blow radiated along the side of his head and down his neck, and then the guy hit him again—

Fucking sonofabitch!

Badger bucked his hips, trying to knock Luis off before finally grabbing him by the lapels of his suit jacket. Badger yanked him forward and head-butted him in the nose. Blood exploded in an arc as the bodyguard flew backward off Badger and stumbled to his feet.

Before Badger could get up off the ground, the dude was coming back at him, blood running from his nose and down his chin. Luis said something Badger could barely make out, thanks to the high-pitched note playing in his head. He could've asked him to repeat himself, but instead, raised his leg and kicked him in the stomach.

The guy shuffled backward, giving Badger the precious seconds he needed to get to his feet. Badger had no idea if Wolf and Rosie were okay, and if she screamed again, he was going to lose his fucking mind. He needed to finish this and get to them both. With the coppery taste of blood in his mouth, Badger gritted his teeth as he raised his fists and stalked after his opponent. "Come on, motherfucker. Let's go!"

Luis waved him forward, and when Badger swung, the guy blocked it and slammed Badger in the ribs. He doubled over, but as he did, he pressed into Luis, planting his shoulder in his stomach and gripped him tight around the waist. Badger took a few hits to his kidneys until he finally spun and shoved Luis away.

The guy stumbled back and crash-landed over a table with junk littering the top of it. Badger dove over the table, gaining the upper hand and slammed the guy in the nose again before cracking him across the jaw. As Luis groaned and tried to gain purchase on Badger's shirt and throat, Badger gripped him by the hair and slammed his head down on the concrete, once, twice…before Luis got lucky and finally landed a punch to the side of Badger's head.

Badger let out a yell as the ringing in his eardrum kicked in again, and he flew to the side. Laying there, he spotted his 9mm on the ground. No shit. Lady Luck was smiling? The table Luis had knocked over was the one he'd placed Badger's weapons on. In the blink of an eye, Badger had the gun in his hand.

He turned just as Luis grabbed him by the shoulder and fired, point-blank, into the bodyguard's stomach.

Badger froze, ready to shoot again, as a look of shock blanketed Luis's features. The man glanced down to where the muzzle of the gun still pointed. Blood oozed quickly from the wound, around the singed fabric from the blast, spreading wide on his white dress shirt.

The fucker hadn't expected that.

After crawling backward a few feet, Badger got to his feet, and Luis fell to his knees, hand covering the wound, eyes still wide with disbelief, before falling to his side on the cold concrete floor. He holstered his gun and turned away from the dying man.

Badger didn't need to watch any longer. He had a brother and his woman to get to.

After finding the leather bag, he weaved around several old shipping crates and various debris in the direction Alvaro had gone in. He spit out a mouthful of blood and swiped his wrist across his lips as he listened for voices or noise of any kind. Though he'd weathered a few hard hits, his wounds were all superficial—he'd survive. Badger just prayed the same would be true for all of them when this was over.

It wasn't until he rounded a corner and found a long corridor lined with offices—or something of the like—that he could finally hear her. The ringing in his ears was still there, but that mouth of hers…Jesus, he loved it and hated it. Potent enough to break through any brain-screeching noise, he was damn sure. The woman lacked an off-switch when she was pissed. But at that moment, it was the best fucking sound in the world.

Badger slowed his steps and pressed his shoulder to the wall, gun at the ready, as he passed several closed doors. Each office had a tall but narrow window. Glancing in each, he noticed some empty, some cluttered with old office furniture, trash, and boxes. Badger heard her again and moved farther down the hall.

Tamping down the desperation rising inside him to run to her or yell her name, Badger drew in a deep breath and focused on keeping his steps light as he approached the doorway to the office she was in. With his back pressed against the wall just before the door, he listened, trying to get a feel for what awaited him.

"You cold-hearted fucking monster! Say something!" She let out a frustrated growl, and Badger's lips twitched with a grin. "Such a badass with your gun to my head, right? I have no weapon. It's not like I can do anything, so just let me go back to the other room and see if he's okay! You can even come with me."

Holy shit, Badger loved this woman. He realized she was talking about Wolf, which didn't bode well, and likely she'd heard the gunshots ring out from the other part of the warehouse. She was probably terrified. Badger had been on the receiving end of those bullets, but she didn't sound terrified. No, she sounded pissed, and she was still calling out the scene for him…just in case. Just in case he was coming to get her.

Alvaro wasn't saying anything. The man was smart but insane and was probably patiently waiting for whoever survived the fight to show their face. Badger bet the guy had laid odds on his boy coming out on top. Too bad, so sad. The better man had won, and Alvaro was about to find that out.

Shifting his grip on his weapon, Badger drew in a deep breath. He only had the 9mm. His .22 had been left downstairs, and he was likely insane for even going this route, but fuck it. Go big and badass, or go home. With his gun upside down in his grip and held out to one side, bag held out to the other, Badger pivoted and stepped in front of the open doorway of the room. "Honey, I'm home."

Alvaro jerked Rosie closer to him, the muzzle of his gun pressed to her temple. "Ah, my friend. I see you've been victorious."

He caught Rosie's gaze, pleading with her with his eyes to follow his lead. She raised one single brow and then blinked. Yeah, totally fucking loved her. He focused on Alvaro again and kept his tone even. "Yeah, well, you underestimated me, apparently. Now, let her go, Alvaro. I have your money. Even trade, remember?"

Alvaro smiled. "You and your partner seem to have taken both of my men. Not very even in my book, my friend. Though—" Alvaro jerked his chin, "—by the looks of him in the other room, we're almost even."

"Let's not play games, Alvaro. I'll give you the advantage." Badger had no idea where Wolf was…or if he was still breathing. *Motherfucking-cocksucking-sonofabitch!* Knowing he could do nothing to help his brother, he swallowed the rage that threatened to emerge and, focused on Rosie…and made his next move.

Badger squatted slowly and placed his gun on the ground. Reasoning with an insane person was, well…insane, but

Badger was banking on the guy being focused on the cash, even if only long enough for Badger to get Rosie safe. He stood again and held the bag out in front of him. "You wanted your money. I got it for you. Give me the girl."

"It makes no difference to me if you have no weapon. The money is good. Thank you. However, I certainly will enjoy listening to you scream as you watch her brains spill out of her pretty skull." He smoothed his free hand over the side of Rosie's head and looked back to Badger. "Toss the bag to me, my friend."

Badger looked at Rosie again; her eyes flared, and he blinked, willing her to trust him. There was no fucking way in hell he was going to let that threat come to fruition. The temptation to keep the dealer talking until he talked himself in a circle was huge, but Badger had a feeling going that route would only fan the flames of madness already licking at Alvaro's heels. "I know you're a man of your word, Alvaro."

He swung the bag backward and then tossed it to the left and deliberately short of where Alvaro stood. It landed with a thud, and as Alvaro took a step to move toward it, Rosie yanked herself away from him.

Badger charged for Alvaro. "Rosie! Run!"

"*Noooo!*" Alvaro turned to grab for Rosie. He caught her shirt, but she slipped free and kept moving.

"Go! Deuce is outside!" Badger got to Alvaro, tackling him to the ground, praying he'd lose his grip on the gun. As he rolled with the dealer, struggling for the upper hand, he caught a glimpse of Rosie running out of the room. Thank fuck!

A hard punch to the neck caught Badger's attention, and his eyes went wide as a yell burst out of him. Goddammit, that fucking hurt! He grabbed Alvaro by the throat with both hands and squeezed. It took a moment for Badger to realize the numb, cool feeling he felt on his shoulder, far too close to his neck, damn near in his neck…was a knife. The wetness he felt was blood.

Motherfucker had stabbed him and was coming back for another slice.

ROSIE RAN out of the room Alvaro had brought her into after Wolf had shot his bodyguard. Much needed oxygen had filled her lungs the moment Badger had stepped into the doorway, as relief spilled through her like a cool drink. Finally, she could breathe again. Her man was okay, thank God.

But Wolf had been shot, and Rosie needed to see if he was okay and somehow find a way out. Before she made it into the office where Wolf still laid, a loud yell that sounded a whole lot like a growl reached her ears. She skidded to a halt. *Oh God!* That was Badger. She knew it was. What the hell was she doing? No matter what he told her to do, she couldn't just leave. She would not just leave Wolf, and she sure as hell wasn't going to leave Badger.

Jesus Christ, this was insane. Continuing forward, she moved into the room and straight for Wolf. *God, Wolf…* Rosie swallowed the wave of emotion threatening to spill out of her. She bent to her knees at his side. "Wolf?" She cupped his warm cheek, then slid her fingers to his neck.

His pulse hammered hard against her fingertips, and Rosie had to bite back her cry of relief. Scanning down his body, she noticed there was no blood, but there was a bullet hole. The fabric of his navy blue Henley frayed where it'd entered. She tugged his shirt up.

Vest! Holy fucking hell—he was wearing what she assumed was a bulletproof vest. Thank God. Rosie hoped like hell Badger had one on, too. Glancing back to his face, Rosie shook his shoulder. "Wolf? Wake up."

Nothing. What the hell? Rosie slid her fingers behind his head, and when they met with wetness, she realized why. The fear was back, racing through her veins, making her skin itch. He'd cracked his head. Apparently, hard enough, he was bleeding. And he was out cold. None of that was good. Goddammit…

Rosie turned and glanced around the room as the sound of something crashing to the ground echoed from the other office. *Oh God, think*! Before panic took over completely, Rosie scanned the room, searching for a gun, any fucking gun.

The *Men in Black* ass-kissing bodyguard's dead body was just inside the doorway to the left—the gun he'd shot Wolf with still locked in the grip of his right hand. And she planned to leave that gun right where it was. She looked back to Wolf and then past his body to where his weapon lay. Leaning over him, she wrapped her fingers around the butt of his gun. "Need to borrow this, honey. Promise I'll give it back, though."

Rosie stood and ran back toward the room Badger was in, but slowed as she got closer. The grunts, groans, and random crashes coming from the room made her flinch. God help her, Badger was going to be furious that she'd come back for him. Fuck it, he could be mad all he wanted, punish her for it, too. She'd take it, with a smile no less, because that would mean he'd be alive to deliver the ass-whooping.

Drawing in a deep breath, Rosie blew it out slowly as she crouched low to the ground and peered around the doorframe.

Badger was on his feet, left hand clasped to the left side of his neck where it met his shoulder—fingers coated with blood. His blood. *Oh God!* Too much blood!

Rosie sucked in a breath, almost choking on her own saliva. She was ready to scream his name, but somehow got control of herself and bit down on her tongue when Badger swung at Alvaro, landing a punch with his right fist and knocking the bastard back a few steps.

Alvaro came right back at him, though, swinging a small

knife near Badger's midsection. Badger managed to knock his arm away and countered by tackling the guy using his sheer mass and brute strength. When they landed, both men groaned, and Rosie cringed but spotted the knife as it skidded across the floor. Thank God!

Alvaro landed a punch to Badger's ribs, and Rosie flinched as a harsh groan shot out of her man. Badger recovered, gaining the upper hand again. He grabbed Alvaro by the hair, raised his head off the ground and slammed it down on the concrete. Alvaro let out a yell before bucking Badger off him.

Keeping her movement slow—as Badger and Alvaro continued to beat the ever-loving piss out of each other—she squatted down, trying to gain entry into the room without being noticed. As she shifted her weight to her other foot—

Rosie flinched at the loud pop and snapped her attention back to where both men were. Not more than six feet away, Alvaro stood with his back to her. His arm still raised in the air, gun pointed at Badger...and fired again.

No! Noooooo! Oh God, how was this happening?

The bullet hit Badger in the right shoulder, far too close to his chest, and his body jerked back, listing to one side from the impact. The spot immediately turned red, filling with blood and then trickling down his shirt. Rosie sucked in a deep breath and... *"Baaaaadddddddggggeerrrrrrr!"*

Alvaro had just shot her man and, by the looks of it, was about to pull that trigger again. He'd already taken so much from her. It would be the end of the world as she knew it if he took Badger, too.

Her new world.

Her perfect world.

Raw, blistering fear raced through Rosie's bloodstream at the thought of losing him. There was no way in hell she was going to let Alvaro rob her of anything more. *"Nooooooo!"*

"Rosie!"

She had a moment to glance to her left and see Wolf staggering toward her. His arm out, reaching for her. A deadly calm came over her as she looked back to Badger, and then all her focus landed on Alvaro. With Wolf's gun tight in her fist, as if driven by pure animalistic instinct, she raised her arm and gripped the butt of the gun with both hands...and squeezed the trigger.

The bullet entered the back of Alvaro's head and exited the front, bone and brain matter expelling outward—some of it landing on Badger.

Not really comprehending the damage she'd just done, Rosie screamed, ready to shoot again, until she saw Badger stumble to his side before falling to the ground, as Alvaro's lifeless body fell face-first onto the concrete floor.

Wolf got to her. His fingers clamped loose around the wrist of the hand she still held the gun in. "Let it go, darlin'."

On autopilot mode, Rosie looked to his face.

"Let it go, darlin'. It's okay." The expression in Wolf's bright blue eyes soft and comforting.

Rosie swallowed before nodding, then released her grip and let Wolf take the gun from her hands. She ran to her man, sliding to her knees beside him. "Badger..." She pressed her palm to the bleeding puncture at the base of his neck, where it met his shoulder. There was so much blood from the knife wound, more than where he'd been shot, even. God, why was there so much blood?

"Fuuuckkk! This sucks." Badger glanced up at her, his face far too pale.

"Hold still, honey. Please?"

He cupped her cheek and managed a weak smile. "You got him, baby. That's my woman. So proud of you." He drew in a strangled breath. "Fuck that hurts."

Tears trickled down Rosie's cheeks. "Just...dammit, Badger. Hold still. Stop moving and look at me. Please? I can't lose you."

"I am looking at you, baby. Always looking at you. You're beautiful. Most beautiful thing I ever had."

"Shh…honey please—" Rosie sobbed as she bent forward and pressed a soft kiss to his forehead, "—just breathe. I can hear sirens. Help is coming."

"Most beautiful thing I ever got to have in my life. Didn't deserve it, but got it anyway. So perfect. So different." He sucked in a hard breath. "I love you, Rosie."

Sobbing, she found his other hand and clasped it. Adrenaline pulsed through her system in time with her heart. "Please, Badger. Oh God, don't leave me!"

"Never gonna leave you. It's okay, baby. Just need to rest…" Badger squeezed her hand and closed his eyes.

"No!" She dropped his hand and gripped his jaw between her fingers, shaking him. "Stay with me, dammit!"

How could this be happening? How could she lose him now, after everything they'd gone through? She should've stayed home like he'd wanted her to. She should've listened and let him take her on vacation. She should've done a lot of things.

And it was too late now. The damage was done.

There was so much blood—he was so pale. Rosie pressed down harder on the wound, trying to stem the steady stream. Badger could bleed out right before her eyes, and she had no idea what to do.

Sheer terror brought more tears as it swamped her system, and she became near hysterical. "*Wolf! Do something!*"

"Darlin', you gotta breathe." Wolf's hand landed on her shoulder and gave a squeeze. "And not for nothing, but I get knocked unconscious for what, five minutes? And mayhem ensues? You shoot a drug dealer in the back of the head and, fast as lightning, go into a dramatic display of hysterics. Although this is damn exciting to watch, buck up and get your shit in check. Your man needs you."

"Are you crazy?" she said through a sob.

"Might be. But it's a fun ride." He smiled that smile of his, crinkles forming around his gorgeous eyes.

Rosie shook her head and started to laugh. "Yep, crazy." Drawing in a deep breath, she got a grip on her hysterics. "But you're my kind of crazy. Thanks, Wolf."

"Anytime, darlin'." He gave her a wink.

She smiled up at him before turning back to Badger. Wolf gave her exactly what she needed in that moment. Humor amidst the insanity, which brought her right back to where she needed to focus. And that was stopping Badger's bleeding; however she could do that. Pulling her hand away, she yanked her shirt over her head, balled up the fabric and pressed it against the wound. His breaths were so shallow as he shivered. "Badger, listen to me. Honey, please open your eyes."

No response. No nothing. Just her and him and what was left between them. God, she loved him, and she was losing him. She was losing everything.

CHAPTER THIRTY-THREE

 the cops had given her wrapped around her shoulders, Rosie watched the ambulance pull away from the sidewalk, her hands cuffed in front of her body from the backseat of a patrol car. Badger was inside it on his way to the hospital. Phoenix officers, as well as the Crime Scene Response unit, were crawling all over the scene. They'd cuffed her and Wolf when they'd first invaded the building.

It was to be expected. How in the hell did they know who shot who and who might do more shooting? Three dead bodies and two injured at the scene? Damn right, she was first in line for cuffs; Wolf had been second.

Rosie let out a sigh and glanced to the right. Another team of paramedics were attending to Wolf, though he was still in his cuffs. Thanks to the body armor beneath his shirt, the bullet hadn't entered his body. But he'd cracked his head so hard when he tripped and fell backward that he needed stitches, and the medics were concerned he had a concussion.

With the back passenger window open just far enough so she could hear, he was refusing to go to the hospital and trying to just get them to stitch his "noggin" up right then and there. Which pretty much told Rosie he was going to be fine. Too ornery to not be. Fortunately for him, one of the medics was female and apparently not immune to the beautiful toxicity of Wolf's blue eyes and perfect smile, so it looked like he was going to get his way.

Badger had been wearing body armor, too, but it'd done little to protect the curve of his neck from a knife wound and his shoulder from the bullet Alvaro had planted there.

Unlike Wolf, she had no idea if Badger was going to be fine.

The officer that had cuffed her had said they'd be questioning her shortly. She had to wait. Something she was definitely not good at. Wait while they got some of the particulars uncovered and sorted, like the fact that Alvaro was still holding his gun in his dead hand but was also facing a murder charge for the murder of her husband, as well as being a known drug dealer, who had left the state, violating the terms of his bail—something she'd advised them of as they'd cuffed her and walked her to the police car.

A man in a gray suit, white dress shirt, and tie approached the car and opened the back door. "Mrs. Santini. I'm Detective Hammel. May I have a word, please?"

"Sure. Not like I have a choice." She raised her cuffed hands.

"Yes, well. I'm sure you understand the reason for those." He helped her from the backseat, uncuffed her, and walked her away from the police car. "I'm hoping you're still in a cooperative mood. If so, based on what your friend Mr. Stevens advised the nine-one-one operator and what I've seen upstairs, as well as the details around Mr. Alvaro that he provided, we should be able to handle this without going down to the station."

Relief washed through her as she thanked God that Deuce had been outside and called the cops. "Thank you. Sorry, I know you're just doing your job. Of course, I'll cooperate. There's no reason not to."

They needed the details now, the ugly nitty-gritty of it. She'd killed a man, after all. And not just any man, the man that'd murdered her husband. Rosie's actions still hadn't quite sunk in because she felt nothing about what she'd done…or maybe she just didn't care? Her whole focus had been on Badger when she'd pulled that trigger. And then, even after Alvaro had fallen to the ground, Rosie had been preoccupied with getting to Badger…helping him. Trying to save him.

She hoped to God she had.

The detective led her to the Crime Scene Response van, where they'd set up a couple of chairs. "Have a seat, please. Can I get you anything?"

"A shirt would be nice. Bottle of water would be good, too."

"Sorry, no spare shirts. But water, I can do." He signaled to one of the officers nearby. "Why don't you tell me what happened."

An officer came over and handed her a bottle of water. She thanked him, took a long swallow and then began telling the story. The only part she left out was the money. Wolf had told her, before the cops got there, that Badger hadn't actually brought the money but had stuffed the bag full of old newspapers.

Instead, she made sure to let them know that Wolf had acted in defense of her as well as his own life. She couldn't offer any info about the other bodyguard that Badger had taken out, and assumed that if they hadn't already spoken to Badger about the other dead man, they'd be doing it at the hospital.

All through her detailed disclosure to the detective, Rosie kept searching her soul for even a splinter of guilt for what she'd done, but it was nowhere to be found. After everything Alvaro had taken from her, she couldn't feel bad for taking his life from him. Granted, he was someone's son, and a parent should never have to suffer the loss of a child. It was possible he was someone's husband, father, or brother, too. If that was the case, she did feel bad for them, but that was it. That was as far as it went.

Only God knew how many other people had suffered at Alvaro's hand or how many addicts died from the drugs he pushed. There was no way to know. And maybe that was all just her way of justifying what she'd done.

Aside from letting her know that Badger had regained enough consciousness to advise them that she pulled the trigger, shooting Alvaro in defense of Badger's life, he refused to discuss Wolf or Badger further or if any charges could be brought against them. But they'd both acted in self-defense, so for now, she was going to tell herself they wouldn't.

The detective asked her a few more questions before finally releasing her. He didn't feel they would be pressing charges, considering she'd been kidnapped and assaulted, and Alvaro was about to kill Badger. Never mind the fact that the man was to stand trial for the murder of her husband. But regarding her, she'd have to wait and see if the DA agreed. Yay, something new to look forward to. A couple of officers showing up at her door to take her to jail. Or even Badger to jail. God, how she would so much rather just look forward to something simple like…going on a date with her man. Going to the movies or even going to work, for fuck's sake. Rosie shook her head at the randomness of her thoughts as she stepped away from the detective in search of Wolf.

She found Deuce instead, standing outside the police barricade tape. With a big smile, he held his arms out to his sides. "Hey, little lady."

Rosie did a face plant into his chest and wrapped her arms around his waist. "I'm really glad you're here, but Deuce, why didn't you go to the hospital with Badger?"

"Nope." He gave her a squeeze before letting her go. "Badger would kick my ass if I left you alone. Not happening. The ass-kicking or the leaving you alone part."

"But I don't want him to be alone. What if he…" Rosie sucked back a sob and wiped a tear away that escaped.

"What if, nothing. He's gonna be fine." He leaned in and pressed a kiss to the side of her head. "Besides, Evie'd kick my ass harder than Badger if I left you. So, little lady, it ain't happening."

Rosie turned and hugged him again. He was such a good man. "I'm so glad you weren't in there. I'd never forgive myself if something happened to you and Evie was left on her own."

"I should've been in there, but Badger, the stubborn ass that he is, banished me to wait outside."

"Stubborn but smart." She pulled back, a small smile curving her lips.

Deuce gave her another one of his big smiles. "He's a good man."

"Better than good. We need to get to him now, though. Do you know if they're done with Wolf?"

"Not sure. Since you're on the other side of the tape, you might have better luck finding out if they're letting him go."

"Got it. Back in a bit." Rosie stepped away from Deuce, fear and concern racing through the back of her mind, almost like a white noise.

Between her worry for Badger's well-being and her confusion regarding her lack of emotions around killing a man, Rosie felt like she was moving through quicksand. Did her lack of guilt or remorse make her just as much a monster as Alvaro? Could she be that cold inside? She hadn't wanted to hurt anyone. But she had…

And she'd do it again if it was necessary.

Rosie got out of the truck and, with both Deuce and Wolf by her side, walked through the emergency room entrance at County Hospital. They'd let Wolf go, which was a good sign, but the fear that had been a constant in the back of her mind kicked into high gear on the drive from the warehouse of horrors to the hospital. And it'd taken what felt like a lifetime to get there. She swore to God they hit every fucking red light possible along the way, and Rosie had bit every one of her fingernails, with each stop, down to stubs. Knowing she must look like hell and not caring, she stepped to the intake window. "Drew Baxter, please?"

"Are you family?"

Wolf came up beside her. "She's his woman. We're his brothers." The growl in his tone was enough to make her nervous.

The young man dressed in scrubs looked up *and up* at Wolf, eyes wide, before a small smirk formed on his lips. "Yeah, okay…just a minute."

"Try not to scare the shit out of the staff." Deuce crossed his arms.

Wolf jerked his chin. "It's County. That's not really possible."

Rosie smoothed her hands over the top of her hair and ran her fingers through the length. "I'm sure I'm not helping the situation. How bad do I look?"

"Rosie, you look beautiful. Fat lip and bruised cheek make no difference, darlin'." Wolf shot her one of his drop-dead gorgeous grins as he made a show of cracking his knuckles.

"Be glad I had an extra T-shirt in the truck. Else you'd be sporting your pretty paper blanket over your bra right now. Though Badger might not complain about that." Deuce laughed.

"Hey, at least I was wearing a bra." She snorted.

Wolf shifted. "Hey now—"

"Excuse me, gentlemen…and ma'am? Go down the hall there and make a left at the end." The kid gestured to his right as a set of double doors opened automatically. "Mr. Baxter is in room eight."

"Thank you!" Rosie grabbed Wolf by the shirt and moved for the door.

"He called us gentlemen. How cute." Wolf chuckled.

Deuce stepped to Rosie's left. "That's because he has manners. Unlike you. Behave, ya big Viking."

"Yeah, yeah." Wolf grinned.

Rosie shook her head and kept moving. "Why is he still in Emergency? Shouldn't they have admitted him by now?" No one answered her, probably because she didn't give them a chance to. She continued down the hall and made the left as the reception kid said to. Room five, six... "Eight!" Hustling, she barreled into the room and stopped short.

Badger was on the gurney, eyes closed, sitting up but at a low angle. His shirt was gone, and there was a pile of gauze taped to where the knife wound was and another secured to where the bullet wound was. An IV bag hung to his right, the tube taped and plugged into his arm. Little plastic monitor on his finger hooked up to a machine on his left pumping out a steady beep. His face was bruised, eyes swollen, and his lips split in a few places from all the hits he'd taken.

Wolf scooted around her and moved to the other side of the gurney. "Sweet Jesus, brother! *Look. At. You.* You *are* a goddamn mess."

"Good to see you too, asshole." Badger opened one eye but didn't raise his head. "Made 'em wait to take me to surgery 'til you all got here."

And Rosie blew out a breath she hadn't realized she was holding before sucking in needed oxygen that was Badger— because one more time, she hadn't lost him.

Deuce came up next to her, and she felt his warm palm on her lower back. "You all right, sweetheart?"

Unable to find her voice, Rosie nodded as she raised her fingers to her mouth. Badger looked so much better than he had when they'd loaded him into that ambulance and taken him away from her.

The relief she felt was instantaneous. But then the whole scene back in that room in the warehouse started to play before her eyes…like some sort of endless rerun of a B horror flick.

Except it wasn't a movie; it was real life—her life, and Badger was about to die, and she'd blown someone's brains out. Rosie flinched and turned away as the sound of the gun in Alvaro's hand going off echoed in her mind.

"Rosie!"

Badger…

With tears dripping down her cheeks, Rosie turned back toward the sound of his voice. He'd raised his head off the pillow and was staring right at her. "Woman, get your ass over here. Now."

Rosie stepped forward, one foot in front of the other, until she was beside him. With a slight cringe, he grabbed her by her T-shirt and pulled her down so she was nearly nose-to-nose with him. Distantly, she was aware of Wolf and Deuce leaving the room, but she didn't dare look away from Badger's gaze.

He stared at her for what seemed like an eternity—his eyes roaming over her face like a physical touch. Until finally, he spoke. "I told you to run. Didn't I?"

Oh fuck, really? Rosie swallowed past the knot in her throat. "Yes, sir."

"Why didn't you run?"

He'd almost died, and this is what he wanted to discuss with her? Seriously? "Honey, I did!" He raised an eyebrow at her and cocked his head to the side. Rosie swallowed again. Fuck's sake. "Okay, fine. I started to, sort of. I was going back to Wolf to help him and get us both out, but then I heard you yell. And I'm sorry, but that yell? Everything I heard in it? I had to come back. I couldn't…" She bit her bottom lip and glanced away from his stare.

"Eyes to me. Couldn't what?"

She looked back at him. "I couldn't let him take you from me, too."

"Why not?"

Christ, what was this, interrogation hour? "Because!"

Badger growled. "Try again."

"Fine. Because that motherfucker already took one man from me, I wasn't about to lose you too."

"Why not?"

"Are you crazy? What do you mean, why not?" Rosie pulled back from him and crossed her arms.

"Why don't you want to lose me, Rosie?"

Rosie shook her head as tears began to flow again. "Because I love you. Is that what you want to hear?" She swiped at one cheek. "I told you in the letter, but I'll say it again. I'm in love with you."

"C'mere, woman."

Rosie bent close again. "What?"

"Who do you belong to?"

Rosie let out a half-laugh, half-cry and then sniffled. "You."

"That's right. And who do I belong to?"

Rosie wiped another tear away. "Me."

"Good answer, baby." He pursed his lips. "Now that we're clear. I need a kiss, but keep it soft."

Rosie couldn't help the smile that arched her lips through her tears. Jesus, he was a pain in the ass, but he was her pain in the ass. She pressed her lips to his, soft like he'd asked, taking little sips of his tongue. When she broke the kiss, she pulled back only slightly. The movie had stopped playing in her mind. Badger had taken care of that, but the emotions the replay stirred in her were still flooding her system, and she let out a small sob. "I was so scared. I was so fucking scared, baby."

"Yeah, I know you were scared. I was scared, too." He

smoothed a lock of her hair between his finger and thumb. "But you were also a fucking badass!"

Rosie shook her head and smiled again. "Well, what do you expect? My man is a major badass. He deserved nothing less from me."

He chuckled but, a moment later, sobered, his expression going serious. "So different. So, perfect. My whole world, woman."

Rosie smiled at him before pressing another kiss to his lips. For their sake, she hoped neither of them were ever in a situation like that again. She wouldn't change what had happened, but she'd much rather prefer life not be that exciting.

She didn't need to be a badass. Rosie just needed to be a good woman to her man. And she knew Badger would be good to her, take care of her.

They'd breathe easy…together.

EPILOGUE

Rosie knelt in the grass of the front yard, surveying the flowers she'd planted in the new flowerbed Badger had built for her last weekend. She'd planted three rose bushes, and around them, scattered throughout the bed, a variety of petunias in pink, white, and purple. It was beautiful and a complete contrast to the desert landscapes she'd seen in many other neighborhoods.

The familiar rumble of loud motorcycle pipes reached her ears from down the street. She smiled, knowing it was Badger making his way through the neighborhood, making his way home to her. After getting to her feet and tossing the small spade, plus her garden gloves, to the ground, Rosie arched her back to stretch. It'd been nine months since the night with Alvaro and his bodyguards when all hell broke loose. That night, Badger had undergone surgery to repair the damage Alvaro had done to him with the knife and bullet.

They'd given the money to the local Salvation Army drug and alcohol rehab center. It was the best thing Rosie felt the money should be used for. But after that, their life began. And Rosie and Badger's relationship went in an entirely new direction. It was September, just about thirteen months since she'd moved to Phoenix from Waterbury. Thirteen months since she'd laid eyes on Drew "Badger" Baxter. The man who would become the love of her life.

Still living together, they'd had nine months of being a real deal, official couple. Nine months of dates, breakfast out on Sunday mornings. Friday night dinners…and shopping, lots of shopping. But more importantly, love. Lots and lots of love —making love too.

Rosie felt her face get warm at the thought of what he'd done to her just the night before. Shifting her hips, she smoothed her palm over one butt cheek, the sting still present. Perfect. She'd loved every minute of it, begging him the whole time for more. The rumble of the pipes on his Harley got louder, drawing her attention, and Rosie watched as her man rounded the corner and rolled up in front of their house. And he'd made it very clear it'd become their house. Rosie smiled again.

After parking in the driveway and dropping the kickstand, he glanced her way, head cocked to the side, chin dipped. And smiled. Cue the swoon and gooey insides… Just like it had the first time she'd ever laid eyes on the man, that look of his took her breath away.

Badger dismounted the cycle and came her way. "How's my baby today?"

"Great!" She circled his neck with her arms. "I planted all the petunias. What do you think?"

He glanced over at the flowerbed. "Huh. Looks great, babe. Nice job. Not doing too much, though, right?"

"Pssshaw. I'm fine."

"Mmmhmm." He slid his hand down to her small, rounding tummy. "Precious cargo in here, woman. Don't forget that."

"Like I *could* forget that. The heartburn alone reminds me daily." She covered his hand with hers.

He grinned as he bent his head and kissed her. Sweet, yet

demanding. Rosie melted against him, loving when he touched her little baby bump. She never thought she'd have kids, never really wanted any…until she found out she was pregnant with Badger's child. Now, she couldn't ever imagine not having a baby. Their baby.

Rosie moaned into his mouth as she tangled her tongue with his. God, she also loved kissing him. She pretty much loved everything with him. She was living a life she'd never imagined possible. Happy.

Rosie was just plain happy and breathing easy.

Needing a breath, she broke from his lips—but only because he let her. She gazed up at him with a smile. "Did you have a good day? Catch any bad guys?"

"Not yet. Close though. You 'bout done out here?"

"Yep. I got it all planted. You have perfect timing. You get to clean up the mess." She laughed.

Taking her hand, he turned and led them to the garage. "Yes, my queen, I shall take care of all of that. Let's get you off your feet, and while I clean up, you decide what you want to feed our baby for dinner."

"Honey, I'm only four months along. I don't think our baby cares yet."

"Oh, she cares." He glanced back at her, lips curved in a grin and continued into the house.

"She?" Rosie rolled her eyes. "I told you, I'm beyond sure *she's a boy.*"

"You can keep telling yourself that all you want, but I'm having a daughter, and she's gonna be as beautiful and badass as you."

Rosie sighed. This had been a debate between them from about five minutes after the pregnancy test had come up positive. In truth, she didn't care what sex the baby was, just as long as it was healthy and had all its fingers and toes. "I guess we'll find out at the ultrasound next month, then." She grinned.

"Guess so." He held the door open for her.

Yep, this was her life. Her man by her side. His child growing inside her belly. A happy home to raise their child in together. The perfect life, perfectly fit for a queen and her king.

Badger was hers, and she was his. And their life was so much more than she could've ever dreamed of, but everything she'd ever wanted.

He was her everything.

Body, heart and soul.

Forever and always.

ABOUT THE AUTHOR

Dorothy F. Shaw lives in Arizona, where the weather is hot, and the sunsets are always beautiful. She's a self-proclaimed sex scene snob and is proud of it. When she's not writing, she's thinking about writing.

With her ever-open heart, bright red hair, and many colorful tattoos, she truly lives and loves in Technicolor!

ALSO BY DOROTHY F. SHAW

Head to my site to find all links to my available backlist:

www.DorothyFShaw.com

Start at the beginning of
The Donnellys series with:
Unworthy Heart

The Donnellys Book 1
© 2019 Dorothy F. Shaw

Opposites not only attract, sometimes they spontaneously combust.

Ryan Donnelly's past relationship may have failed, but he's determined to make single fatherhood and his career a resounding success. He's got his eye on the top of the ladder at an L.A. marketing firm when his gaze snags on co-worker Maiya Rossini.

She's a feisty, witty, tattooed redhead who's nowhere near his type, but she pushes every one of his hot buttons.

Maiya clawed her way out of her dysfunctional, trailer-park childhood to earn a college degree and establish a promising career. Her future dreams are big, bright and packed with full-throttle fun, but when it comes to matters of the heart and men—especially stuffy corporate types like Ryan —her past slams on the emotional brakes.

In the office and in the bedroom, Maiya and Ryan rub each other in all the *right* ways. Though Maiya is everything Ryan didn't know he wanted, he's got his work cut out for him convincing her she's worthy of love—or the bright light she's brought to his life could slip through his fingers.

Turn the page for a sneak peek…

Unworthy Heart

Chapter One

"Cutting it a little close, aren't you, Maiya?"

Dammit, she was. Her hair always took forever when she was in Los Angeles. And the last thing she wanted was to look like crap the first time she met Ryan Donnelly face to face.

"Of course, boss. There's no excitement in actually making it on time." Maiya stepped out of the elevator and pulled off her sunglasses. "Besides, I'm not in the office all that much these days. It takes time to change out of my work-from-home uniform of hair scrunchies, tank tops and boxer briefs to appropriate business attire."

"Very true." Tony tilted his head down, peering at her over the top of his frameless glasses perched on the end of his nose. "Three months is too long for you to not pay a visit."

She brushed her hair away from her face. Relocating from Las Vegas to Los Angeles eight years ago to start her job with Amaryllis Marketing Firm had been a leap of faith for her, but it'd paid off tenfold. And the man in front of her was a huge part of the reason why. Plus, when she had needed to move back to Vegas to care for her mother, Tony had allowed her to stay on, working remotely from home. He'd earned her respect and loyalty in spades, and she couldn't imagine working for anyone else. "Blame the finance group and their travel budgets. You know I'd rather be out here at least once a month."

His handsome smile crinkled the corners of his eyes, and he ushered her into the conference room. "Also true. Regard-less, glad to have you here now."

Maiya entered, and excitement raced through her. "Thanks." They grabbed a seat along the back row against the windows, and she nodded to the familiar faces in attendance around the conference room table. She loved connecting with the people she worked with on a daily basis but rarely saw face-to-face. A sense of comfort spilled through her, like she'd come home again.

The senior marketing executive, Mr. Mawbry, spoke to the room, and the conference phone in the center of the table. "Good morning, everyone. Thank you for joining the monthly project status meeting."

Notebook and pencil in hand, Maiya scanned her surroundings. Taking a deep breath, her excitement settled, and pride took its place. Maiya had done hella good for herself sticking with this company. She'd worked her way up the corporate ladder, rung by rung, and found success.

There were a few new faces in attendance, and curiosity pranced through her mind. Did any of them belong to Ryan? They'd only recently started collaborating on a project together. Their conversations, which had started out professional, had begun to slip into the land of flirtation. Dangerous territory, yes, but regardless, Maiya would kill to know what he looked like. She'd checked his Facebook account—in a purely non-stalkerish way—but had come up empty-handed. His page was locked down like Fort Knox.

Sad thing was, she had a feeling Ryan resembled a corporate Ken Doll. Annnd surprise, surprise, Maiya was *nothing* like Barbie.

At least meeting him face to face would be the dose of reality necessary to evaporate her physical reaction to him and focus on work again. She hoped, anyway.

One of the project managers in attendance kicked the group off and reported on their campaign. Maiya checked her notes for any details she might need to report on for her particular project. At the sound of an additional male voice, her head snapped up. *He sounds familiar.*

The guy turned and looked at her.

Their eyes locked, and a bolt of electricity arced between them. The jolt shot straight to Maiya's toes. *Hello, Gorgeous and totally not my type.* She drew in a deep breath and let her gaze roam over his short, sandy, light-brown hair, high cheekbones and crystal blue-gray eyes. And his lips.

He flashed her a quick smile.

My God, that can't be Ryan. *Jesus, if that's him, I'm in a fuckton of trouble.* Maiya broke their stare and returned her focus to her notepad, tapping it with her pencil—a pale attempt to convince herself the guy *was not* Ryan.

A few minutes later, Mr. Mawbry spoke again. "Ryan, could you please report the status of your campaign?"

Maiya searched the unknown faces, desperate to find him among the team, when Mr. Gorgeous started talking.

"Oh. Shit," she muttered.

Ryan glanced at her, a devilish grin adorning his lips.

Double shit. She couldn't stop herself from staring while he spoke. Especially at his lips. She really liked his lips. This was *so* not good. This wasn't in the plan. It was bad enough his voice got her aching and wet, but…his face. That mouth. Those lips—she could *not* be attracted to him. Absolutely out of the question.

She had to work with him, for fuck's sake!

As the Senior Project Manager assigned, Ryan gave his report. Maiya answered the few questions some of the other executives in attendance had. She had to pry her tongue off the roof of her mouth in order to speak, but she'd managed. Maybe the corporate ladder hadn't paid off as well as she thought.

The group moved on to the next project on the agenda. Still warm and tingling from the intense eye lock with Ryan, Maiya blew out a harsh breath, trying to cool down. After a few more projects were discussed, the meeting adjourned. She bent to retrieve her things from the floor by her seat. If she didn't get some air and fast, she might spontaneously combust.

A set of long legs entered her line of sight.

Her gaze traveled up his casual khaki pants, over his chest, clad in a pale blue Polo shirt—the color emphasizing the blue in his eyes—and then settled on his lips. *Dammit.* With burning cheeks, she stood and raised her eyes to meet his.

"Maiya Rossini, I assume." Ryan extended his hand to shake hers. "Nice to finally meet you."

She placed her palm in his and drank him in. In hopes of playing it cool, she cleared her throat before speaking. "Ryan Donnelly. Yes, it's nice to meet you, too."

His long fingers curled around her hand, and he smiled. Tingles danced up her arm. Being right in front of him now and touching him, queued up every hormone in her body. *This is crazy!* She was caught between wanting to run in the other direction or throw herself at him and beg him to drag her somewhere private.

They assessed each other for a moment, saying nothing before she mentally kicked herself in the ass and broke the silence. "My team is having a gathering tonight. You joining us?" With regret, she extricated her hand from his very warm one.

"I'll have to see if I can make it. What time again?"

"Thinking of blowing off fun team-building time?" She raised her brows. "Six, I believe. Check your calendar. I'm sure you were sent an invite."

He tilted his head to the side. "I wouldn't dream of blowing off 'fun team time'. As if you'd let me get away with doing that anyway."

"Good to know." Unable to help herself, she glanced at his lips again. With mammoth effort, she forced her gaze away, took her seat and finished gathering her things.

She was having a hell of a time looking him in the eye, and making small talk wasn't any easier. Her skin was tight all over, and her cheeks were flaming hot. Struck stupid was a damn understatement.

Her reaction bothered her.

And he bothered her.

Ryan stepped a couple feet away to talk to another team member.

Maiya took the opportunity to escape. She needed air. And a cigarette. Maybe a cold drink of water, too. "See you later, Ryan. I gotta run."

"Bye, Maiya. Guess I'll see you la—"

Ducking her head, Maiya rushed from the room.

Want more?

Head to my site to find all links to my available backlist:

www.DorothyFShaw.com

Available from all major e-sellers in digital and print.

Dorothy F. Shaw
Phoenix, Arizona
STRIPPED BOUNTY
Copyright © 2016 by Dorothy F. Shaw
ISBN-10: 0-9978310-0-6
ISBN-13: 978-0-9978310-0-9
Draft2Digital ISBN-13: 978-1-3701445-5-6
Edited by Tera Cuskaden
Cover by Kelli Martin and Terry "Wookie" Hoffman

Red Queen Publications electronic and print publication: August 2016

Publishing History
Digital/Print 1.0 editions /August 2016

Red Queen
Publications

www.ingramcontent.com/pod-product-compliance
Lightning Source LLC
Chambersburg PA
CBHW031218120726
47905CB00002B/377